THE ROYAL SUCCESSION

Maurice Druon was a French resistance hero, a Knight of the British Empire and a holder of the Grand Croix de la Légion d'Honneur. He was also a member of L'Académie française and a celebrated novelist, best known for his series of seven historical novels under the title of *The Accursed Kings*, which were twice adapted for television. A passionate Anglophile, he was a great expert on all things English, including its medieval history, which provides great inspiration for the series. His many and diverse fans include George R.R. Martin, Nicolas Sarkozy and Vladimir Putin.

BY MAURICE DRUON

The Accursed Kings

The Iron King

The Strangled Queen

The Poisoned Crown

The Royal Succession

The She-Wolf

The Lily and the Lion

The King Without a Kingdom

THE ROYAL SUCCESSION

Book Four of The Accursed Kings

MAURICE DRUON

Translated from French by
Humphrey Hare

HarperCollins*Publishers*

HarperCollins*Publishers*
77–85 Fulham Palace Road,
Hammersmith, London W6 8JB

www.harpercollins.co.uk

First published in Great Britain by Rupert Hart-Davis 1958
Century edition 1972
Arrow edition 1988

This paperback editon 2014

1

A catalogue record for this book
is available from the British Library

ISBN: 978-0-00-749132-2

Printed and bound in the United States of America

'History is a novel that has been lived'
E. & J. DE GONCOURT

'It is terrifying to think how much research
is needed to determine the truth of even
the most unimportant fact'
STENDHAL

Foreword

GEORGE R.R. MARTIN

Over the years, more than one reviewer has described my fantasy series, *A Song of Ice and Fire*, as historical fiction about history that never happened, flavoured with a dash of sorcery and spiced with dragons. I take that as a compliment. I have always regarded historical fiction and fantasy as sisters under the skin, two genres separated at birth. My own series draws on both traditions . . . and while I undoubtedly drew much of my inspiration from Tolkien, Vance, Howard, and the other fantasists who came before me, *A Game of Thrones* and its sequels were also influenced by the works of great historical novelists like Thomas B. Costain, Mika Waltari, Howard Pyle . . . and Maurice Druon, the amazing French writer who gave us the *The Accursed Kings*, seven splendid novels that chronicle the downfall of the Capetian kings and the beginnings of the Hundred Years War.

Druon's novels have not been easy to find, especially in English translation (and the seventh and final volume was never translated into English at all). The series has *twice* been made into a television series in France, and both versions are available on DVD . . . but only in French, undubbed, and without English subtitles. Very frustrating for English-speaking Druon fans like me.

The Accursed Kings has it all. Iron kings and strangled queens, battles and betrayals, lies and lust, deception, family rivalries, the curse of the Templars, babies switched at birth, she-wolves, sin, and swords, the doom of a great dynasty . . . and all of it (well, most of it) straight from the pages of history. And believe me, the Starks and the Lannisters have nothing on the Capets and Plantagenets.

Whether you're a history buff or a fantasy fan, Druon's epic will keep you turning pages. This was the original game of thrones. If you like *A Song of Ice and Fire*, you will love *The Accursed Kings*.

George R.R. Martin

Author's Acknowledgments

I AM most grateful to Georges Kessel, Edmonde Charles-Roux, Christiane Grémillon and Pierre de Lacretelle for the assistance they have given me with the material for this book; and to the *Bibliothèque Nationale* in Paris, the *Bibliothèque Méjanes* in Aix-en-Provence, and the Municipal Library of Florence for indispensable aid in research.

Contents

The Characters in this Book

THE QUEEN OF FRANCE:

CLÉMENCE OF HUNGARY, grand-daughter of Charles II of Anjou-Sicily and of Marie of Hungary, second wife and widow of Louis X, the Hutin, King of France and Navarre, aged 23.

LOUIS X'S CHILDREN:

JEANNE OF NAVARRE, daughter of Louis X and his first wife, Marguerite of Burgundy, aged 5. JEAN I, called THE POSTHUMOUS, son of Louis X and Clémence of Hungary, King of France.

THE REGENT:

PHILIPPE, second son of Philip IV, the Fair, and brother to Louis X, Count of Poitiers, Peer of the Kingdom, Count Palatine of Burgundy, Lord of Salins, Regent, then Philippe V, the Long, aged 23.

HIS BROTHER:

CHARLES, third son of Philip the Fair, Count de La Marche and future King Charles IV, the Fair, aged 22.

HIS WIFE:

JEANNE OF BURGUNDY, daughter of Count Othon of Burgundy and of the Countess Mahaut of Artois, heiress to the County of Burgundy, aged 23.

HIS CHILDREN:

JEANNE, also called of Burgundy, aged 8.

MARGUERITE, aged 6.

ISABELLE, aged 5.

LOUIS-PHILIPPE of France.

THE VALOIS BRANCH:

MONSEIGNEUR CHARLES, son of Philippe III and of Isabella of Aragon, brother of Philip the Fair, Count of the Appanage of Valois, Count of Maine, Anjou, Alençon, Chartres, Perche, Peer of the Kingdom, ex-Titular Emperor of Constantinople, Count of Romagna, aged 46.

PHILIPPE OF VALOIS, son of the above and of Marguerite of Anjou-Sicily, the future King Philippe VI, aged 23.

THE EVREUX BRANCH:

MONSEIGNEUR LOUIS OF FRANCE, son of Philippe III and of Marie of Brabant, half-brother of Philip the Fair and of Charles of Valois, Count of Evreux and Etampes, aged 40.

PHILIPPE OF EVREUX, his son.

THE CLERMONT-BOURBON BRANCH:

ROBERT, COUNT OF CLERMONT, sixth son of Saint Louis, aged 60.

LOUIS OF BOURBON, son of the above.

THE ARTOIS BRANCH, DESCENDED FROM A BROTHER OF SAINT LOUIS:

THE COUNTESS MAHAUT OF ARTOIS, Peer of the Kingdom, widow of the Count Palatine Othon IV, mother of Jeanne and Blanche of Burgundy, mother-in-law of Philippe of Poitiers and of Charles de La Marche, aged about 45.

ROBERT III OF ARTOIS, nephew of the above, Count of Beaumont-le-Roger, Lord of Conches, aged 29.

THE DUCHY OF BURGUNDY FAMILY:

AGNÈS OF FRANCE, youngest daughter of Saint Louis, dowager Duchess of Burgundy, widow of Duke Robert II, mother of Marguerite of Burgundy, aged about 57.

EUDES V, her son, Duke of Burgundy, brother of Marguerite and uncle of Jeanne of Navarre, aged about 35.

THE COUNTS OF VIENNOIS:

THE DAUPHIN JEAN II de la Tour du Pin, brother-in-law of Queen Clémence.

THE DAUPHINIET GUIGUES, his son.

THE GREAT OFFICERS OF THE CROWN:

GAUCHER DE CHÂTILLON, Constable of France.

RAOUL DE PRESLES, jurist, one-time Councillor to Philip the Fair.

MILLE DE NOYERS, jurist, one-time Marshal of the Army, brother-in-law of the Constable.

HUGUES DE BOUVILLE, one-time Grand Chamberlain to Philip the Fair.

THE SENESCHAL DE JOINVILLE, companion-in-arms to Saint Louis, a chronicler.

ANSEAU DE JOINVILLE, son of the above, Councillor to the Regent.

ADAM HÉRON, Grand Chamberlain to the Regent.

COUNT JEAN DE FOREZ.

JEAN DE CORBEIL and JEAN DE BEAUMONT, called the Déramé, Marshals.

PIERRE DE GALARD, Grand Master of the Crossbowmen.

ROBERT DE GAMACHES and GUILLAUME DE SERIZ, Chamberlains.

GEOFFROY DE FLEURY, Bursar.

THE CARDINALS:

JACQUES DUÈZE, Cardinal in Curia, then Pope Jean XXII, aged 72.

FRANCESCO CAETANI, nephew of Pope Boniface VIII.

ARNAUD D'AUCH, Cardinal Camerlingo.

NAPOLÉON ORSINI, JACQUES and PIERRE COLONNA, BÉRENGER FRÉDOL, elder and younger brothers, ARNAUD DE PÉLAGRUE, STEFANESCHI, and MANDAGOUT, etc.

THE BARONS OF ARTOIS:

The Lords of VARENNES, SOUASTRE, CAUMONT, FIENNES, PICQUIGNY, KIÉREZ, HAUTPONLIEU, BEAUVAL, etc.

THE LOMBARDS:

SPINELLO TOLOMEI, a Siennese banker living in Paris.

GUCCIO BAGLIONI, his nephew, aged 20.

BOCCACCIO, a traveller, father of the poet Boccaccio.

THE CRESSAY FAMILY:

DAME ELIABEL, widow of the Lord of Cressay.

JEAN and PIERRE, her sons, aged 24 and 22 respectively.

MARIE, her daughter, aged 18.

Robert de Courtenay, Archbishop of Rheims.

Guillaume de Mello, Councillor to the Duke of Burgundy.

Messire Varay, Consul of Lyons.

Geoffroy Coquatrix, a Burgess of Paris, an army contractor.

Madame de Bouville, wife of the one-time Chamberlain.

Béatrice d'Hirson, niece of the Chancellor of Artois, Lady-in-Waiting to the Countess Mahaut.

All the above names have their place in history.

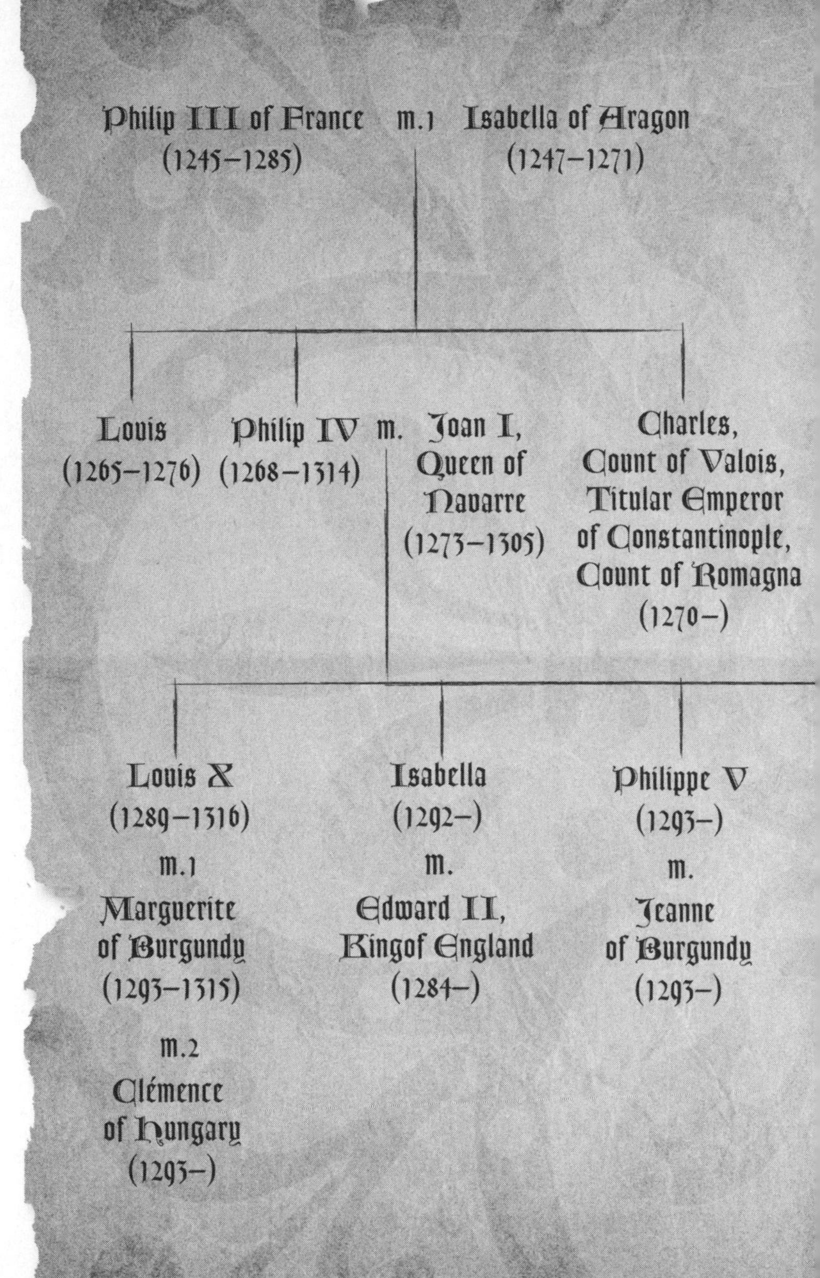
Philip III of France
(1245–1285)
m.1
Isabella of Aragon
(1247–1271)
Louis
(1265–1276)
Philip IV
(1268–1314)
m.
Joan I,
Queen of
Navarre
(1273–1305)
Charles,
Count of Valois,
Titular Emperor
of Constantinople,
Count of Romagna
(1270–)
Louis X
(1289–1316)
m.1
Marguerite
of Burgundy
(1293–1315)
m.2
Clémence
of Hungary
(1293–)
Isabella
(1292–)
m.
Edward II,
Kingof England
(1284–)
Philippe V
(1293–)
m.
Jeanne
of Burgundy
(1293–)

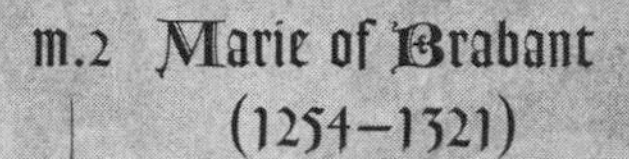

(1254–1321)

Louis Capet,
Count of Evereux
(1276–)

Blanche
(1278–1305)

Margaret
of France
(1282–)

Charles IV
(1294–)
m.
Blanche
of Burgundy
(1296–)

The House of Capet 1316

NORTH
KINGDOM of ENGLAN
ENGLISH CHANNEL
Cherbourg
Brittany
Le Mans
Anjou
Poitou
BAY of BISCAY
Saintonge
Bordeaux
Gascony
Bearn

NORTH SEA
Calais
Flanders
Artois
Crécy
Somme R.
Amiens
ormandy
Coucy
Champagne
reux
Paris
rtres
Seine R.
Reims
Meuse R.
Orléans
Loire R.
DOM of FRANCE
Dijon
Burgundy
aine
Berry
rs
Bourbon
Limoges
Lyon
Dauphiny
nne
Avignon
Toulouse
Languedoc
Foux
MEDITERRANEAN SEA

The Royal Succession

Queens wore white mourning.

The wimple of fine linen, enclosing her neck and imprisoning her chin to the lip, revealing only the centre of her face, was white; so was the great veil covering her forehead and eyebrows; so was the dress which, fastened at the wrists, reached to her feet. Queen Clémence of Hungary, widowed at twenty-three after ten months of marriage to King Louis X, had donned these almost conventual garments and would doubtless wear them for the rest of her life.

Prologue

In three hundred and twenty-seven years, from the election of Hugues Capet to the death of Philip the Fair, only eleven Kings had reigned in France and each one had left a son to ascend the throne.

It was a prodigious dynasty, which Providence seemed to have marked out for duration and permanence. Only two of the eleven reigns had covered less than fifteen years.

This singular continuity in the exercise and transmission of power had allowed, if not determined, the formation of national unity.

For the feudal link, a purely personal one between vassal and suzerain, between the weaker and the stronger, was substituted gradually another relationship, another compact uniting the members of a vast human community which had for long been subject to similar vicissitudes and an identical law.

If the concept of the nation had not yet become evident, its symbol already existed in the person of the sovereign, the supreme source of authority and the ultimate court of appeal. Whoever thought of the King also thought of France.

And Philip the Fair, throughout his life, had set himself to cement this nascent unity with a powerful centralized administration and the systematic destruction of external and internal rivalry.

Hardly had the Iron King died, when his son, Louis X, followed him to the grave. The population could not help but see in these two deaths, kings struck down in their prime, one following so quickly on the other, the finger of fate.

Louis X, the Hutin, had reigned eighteen months, six days and ten hours. During this short period of time, this pitiful monarch had destroyed the greater part of his father's achievement. His reign had seen the murder of his Queen and the hanging of his first minister; famine had ravaged France; two provinces had rebelled; and an army had been engulfed in the Flanders mud. The great nobles were infringing on the royal prerogatives once more; reaction was all-powerful; and the Treasury empty.

Louis X had ascended the throne at a moment when the world lacked a Pope; he died before a Pontiff had been elected, and Christendom trembled on the verge of schism.

And now France was without a king.

For Louis X, by his marriage to Marguerite of Burgundy, had left only a daughter of five years of age, Jeanne of Navarre, who was suspected strongly of bastardy. By his second marriage, he had bequeathed but an expectation: Queen Clémence was pregnant; but would not be brought to bed for five months. Moreover, it was being canvassed openly that the Hutin had been poisoned.

No disposition had been made for a regency; and personal

ambitions resulted in individual attempts to seize power. In Paris the Count of Valois endeavoured to have himself proclaimed Regent. At Dijon the Duke of Burgundy, brother of the murdered Marguerite and the powerful head of a baronial league, undertook to avenge the memory of his sister by championing the rights of his niece. At Lyons the Count of Poitiers, elder surviving brother of the Hutin, was grappling with the intrigues of the Cardinals and vainly striving to force the Conclave to a decision. The Flemings were but awaiting the occasion to take up arms again; while the nobility of Artois was pertinaciously conducting a civil war.

All this was enough to remind the people of the curse pronounced two years before by the Grand Master of the Templars from among the faggots of his pyre. In that age of superstition, it might well have seemed, in the first week of June 1316, that the Capets were an accursed race.

PART ONE

PHILIPPE AND THE CLOSED GATES

I

The White Queen

QUEENS WORE white mourning.

The wimple of fine linen, enclosing her neck and imprisoning her chin to the lip, revealing only the centre of her face, was white; so was the great veil covering her forehead and eyebrows; so was the dress which, fastened at the wrists, reached to her feet. Queen Clémence of Hungary, widowed at twenty-three after ten months of marriage to King Louis X, had donned these almost conventual garments and would doubtless wear them for the rest of her life.

Henceforth no one would look on her wonderful golden hair, on the perfect oval of her face, and on the calm, lustrous splendour which had struck all beholders and made her beauty famous.

The narrow and pathetic mask, framed in its immaculate linen, bore the marks of sleepless nights and days of weeping. Even her gaze had altered, never coming to rest but seeming to flutter across the surface of people and of things. The lovely Queen Clémence already looked like the effigy on her tomb.

Nevertheless, beneath the folds of her dress, a new life was forming: Clémence was pregnant; and she was obsessed by the thought that her husband would never know his child.

'If only Louis had lived long enough to see his child born!' she thought. 'Five months, only five months longer! How happy he would have been, particularly if it is a son. If I had only become pregnant on our wedding night!'

The Queen turned wearily to look at the Count of Valois, who was strutting up and down the room like a cock on a dunghill.

'But why, Uncle, why should anyone have been so wicked as to poison him?' she asked. 'Did he not do all the good in his power? Why are you always searching for the wickedness of man where, doubtless, there is but a manifestation of the Divine Will?'

'You are on this occasion alone in rendering to God that which seems rather to belong to the machinations of the Devil,' replied Charles of Valois.

The great crest of his hood falling on his shoulder, his nose strong, his cheeks bloated and high of colour, his stomach thrust well to the fore, dressed in the same suit of black velvet with silver clasps which he had worn eighteen months earlier at the funeral of his brother Philip the Fair, Monseigneur of Valois had just returned from Saint-Denis, where he had been burying his nephew, Louis X. The ceremony had created a problem or two for him, because, for the first time since the ritual of royal burials had been established, the officers of the household, having cried: 'The King is dead!' had been unable to add: 'Long live the King!'; and no one knew before whom the various rites, normally appropriate to the new sovereign, should be performed.

'Very well! Break your wand before me,' Valois had said to the Grand Chamberlain, Mathieu de Trye. 'I am the eldest of the family and take precedence.'

But his half-brother, the Count of Evreux, had taken exception to this peculiar innovation, for Charles of Valois would certainly have taken advantage of it as an argument for his being recognized as Regent.

'The eldest of the family, if you mean it in that sense,' the Count of Evreux had said, 'is not you, Charles. Our Uncle Robert of Clermont is the son of Saint Louis. Have you forgotten that he is still alive?'

'You know very well that poor Robert is mad and that his clouded mind cannot be relied on in anything,' Valois had replied, shrugging his shoulders.

In the end, after the funeral feast, which had been held in the abbey, the Grand Chamberlain had broken the insignia of his office before an empty chair.

'Did not Louis give alms to the poor? Did he not pardon many prisoners?' Clémence went on, as if she were trying to convince herself. 'He had a generous heart, I assure you. If he sinned, he repented.'

It was clearly not the moment to contest the virtues with which the Queen embellished the recent memory of her husband. Nevertheless, Charles of Valois found it impossible to control an outburst of ill-humour.

'I know, Niece, I know,' he replied, 'that you had a most pious influence on him, and that he was extremely generous . . . to you. But one cannot rule by Paternosters alone, nor by heaping presents on those one loves. Repentance is not enough to disarm the hatreds one has sown.'

'So now,' Clémence thought, 'Charles, who laid a claim to

power while Louis was alive, is denying him already. And soon I shall be reproached with all the presents he gave me. I have become the foreigner.'

She was too weak, too overcome to find the strength for indignation. She merely said: 'I cannot believe that Louis was so hated that anyone would wish to kill him.'

'All right, don't believe it, Niece,' cried Valois; 'but it's the fact! There's the proof of the dog that licked the linen used for removing the entrails during the embalming and died an hour later. There's . . .'

Clémence closed her eyes and clutched the arms of her chair in order not to reel at the vision it conjured up in her mind. How could anyone speak so cruelly of her husband, the King who had slept beside her, the father of the child she carried, compelling her to imagine the corpse beneath the knives of the embalmers?

Monseigneur of Valois continued to develop his macabre thesis. When would he stop talking, that fat, restless, vain authoritarian who, dressed sometimes in blue, sometimes in red, sometimes in black, had appeared at every important or tragic hour in Clémence's life during the ten months she had been in France, to lecture her, deafen her with words and compel her to act against her will? Even on the morning of her marriage at Saint-Lyé, Uncle Valois, whom Clémence had scarcely ever seen, had almost spoiled the ceremony by instructing her in court intrigues of which she understood nothing. Clémence remembered Louis coming to meet her on the Troyes road, the country church, the room in the little castle, so hastily furnished as a nuptial chamber. 'Did I realize my happiness? No, I must not weep in front of him,' she thought.

'Who the author of this appalling crime may be,' went on Valois, 'we do not yet know; but we shall discover him, Niece, I give you my solemn promise. If I am given the necessary powers, that is. We kings . . .'

Valois never lost an opportunity of reminding people of the fact that he had worn two crowns, which, though they were purely nominal, still put him on an equal footing with sovereign princes.[1]*

'We kings have enemies who are less hostile to our persons than to the decisions of our power; and there are many people who might have an interest in making you a widow. There are the Templars, whose Order, as I said at the time, it was a great mistake to suppress. They formed a secret conspiracy and swore to kill my brother and his sons. My brother is dead, his eldest son has followed him. There are the Roman Cardinals. Do you remember Cardinal Caetani's attempt to cast a spell on Louis and your brother-in-law of Poitiers, both of whom he wished to destroy? The attempt was discovered, but Caetani may well have struck by other means. What do you expect? One cannot remove the Pope from the throne of Saint Peter, as my brother did, without arousing resentment. It is also possible that supporters of the Duke of Burgundy may still feel bitter about Marguerite's punishment, to say nothing of the fact that you replaced her.'

Clémence looked Charles of Valois straight in the eye, which embarrassed him and made him flush a little. He had had some hand in Marguerite's murder. He now realized that Clémence knew it; through Louis's rash confidences no doubt.

But Clémence said nothing; it was a subject she was chary

---

*The numbers in the text refer to historical notes at the end of the book.

of broaching. She felt that she was involuntarily to blame. For her husband, whose virtues she boasted, had nevertheless had his first wife strangled so that he might marry her, Clémence, the niece of the King of Naples. Need one look further for the cause of God's punishment?

'And then there is your neighbour, the Countess Mahaut,' Valois hurried on, 'who is not the woman to shrink from crime, even the worst . . .'

'How does she differ from you?' thought Clémence, not daring to reply. 'Nobody seems to shrink much from killing at this Court.'

'And less than a month ago, to compel her to submit, Louis confiscated her county of Artois.'

For a moment Clémence wondered if Valois were not inventing all these possible culprits in order to conceal the fact that he was himself the author of the crime. But she was immediately horror-struck at the thought, for which there was indeed no possible basis. No, she refused to suspect anyone; she wanted Louis to have died a natural death. Nevertheless, Clémence gazed unconsciously out of the open window towards the south where, beyond the trees of the Forest of Vincennes, lay the Château of Conflans, Countess Mahaut's summer residence. A few days before Louis's death, Mahaut, accompanied by her daughter, the Countess of Poitiers, had paid Clémence a visit: an extremely polite visit. Clémence had not left them alone for a single instant. They had admired the tapestries in her room.

'Nothing is more degrading than to imagine that there is a criminal among the people about one,' thought Clémence, 'and to start looking for treason in every face.'

'That is why, my dear Niece,' went on Valois, 'you must

return to Paris as I asked you. You know how fond of you I am. I arranged your marriage. Your father was my brother-in-law. Listen to me as you would have listened to him, had God spared him. The hand that struck down Louis may intend pursuing its vengeance on you and on the child you carry. I cannot leave you here, in the middle of the forest, at the mercy of the machinations of the wicked, and I shall be easy only when you are living close to me.'

For the last hour Valois had been trying to persuade Clémence to return to the Palace of the Cité, because he had decided to go there himself. It formed part of his plan for assuming the regency and facing the Council of Peers with the accomplished fact. Whoever was master in the Palace had the trappings of power. But to install himself there on his own might look as if he were usurping it by force. If, on the other hand, he entered the Cité in his niece's wake, as her nearest relative and protector, no one could oppose it. The Queen's condition was, at this moment, the best pledge of respect and the most effective instrument of government.

Clémence turned her head, as if to ask for help, towards a third person who was standing silently a few paces from her, his hands crossed on the hilt of a long sword, as he listened to the conversation.

'Bouville, what should I do?' she murmured.

Hugues de Bouville, ex-Grand Chamberlain to Philip the Fair, had been appointed Curator of the Stomach by the first Council which had followed on the death of the Hutin. This good man, now growing stout and grey, but still extremely alert, who had been an exemplary royal servant for thirty years, took his new duties most seriously, if not tragically. He had formed a corps of carefully picked gentlemen, who mounted guard in detachments of twenty-four over the Queen's door. He himself had donned his armour and, in the heat of June, large drops of sweat were running down under his coat of mail. The walls, the courtyards, indeed the whole perimeter of Vincennes, were stuffed with archers. Every kitchen-hand was constantly escorted by a sergeant-at-arms. Even the ladies-in-waiting were searched before entering the royal apartments. Never had a human life been guarded so closely as that which slumbered in the womb of the Queen of France.

In theory Bouville shared his duties with the old Sire de Joinville, who had been appointed Second Curator; the latter had been selected because he happened to be in Paris where he had come to draw, as he did twice a year, with the fussy punctuality of an old man, the income from the endowments conferred on him in three successive reigns, and in particular when Saint Louis was canonized. But the Hereditary Seneschal of Champagne was now ninety-two years old; he was practically the doyen of the high French nobility. He was half-blind and this last journey from his Château de Wassy in the Haute-Marne had tired him out. He spent most of his time dozing in the company of his two white-bearded equerries, so that all the duties had to be performed by Bouville alone.

For Queen Clémence, Bouville was linked with all her happiest memories. He had been the ambassador who had come to ask her hand in marriage and had escorted her from Naples; he was her utterly devoted confidant and probably the only true friend she had at the French Court. Bouville had perfectly understood that Clémence did not wish to leave Vincennes.

'Monseigneur,' he said to Valois, 'I can better assure the safety of the Queen in this manor with its close, surrounding walls than in the great Palace of the Cité, open to all comers. And if you are worried about the Countess Mahaut being near, I can inform you, for I am kept in touch with everything that goes on in the neighbourhood, that Madame Mahaut's wagons are at this moment being loaded for Paris.'

Valois was considerably annoyed by the air of importance Bouville had assumed since he had become Curator, and by his insistence on remaining there, stuck to his sword, by the Queen's side.

'Monsieur Hugues,' he said haughtily, 'your duty is to watch over the stomach, not to decide where the royal family shall reside, nor to defend the whole kingdom on your own.'

Not in the least perturbed, Bouville replied: 'I must also remind you, Monseigneur, that the Queen cannot appear in public until forty days have elapsed since her bereavement.'

'I know the custom as well as you do, my good man! Who said that the Queen would show herself in public? She shall travel in a closed coach. Really, Niece,' Valois cried, turning to Clémence, 'anyone would think that I was trying to send you to the country of the Great Khan, and that Vincennes was two thousand leagues from Paris!'

'You must understand, Uncle,' Clémence replied weakly, 'that living at Vincennes is my last gift from Louis. He gave me this house, in there, and you were present' – she fluttered her hand towards the room in which Louis X had died – 'that I might live in it. It seems to me that he has not really departed. You must understand that it's here that we had . . .'

But Monseigneur of Valois could not understand the claims of memory or the imaginings of sorrow.

'Your husband, for whom we pray, my dear Niece, belongs henceforth to the kingdom's past. But you carry its future. By exposing your life, you expose that of your child. Louis, who sees you from on high, would never forgive you.'

The shot went home, and Clémence sank back in her chair without another word.

But Bouville declared that he could decide nothing without the agreement of the Sire de Joinville, and sent someone to look for him. They waited several minutes. Then the door opened, and they waited again. At last, dressed in a long robe such as had been worn at the time of the Crusade, trembling in every limb, his skin mottled and like the bark of a tree, his eyes with their faded irises watering, Saint Louis's last companion-at-arms entered, dragging his feet, supported by his equerries, who tottered almost as much as he did. He was given a seat with all the respect to which he was entitled, and Valois began to explain his intentions about the Queen. The old man listened, solemnly nodding his head, obviously delighted still to have some part to play. When Valois had finished, the Seneschal fell into a meditation they were careful not to disturb; they waited for the oracle to speak. Suddenly he asked: 'But where is the King then?'

Valois looked crestfallen. So much useless trouble, and when time pressed! Did the Seneschal still understand what was said to him?

'But the King is dead, Messire de Joinville,' he replied, 'and we buried him this morning. You know that you have been appointed Curator.'

The Seneschal frowned and seemed to be making a great effort to recollect. Indeed, failure of memory was no new thing with him; when he was nearly eighty and dictating his famous *Memoirs,* he had not realized that towards the end of the second part he was repeating almost word for word what he had already said in the first.

'Yes, our young Sire Louis,' he said at last. 'He is dead. It was to himself that I presented my great book. Do you know that this is the fourth king I have seen die?'

He announced this as if it were an exploit in itself.

'Then, if the King is dead, the Queen is Regent,' he declared.

Monseigneur of Valois turned purple in the face. He had had appointed as Curators a senile idiot and a mediocrity, believing he could manage them as he wished; but he was hoist with his own petard, for it was they who were creating his worst difficulties.

'The Queen is not Regent, Messire Seneschal; she is pregnant,' he cried. 'She cannot in any circumstances be Regent until it is known whether she will give birth to a king! Look at her condition, see if she is in a fit state to carry out the duties of the kingdom!'

'You know that I see very little,' replied the old man.

With her hand to her forehead, Clémence merely thought: 'When will they stop? When will they leave me in peace?'

Joinville began explaining in what circumstances, after the death of King Louis VIII, Queen Blanche of Castile had assumed the regency, to the satisfaction of all.

'Madame Blanche of Castile, and this was only whispered, was not as pure as the image that has been created of her. It appears that Count Thibaut of Champagne, who was a good friend of Messire my father's, served her even in her bed . . .'

They had to let him talk. Though the Seneschal easily forgot what had happened the day before, he had a precise memory for the things he had been told as a small child. He had found an audience and was making the most of it. His hands, shaking with a senile trembling, clawed unceasingly at the silk of his robe over his knees.

'And even when our sainted King left for the Crusade, where I was with him . . .'

'The Queen resided in Paris during that time, did she not?' interjected Charles of Valois.

'Yes, yes . . .' said the Seneschal.

Clémence was the first to give way.

'Very well, Uncle, so be it!' she said. 'I will do as you wish and return to the Cité.'

'Ah! A wise decision at last, which I am sure Messire de Joinville approves.'

'Yes, yes . . .'

'I shall go and take the necessary measures. Your escort will be under the command of my son, Philippe, and our cousin, Robert of Artois.'

'Thank you, Uncle, thank you,' said Clémence, on the verge of collapse. 'But now, I ask you, please, let me pray.'

An hour later, the Count of Valois's orders had set the Château of Vincennes in turmoil. Wagons were being brought out of the coach-house; whips were cracking on the cruppers of the great Percheron horses; servants were running to and fro; the archers had laid down their weapons to lend a hand to the stablemen. Since the King's death they had all felt they should talk in low voices, but now everyone found an occasion to shout; and, if anyone had really wished to make an attempt on the Queen's life, this would have been the very moment to choose.

Within the manor the upholsterers were taking down the

hangings, removing the furniture, carrying out tables, dressers and chests. The officers of the Queen's household and the ladies-in-waiting were busy packing. There was to be a first convoy of twenty vehicles, and doubtless they would have to make two journeys to complete the move.

Clémence of Hungary, in the long white robe to which she was not yet accustomed, went from room to room, escorted always by Bouville. There were dust, sweat and tumult everywhere, and that sense of pillage that goes with moving house. The Bursar, inventory in hand, was superintending the dispatch of the plate and valuables which had been collected together and now covered the whole floor of a room: dishes, ewers, the dozen silver-gilt goblets Louis had had made for Clémence, the great gold reliquary containing a fragment of the True Cross, which was so heavy that the man carrying it staggered as if he were on his way to Calvary.

In the Queen's chamber the first linen-maid, Eudeline, who had been the mistress of Louis X before his marriage to Marguerite, was in charge of packing the clothes.

'What is the use of taking all these dresses, since they will never be of any use to me again?' said Clémence.

And the jewels too, packed in heavy iron chests, the brooches, rings and precious stones Louis had lavished on her during the brief period of their marriage, were all henceforth useless objects. Even the three crowns, laden with emeralds, rubies and pearls, were too high and too ornate for a widow to wear. A simple circlet of gold with short lilies, placed over her veil, would be the only jewel to which she would ever have a right.

'I have become a white Queen, as I saw my grandmother, Marie of Hungary, become,' she thought. 'But my grandmother was over sixty and had borne thirteen children. My husband will never even see his.'

'Madame,' asked Eudeline, 'am I to come with you to the Palace? No one has given me orders.'

Clémence looked at the beautiful, fair woman who, forgetting all jealousy, had been of such great help to her during the last months and particularly during Louis's illness. 'He had a child by her, and he banished her, shut her up in a nunnery. Is that why Heaven has punished us?' She felt laden with all the sins Louis had committed before he knew her, and that she was destined to redeem them by her suffering. She would have her whole life in which to pay God, with her tears, her prayers and her charity, the heavy price for Louis's soul.

'No,' she murmured, 'no, Eudeline, don't come with me. Someone who loved him must remain here.'

Then, dismissing even Bouville, she took refuge in the only quiet room, the only room left undisturbed, the chamber in which her husband had died.

It was dark behind the drawn curtains. Clémence went and knelt by the bed, placing her lips against the brocade coverlet.

Suddenly she heard a nail scratching against cloth. She felt a terror which proved to her that she still had a will to live. For a moment she remained still, holding her breath, while the scratching went on behind her. Warily she turned her head. It was the Seneschal de Joinville, who had been put in a corner of the room to wait till it was time to leave.

2

The Cardinal who Did not Believe in Hell

THE JUNE NIGHT WAS beginning to grow pale; already in the east a thin grey streak low in the sky was the harbinger of the sun, soon to rise over the city of Lyons.

It was the hour when the wagons set out for the city, bringing fruit and vegetables from the neighbouring countryside; the hour when the owls fell silent and the sparrows had not yet begun to twitter. It was also the hour when Cardinal Jacques Duèze, behind the narrow windows of one of the apartments of honour in the Abbey of Ainay, thought about death.

The Cardinal had never had much need of sleep; and as he grew older he needed still less. Three hours of sleep were quite enough. A little after midnight he rose and sat at his desk. A man of quick intellect and prodigious knowledge, trained in all the intellectual disciplines, he had composed treatises on theology, law, medicine and alchemy which carried weight among the scholars and savants of his time.

In this period, when the great hope of poor and princes

alike was the manufacture of gold, Duèze's doctrines on the elixirs for the transmutation of metals were much referred to.

'The materials from which elixirs can be made are three,' could be read in his work entitled *The Philosophers' Elixir*, 'the seven metals, the seven spirits and other things . . . The seven metals are sun, moon, copper, tin, lead, iron, and quicksilver; the seven spirits are quicksilver, sulphur, sal-ammoniac, orpiment, tutty, magnesia, marcasite; and the other things are quicksilver, human blood, horses's blood and urine, and human urine.'[2]

At seventy-two the Cardinal was still finding fields in which he had not given his thought expression, and was completing his work while others slept. He used as many candles as a whole community of monks.

During the nights he also worked at the huge correspondence which he maintained with numerous prelates, abbots, jurists, scholars, chancellors and sovereign princes all over Europe. His secretary and his copyists found their whole day's work ready for them in the morning.

Or again, he might consider the horoscope of one of his rivals in the Conclave, comparing it to his own sky, and asking the planets whether he would don the tiara. According to the stars, his greatest chance of becoming Pope was between the beginning of August and the beginning of September of the present year. And now it was already the 10th of June and nothing seemed to be shaping to that end.

Then came that painful moment before the dawn. As if he had a premonition that he would leave the world precisely at that hour, the Cardinal felt a sort of diffused distress, a vague unease both of body and of mind. In his fatigue he questioned his past actions. His memories were of an extraordinary destiny. A member of a family of burgesses of Cahors, and still completely unknown at an age at which most men in those times had already made their career, his life seemed to have begun only at forty-four, when he had left suddenly for Naples in the company of an uncle, who was going there on business. The voyage, being away from home, the discovery of Italy, had had a curious effect on him. A few days after landing, he had become the pupil of the tutor to the royal children and had thrown himself into abstract study with a passion, a frenzy, a quickness of comprehension and a precision of memory which the most intelligent adolescent might have envied. He was no more subject to hunger than he was to the need for sleep. A piece of bread had often sufficed him for a whole day, and prison life would have been perfectly agreeable to him provided he had been furnished with books. He had soon become a doctor of canon law, then a doctor of civil law, and his name had begun to be known. The Court of Naples sought the advice of the cleric from Cahors.

This thirst for knowledge was succeeded by a thirst for power. Councillor to King Charles II of Anjou-Sicily (the grandfather of Queen Clémence), then Secretary to the Secret Councils and the holder of numerous ecclesiastical benefices, he had been appointed Bishop of Fréjus ten years after his arrival, and a little later succeeded to the post of Chancellor of the kingdom of Naples, that is to say, first minister of a state which included both southern Italy and the whole county of Provence.

So fabulous a rise among the intrigues of courts had not been accomplished merely with the talents of a jurist or a theologian. An event known to but few people, since it was a secret of the Church, shows the cunning and impudence of which Duèze was capable.

A few months after the death of Charles II he had been sent on a mission to the Papal Court, at a time when the bishopric of Avignon – the most important in Christendom because it was the seat of the Holy See – happened to be vacant. Still Chancellor, and therefore the repository of the seals, he disingenuously wrote a letter in which the new King of Naples, Robert, asked for the episcopate of Avignon for Jacques Duèze. This he did in 1310. Clement V, anxious to acquire the support of Naples at a time when his relations with Philip the Fair were somewhat uneasy, had immediately acceded to the request. The fraud was discovered only when Pope Clement and King Robert met with mutual surprise, the first because he had received no thanks for so great a favour, the second because he considered the unexpected appointment, which deprived him of his Chancellor, somewhat cavalier. But it was too late. Rather than create useless scandal, King Robert turned a blind eye, preferring to keep a hold over a man who was to occupy one of the highest of ecclesiastical positions. Each had done well out of it. And now Duèze was Cardinal in Curia, and his works were studied in every university.

Yet, however astonishing his career might be, it appeared so only to those who looked on it from the outside. Days lived, whether full or empty, whether busy or serene, are but days gone by, and the ashes of the past weigh the same in every hand.

Had so much activity, ambition and expended energy any meaning, when it must all inevitably end in that Beyond of which the greatest intellects and the most abstruse of human sciences could glimpse no more than indecipherable fragments? Why should he wish to become Pope? Would it not have been wiser to retire to a cloister in detachment from the world; lay aside the pride of knowledge and the vanity of power; and acquire the humility of simple faith in order to prepare himself for death? But even meditating thus, Cardinal Duèze turned perforce to abstract speculation; and his concern with death became transformed into a juridical argument with the Deity.

'The doctors assure us,' he thought that morning, 'that the souls of the just, immediately after death, enjoy the beatific vision of God, which is their recompense. So be it, so be it. But after the end of the world, when the bodies of the dead have risen again to rejoin their souls, we are to be judged at the Last Judgment. Yet God, who is perfect, cannot sit in appeal on His own judgments. God cannot commit a mistake and be thereby compelled to cast out of Paradise the elect He has admitted already. Moreover, would it not be proper for the soul to enter into possession of the joy of the Lord only at the moment when, reunited with its body, it is itself in its nature perfect? Therefore the doctors must be wrong. Therefore there cannot be either beatitude, as such, nor the beatific vision before the end of time, and God will permit Himself to be looked on only after the Last Judgment. But, till then, where are the souls of the dead? Do we wait perhaps *sub altare Dei*, beneath that altar of God of which Saint John the Divine speaks in his Apocalypse?'

The noise of horses' hooves, a most unusual sound at that hour, echoed along the abbey walls and across the little round cobbles with which the best streets in Lyons were paved. The Cardinal listened for a moment, then relapsed into the reasoning whose consequences were indeed surprising.

'For if Paradise is empty,' he said to himself, 'it creates a singular modification in the condition of those whom we decree to be saints or blessed. And what is true for the souls of the just must necessarily be true also for the souls of the unjust. God could not punish the wicked before He has recompensed the just. The labourer receives his hire at the end of the day; and it must be at the end of the world that the wheat will be separated finally from the tares. There can be no soul at this moment living in Hell, since sentence has not yet been pronounced. And that is as much as to say that Hell, till then, does not exist.'

This proposition was peculiarly reassuring to someone thinking of death; it postponed the date of the supreme trial without destroying the prospect of eternal life, and was more or less in keeping with the intuition, common to the greater part of men, that death is a falling into a dark and immense silence, into an indefinite unconsciousness.

Clearly such a doctrine, if it were to be openly professed, could not fail to arouse violent attack both among the doctors of the Church and among the pious populace, and the moment was ill-chosen for a candidate to the Holy See to preach the inexistence of both Heaven and Hell, or their emptiness.[3]

'We shall have to await the end of the Conclave,' the Cardinal thought. He was interrupted by a monk in attendance who knocked on his door and announced the arrival of a courier from Paris.

'Whom does he come from?' asked the Cardinal.

Duèze had a smothered, strangled, utterly toneless voice, though it was perfectly distinct.

'From the Count de Bouville,' replied the monk. 'He must have ridden fast, for he looks very tired; when I went to open to him, I found him half-asleep, his forehead against the door.'

'Bring him to me at once.'

And the Cardinal, who had been meditating a few minutes before on the vanity of the ambitions of this world, immediately thought: 'Can it be on the subject of the election? Is the Court of France openly supporting my candidature? Is someone going to offer me a bargain?'

He felt excited, full of hope and curiosity; he walked up and down the room with little, rapid steps. Duèze was no taller than a boy of fifteen, and had a mouse-like face beneath thick white eyebrows and fragile bones.

Beyond the windows the sky was beginning to turn pink; it was already dawn but not yet light enough to snuff the candles. His bad hour was over.

The courier entered; at first glance, the Cardinal knew that this was no usual courier. In the first place, a professional would immediately have gone down on his knee and handed over his message-box, instead of remaining on his feet, bowing and saying, 'Monseigneur . . .' Besides, the Court of France sent its messages by strong, solidly built horsemen, well inured to hardship, such as big Robin-Cuisse-Maria, who often made the journey between Paris and Avignon, and not a stripling with a pointed nose, who seemed hardly able to keep his eyes open and reeled in his boots from fatigue.

'It looks very like a disguise,' Duèze thought. 'And what's more, I've seen that face somewhere before.'

He broke the seals of the letter with his thin short hands

and was at once disappointed. It did not concern the election. It was merely a plea for protection for the messenger. Nevertheless, he saw a favourable sign in this; when Paris desired some service from the ecclesiastical authorities, they now looked to him.

'Allora, lei è il signore Guccio Baglioni?'* he said, when he had finished reading.

The young man started to hear himself addressed in Italian.

'Si, Monsignore.'

'The Count de Bouville recommends you to me that I may take you under my protection and conceal you from the enemies who are searching for you.'

'If you will do me that favour, Monseigneur.'

'It appears that you have had an unfortunate adventure which has compelled you to fly in that livery,' went on the Cardinal in his rapid, toneless voice. 'Tell me about it. Bouville says that you formed part of his escort when he brought Queen Clémence to France. Indeed, I remember now. I saw you with him. And you are the nephew of Messire Tolomei, the Captain-General of the Lombards of Paris. Excellent, excellent! Tell me your troubles.'

He had sat down and was toying mechanically with a revolving reading-desk on which were a number of the books he used in his work. He now felt calm and relaxed, ready to distract his mind with other people's little problems.

Guccio Baglioni had ridden three hundred miles in less than four days. He could no longer feel his limbs; there was a thick fog in his head and he would have given anything in the world to stretch himself out on the floor and sleep and sleep.

* 'So you are Messire Guccio Baglioni?'

He managed to master himself; his safety, his love and his future all made it necessary that he should control his fatigue for a little longer.

'Well, Monseigneur, I married a daughter of the nobility,' he replied.

It seemed to him that these words had issued from another's lips. They were not those he would have wished to utter. He would have liked to explain to the Cardinal that an unparalleled disaster had overtaken him, that he was the most crushed and harrowed of men, that his life was threatened, that he had been separated, perhaps for ever, from the one woman without whom he could not live, that this woman was to be shut up in a convent, that events had befallen them during the last two weeks with such sudden violence that time seemed to have lost its normal dimensions, and that he felt he was hardly still living in the world he knew. And yet his whole tragedy, when it had to be put into words, was reduced to the single phrase: 'Monseigneur, I married a daughter of the nobility.'

'Indeed,' said the Cardinal, 'and what is her name?'

'Marie de Cressay.'

'Oh, Cressay; I don't know it.'

'But I had to marry her secretly, Monseigneur; her family were opposed to it.'

'Because you're a Lombard? Naturally; they're still rather old-fashioned in France. In Italy, of course . . . So you wish to obtain an annulment? Well . . . if the marriage was secret . . .'

'No, Monseigneur, I love her and she loves me,' said Guccio. 'But her family has discovered that she is with child, and her brothers have pursued me to try and kill me.'

'They may do so, they have a customary right to do so.

You have put yourself in the position of a ravisher. Who married you?'

'Father Vicenzo.'

'Fra Vicenzo? I don't know him.'

'The worst of it is, Monseigneur, that the priest is dead. So I can never prove that we are really married. But don't think I'm a coward, Monseigneur; I wanted to fight. But my uncle went and asked the advice of Messire de Bouville . . .'

'. . . who wisely advised you to go away for a time.'

'But Marie is going to be shut up in a convent! Do you think, Monseigneur, that you will be able to get her out? Do you think I shall ever see her again?'

'One thing at a time, my dear son,' replied the Cardinal, still revolving his reading-desk. 'A convent? What better place could she be in at the moment? You must trust in God's infinite mercy, of which we all stand in such great need.'

Guccio lowered his head with an exhausted air. His black hair was covered with dust.

'Has your uncle good commercial relations with the Bardi?' went on the Cardinal.

'Indeed yes, Monseigneur. The Bardi are your bankers, I believe,' replied Guccio with automatic politeness.

'Yes, they are my bankers. But I find them less easy to deal with these days than they were in the past. They've become such an enormous concern! They have branches everywhere. And they have to refer to Florence for the smallest demand. They're as slow as an Ecclesiastical Court. Has your uncle many prelates among his customers?'

Guccio's cares were far removed from the bank. The fog was growing thicker in his head; his eyelids were burning.

'We have mostly the great barons,' he said, 'the Count of

Valois, the Count of Artois. We should be greatly honoured, Monseigneur . . .'

'We'll talk of that later. For the moment you're in the shelter of this monastery. You will pass for a man in my employ; perhaps we'll make you wear a clerk's robe. I'll talk to my chaplain about it. You can take off that livery and go and sleep in peace; that appears to be what you need the most.'

Guccio bowed, muttered a few words of gratitude and went to the door. Then, coming to a halt, he said: 'I can't undress yet, Monseigneur; I've got another message to deliver.'

'To whom?' asked Duèze somewhat suspiciously.

'To the Count of Poitiers.'

'Give me the letter; I'll send it later by one of the brothers.'

'But, Monseigneur, Messire de Bouville was very insistent . . .'

'Do you know if the message concerns the Conclave?'

'Oh, no, Monseigneur! It's about the King's death.'

The Cardinal leapt from his chair.

'King Louis is dead? But why didn't you say so at once?'

'Isn't it known here? I thought you would have been informed, Monseigneur.'

In fact, he wasn't thinking at all. His misfortunes and his fatigue had made him forget this capital event. He had galloped all the way from Paris, changing horses in the monasteries whose names he had been given, eating hastily and talking as little as possible. Without knowing it, he had forestalled the official couriers.

'What did he die of?'

'That's precisely what Messire de Bouville wants to tell the Count of Poitiers.'

'Murder?' whispered Duèze.

'It seems the King was poisoned.'

The Cardinal thought for a moment.

'That may alter many things,' he murmured. 'Has a regent been appointed?'

'I don't know, Monseigneur. When I left, everyone was talking of the Count of Valois.'

'All right, my dear son, go and rest.'

'But, Monseigneur, what about the Count of Poitiers?'

The prelate's thin lips sketched a rapid smile, which might have passed for an expression of goodwill.

'It would not be prudent for you to show yourself; moreover, you're dropping with fatigue,' he said. 'Give me the letter; and so that no one can reproach you, I'll give it him myself.'

A few minutes later, preceded by a linkman, as his dignity required, and followed by a secretary, the Cardinal in Curia left the Abbey of Ainay, between the Rhône and the Saône, and went out into the dark alleys, which were often made narrower still by heaps of filth. Thin and slight, he seemed to skip along, almost running in spite of his seventy-two years. His purple robe appeared to dance between the walls.

The bells of the twenty churches and forty-two monasteries of Lyons rang for the first office. Distances were short in this city, which numbered barely twenty thousand inhabitants, of whom half were engaged in the commerce of religion and the other half in the religion of commerce. The Cardinal soon reached the house of the Consul, where lodged the Count of Poitiers.

3

The Gates of Lyons

THE COUNT OF POITIERS was just finishing dressing when his chamberlain announced the Cardinal's visit.

Very tall, very thin, with a prominent nose, his hair lying across his forehead in short locks and falling in curls about his cheeks, his skin fresh as it may be at twenty-three, the young Prince, clothed in a dressing-gown of shot *camocas*, greeted Monseigneur Duèze, kissing his ring with deference.

It would have been difficult to find a greater contrast, a more ironical dissimilarity than between these two figures, one like a ferret just emerged from its earth, the other like a heron stalking haughtily across the marshes.

'In spite of the early hour, Monseigneur,' said the Cardinal, 'I did not wish to defer bringing you my prayers in the loss you have suffered.'

'The loss?' said Philippe of Poitiers with a slight start.

His first thought was for his wife, Jeanne, whom he had left in Paris and who had been pregnant for eight months.

'I see that I have done well to come and tell you,' went

on Duèze. 'The King, your brother, died five days ago.'

Philippe stood perfectly still; his chest barely moved as he drew a deep breath. His face was expressionless, showing no surprise or emotion – or even impatience for further details.

'I am grateful to you for your alacrity, Monseigneur,' he replied. 'But how have you managed to hear the news before myself?'

'From Messire de Bouville, whose messenger has ridden in haste so that I may give you this letter secretly.'

The Count of Poitiers broke the seals and read the letter, holding it close to his nose for he was very short-sighted. Again, he betrayed no sign of emotion; when he had finished reading, he merely slipped the letter into his gown. But he said no word.

The Cardinal also remained silent, pretending to respect the Prince's sorrow, although he showed no great signs of affliction.

'God preserve him from the pains of Hell,' said the Count of Poitiers at last, to complement the prelate's devout expression.

'Yes . . . Hell,' Duèze murmured. 'Anyway, let us pray to God. I am also thinking of the unfortunate Queen Clémence, whom I saw grow up when I was with the King of Naples. So sweet and perfect a Princess . . .'

'Yes, it's a great misfortune for my sister-in-law,' said Poitiers. And as he said it, he thought: 'Louis has left no testamentary disposition for a regency. Already, from what Bouville writes, my Uncle Valois is at work . . .'

'What are you going to do, Monseigneur? Will you return to Paris immediately?' the Cardinal asked.

'I don't know, I don't yet know,' replied Poitiers. 'I shall wait for more information. I shall hold myself at the disposition of the kingdom.'

In his letter Bouville had not concealed the fact that he wished for Poitiers's return. As the elder of the dead King's brothers, and as a peer of the kingdom, Poitiers's place was at the Council of the Crown in which, at the very first meeting, dissension had broken out over the appointment of a regent.

But, on the other hand, Philippe of Poitiers felt regret, even reluctance, at having to leave Lyons before he had completed the tasks he had undertaken.

In the first place he had to conclude the contract of betrothal between his third daughter, Isabelle, who was barely five years of age, and the Dauphiniet of Viennois, the little Guigues, who was six. He had negotiated this marriage, at Vienne itself, with the Dauphin Jean II de la Tour du Pin and the Dauphine Beatrice, sister of Queen Clémence. It was a good alliance, which would allow the Crown of France to counterbalance the influence of Anjou-Sicily in this region. The document was to be signed in a few days' time.[4]

And then, above all, there was the papal election. During the last weeks Philippe of Poitiers had journeyed backwards and forwards across Provence, Viennois and Lyonnais, interviewing each of the twenty-four scattered Cardinals in turn;[5] assuring them that the aggression of Carpentras would not be repeated and that they would be subjected to no violence; giving many of them to understand that they might have a chance of election and pleading for the prestige of the Faith, the dignity of the Church and the interests of the States. Ultimately, as a result of much effort, talk and money, he had succeeded in gathering them at Lyons, a town which had long been under ecclesiastical authority but had passed recently, during the last years of Philip the Fair, into the power of the King of France.

The Count of Poitiers felt that he was on the point of reaching his goal. But if he left, would not the dissensions begin all over again, personal hatreds flourish once more, the influence of the Roman nobility or that of the King of Naples supplant that of France, while the various parties accused each other of heresy? Would not the papacy return to Rome? 'Which my father so much wished to avoid,' Philippe of Poitiers said to himself. 'Is his work, already so much damaged by Louis and by our Uncle Valois, to be destroyed completely?'

For a few moments Cardinal Duèze felt that the young man had forgotten his presence. But suddenly Poitiers asked: 'Will the Gascon party maintain the candidature of Cardinal de Pélagrue? Do you think that your pious colleagues are at last prepared to sit in Conclave? Sit down here, Monseigneur, and tell me your thoughts on the matter. How far have we advanced?'

The Cardinal had seen many sovereigns and ministers during the third of a century he had been concerned with the affairs of kingdoms, but he had never before met one with such self-control. Here was a Prince, aged twenty-three, to whom he had just announced the death of his brother and the vacancy of the throne, and he seemed to have no more urgent concern than the complications of the Conclave.

Sitting side by side near a window, on a chest covered with damask, the Cardinal's feet barely touching the ground and the Count of Poitiers's thin ankle slowly moving from side to side, the two men had a long conversation. It appeared from Duèze's summary of the situation that they were more or less back where they had been two years ago, after the death of Clement V.

The party of the ten Gascon Cardinals, which was also called the French Party, was still the largest, but not large enough by itself to ensure the necessary majority of two-thirds of the Sacred College: sixteen votes. The Gascons considered themselves the depositories of the late Pope's thought. They all owed their hats to him, held out firmly for the see of Avignon and showed themselves remarkably united against the other two parties. But there was a good deal of secret competition among them; the ambitions of Arnaud de Fougères, Arnaud Nouvel and Arnaud de Pélagrue all flourished. They made mutual promises while scheming for one another's downfall.

'The war of the three Arnauds,' said Duèze in his whispering voice. 'Now let's have a look at the Italian Party.'

There were only eight of them, but divided into three sections. The redoubtable Cardinal Caetani, nephew of Pope Boniface VIII, was opposed to the two Cardinals Colonna by a time-honoured family feud which had become an inexorable hatred since the Anagni affair and the blow in the face Colonna had given Boniface. The other Italians wavered between these adversaries. Stefaneschi, from hostility to Philip the Fair's policy, supported Caetani, whose relation moreover he was. Napoléon Orsini tacked about. The eight were only agreed on a single point: the return of the papacy to the Eternal City. On that point they were fiercely determined.

'You know well, Monseigneur,' continued Duèze, 'that at one moment we ran the risk of schism; and indeed we still do so. Our Italians refused to meet in France and they let it be known, but a little while ago, that if a Gascon Pope were elected, they would refuse him recognition and would set up a Pope of their own in Rome.'

'There will be no schism,' said the Count of Poitiers calmly.

'Thanks to you, Monseigneur, thanks to you. I am happy to recognize it, and I tell everyone so. Going, as you have, from town to town with sage advice, if you have not yet found the shepherd, you have at least gathered the flock.'

'Expensive sheep, Monseigneur! Do you know that I left Paris with sixteen thousand *livres*, and that only the other week I had to have as much again sent to me? Jason was nothing compared to me. I hope that all these golden fleeces won't slip through my fingers,' said the Count of Poitiers, screwing up his eyes slightly to look the Cardinal in the face.

The Cardinal, who had done very well out of this largesse by roundabout ways, did not take up the allusion directly but replied: 'I think that Napoléon Orsini and Albertini de Prato, and perhaps even Guillaume de Longis, who was Chancellor to the King of Naples before me, might be fairly easily detached. Avoiding schism is worth the price.'

Poitiers thought: 'He has used the money we gave him to acquire three of the Italian votes. It's clever of him.'

As for Caetani, though he continued to play an implacable game, he was not in so strong a position since his practice of sorcery and his attempt to cast a spell on the King of France and the Count of Poitiers himself had been discovered. The ex-Templar Everard, a half-wit, whom Caetani had used for his devilish work, had talked rather too much before giving himself up to the King's men.

'I am holding that matter in reserve,' said the Count of Poitiers. 'The smell of the faggots might, at the right moment, make Monseigneur Caetani a little more pliant.'

At the thought of seeing another Cardinal grilled, a very slight and furtive smile passed over the aged prelate's thin lips.

'It seems that Francesco Caetani', he went on, 'has quite abandoned God's affairs to devote himself entirely to Satan's. Do you think that, having failed with sorcery, he managed to strike at the King, your brother, with poison?'

The Count of Poitiers shrugged his shoulders.

'Whenever a king dies, it's asserted that he was poisoned,' he said. 'It was said of my ancestor, Louis VIII; it was said of my father, whom God keep. My brother's health was poor enough. Still, one must take the possibility into account.'

'Finally,' Duèze went on, 'there is the third party, which is called Provençal because of the most turbulent among us, Cardinal de Mandagout.'

This last party numbered only six Cardinals of diverse origin; southerners, such as the brothers Bérenger Frédol, were allied in it with Normans and with one member from Quercy, Duèze himself.

The gold lavished on them by Philippe of Poitiers had made them more receptive to the arguments of French policy.

'We are the smallest, we are the weakest,' said Duèze, 'but our votes are decisive in any majority. And since the Gascons and the Italians each refuse to elect a Pope from the other party, then, Monseigneur . . .'

'They'll have to take a Pope from your party, won't they?'

'I believe so, I firmly believe so. I've said so ever since Clement died. No one listened to me; doubtless people thought I was preaching on my own behalf, for indeed my name had been mentioned without my wishing it. But the Court of France has never placed much confidence in me.'

'It was because you were rather too openly supported by the Court of Naples, Monseigneur.'

'And had I not been supported by someone, Monseigneur, who would have paid any heed to me at all? Believe me, I have no other ambition than to see a little order restored to the affairs of Christendom which are in a bad way; it will be a heavy task for the next successor to Saint Peter.'

The Count of Poitiers clasped his long hands together before his face and thought for a few seconds.

'Do you think, Monseigneur,' he asked, 'that the Italians would agree to the Holy See remaining in Avignon in return for the satisfaction of not having a Gascon Pope, and that the Gascons, in return for the certainty of Avignon, would agree to renounce their own candidate and rally to your third party?'

By which he in fact meant: 'If you, Monseigneur Duèze, became Pope with my support, would you formally agree to preserving the present residence of the papacy?'

Duèze perfectly understood.

'It would, Monseigneur,' he replied, 'be the wise solution.'

'I am grateful for your valuable advice,' said Philippe of Poitiers, rising to his feet to put an end to the audience.

He showed the Cardinal out.

When two men, who to all seeming are utterly diverse in age, appearance, experience and position, recognize each other as of similar quality and believe that mutual collaboration and friendship are possible between them, it is due more to the mysterious conjunctions of destiny than to the words they may exchange.

When Philippe bowed to kiss his ring, the Cardinal murmured, 'You would make an excellent regent, Monseigneur.'

Philippe straightened up. 'Does he realize that I have been thinking all this time of nothing else?' he wondered. And he replied: 'Would you not yourself, Monseigneur, make an excellent Pope?'

And they could not help smiling discreetly to each other, the old man with a sort of paternal affection, the young man with friendly deference.

'I will be beholden to you,' Philippe added, 'if you will keep secret the grave news you have brought me until it is publicly announced.'

'I will do so, Monseigneur, in order to serve you.'

Left alone, the Count of Poitiers reflected only for a few seconds. Then he summoned his first chamberlain.

'Adam Héron, has no courier arrived from Paris?' he asked.

'No, Monseigneur.'

'Then close all the gates of Lyons.'

4

Let us Dry our Tears

THAT MORNING THE PEOPLE of Lyons were without vegetables. The market-gardeners' wagons had been stopped outside the walls, and the housewives were clamouring in the empty markets. The only bridge, that over the Saône (for the one over the Rhône had not yet been completed), was barred by soldiery. But if one could not enter Lyons, one could not leave it either. Italian merchants, travellers, itinerant friars, reinforced by loungers and idlers, gathered about the gates and demanded an explanation. The guard invariably replied: 'The Count of Poitiers's orders,' with the distant and important air that agents of authority tend to adopt when executing an order they do not understand.

People were shouting:

'But my daughter is ill at Fouvière . . .'

'My barn at Saint-Just burned down yesterday at vespers . . .'

'The bailiff of Villefranche will have me arrested if I don't take him my poll-tax today . . .'

'The Count of Poitiers's orders!'

And when the crowd began to press forward, the royal sergeants-at-arms raised their maces.

There were strange rumours going round the town.

Some declared that there was going to be war. But with whom? No one could say. Others asserted that a bloody riot had taken place during the night near the Augustinian monastery between the King's men and those of the Italian Cardinals. Horses had been heard going by. Even the number of the dead was mentioned. But at the Augustinians' all was quiet.

The Archbishop, Pierre de Savoie, was very anxious, wondering whether the events which had taken place before 1312 were about to begin all over again and whether he would be compelled to abandon, to the advantage of the archbishopric of Sens, the primacy of the Gaules, the only prerogative he had succeeded in preserving when Lyons had been attached to the Crown.[6] He had sent one of his canons for news; but the canon, having gone to the Count of Poitiers's lodging, had been met by a curtly silent equerry. And now the Archbishop was expecting an ultimatum.

The Cardinals, who were lodged in various religious houses, were no less anxious and, indeed, inclined to panic. Were they to be treated as they had been at Carpentras? But how could they escape this time? Messengers rushed from the Augustinians to the Franciscans and from the Jacobins to the Carthusians. Cardinal Caetani had sent his general assistant, the Abbé Pierre, to Napoléon Orsini, to Albertini de Prato and to Flisco, the only Spaniard, with orders to say to those prelates: 'Look what has happened! You let yourselves be persuaded by the Count of Poitiers. He swore not to molest us, that we should not even have to go into seclusion to vote, and that we should be completely free. And now he has shut us up in Lyons!'

Duèze himself received the visit of two of his Provençal colleagues, Cardinal de Mandagout and Bérenger Frédol, the elder. But Duèze pretended to have but just emerged from his theological studies and to know nothing. During this time, in a cell near the Cardinal's apartment, Guccio Baglioni was sleeping like a log, in no state to speculate what might be the cause of all the panic.

For the last hour Messire Varay, Consul of Lyons,[7] and three of his colleagues, who had come to ask for an explanation in the name of the City Council, had been kept waiting in the Count of Poitiers's antechamber.

The Count was sitting *in camera* with the members of his entourage and the great officers who were part of his delegation.

At last the hangings parted and the Count of Poitiers appeared, followed by his councillors. They all wore the grave expressions of men who had just reached an important political decision.

'Ah, Messire Varay, you have come at the right moment, and you too, Messires Consuls,' said the Count of Poitiers. 'We can give you at once the message we were about to send you. Messire Mille, will you be so good as to read it?'

Mille de Noyers, a jurist, a Councillor of Parliament and Marshal of the East under Philip the Fair, unrolled the parchment and read as follows:

"'To all the Bailiffs, Seneschals, and Councils of loyal towns. We would have you know the great sorrow that has befallen us by the death of our well-beloved brother, the King, our

Lord Louis X, whom God has removed from the affection of his subjects. But human nature is such that no one may outlive the term assigned him. Thus we have decided to dry our tears, to pray with you to Christ for his soul, and to show ourselves assiduous for the government of the Kingdom of France and the Kingdom of Navarre that their rights may not perish, and that the subjects of these two kingdoms may live happily beneath the buckler of justice and of peace.

"The Regent of the two Kingdoms, by the Grace of God.
PHILIPPE"

When they had recovered from their astonishment, Messire Varay immediately came forward and kissed the Count of Poitiers's hand; then the other Consuls unhesitatingly followed suit.

The King was dead. The news was so surprising in itself that no one thought, for several minutes at least, of questioning it. In the absence of an heir who was of age, it seemed perfectly normal that the elder of the sovereign's brothers should assume power. The Consuls did not for a moment doubt that the decision had been taken in Paris by the Chamber of Peers.

'Have this message cried in the town,' Philippe of Poitiers ordered; 'which done, the gates will be immediately opened.'

Then he added: 'Messire Varay, you hold a great position in the cloth trade; I should be glad if you would furnish me with twenty black cloaks which may be placed in the antechamber to clothe those who come to condole with me.'

He then dismissed the Consuls.

The two first acts of his seizure of power had been accomplished. He had been proclaimed Regent by his entourage, who became thereby his Council of Government. He would be recognized by the City of Lyons in which he was staying. He was now in a hurry to extend this recognition over the whole kingdom and thus place the accomplished fact before Paris. It was a question of speed.

Already the copyists were reproducing his proclamation in considerable quantities, and the couriers were saddling their horses to ride with it into every province.

As soon as the gates of Lyons were opened, they hastily set out, passing three couriers who had been kept on the other side of the Saône since morning. The first of them carried a letter from the Count of Valois, announcing himself as the Regent appointed by the Council of the Crown, and asking Philippe to agree, so that the appointment might become effective. 'I am sure that you will wish to help me in my task for the good of the kingdom, and will give me your agreement as soon as possible, like the good and well-beloved nephew you are.'

The second message came from the Duke of Burgundy, who also claimed the regency in the name of his niece, the little Jeanne of Navarre.

Finally, the Count of Evreux informed Philippe of Poitiers that the peers had not sat in accordance with custom and precedent, and that Charles of Valois's haste to seize the reins of government was supported by no legal document or assembly.

The Count of Poitiers had immediately gone into council again with his entourage. It was composed of men who were hostile to the policies pursued by the Hutin and the Count of Valois during the last eighteen months. In the first place, there was the Constable of France, Gaucher de Châtillon,

Commander of the Armies since 1302, who could not forgive the ridiculous campaign of the 'Muddy Army' which he had been compelled to conduct in Flanders the preceding summer. Then there was his brother-in-law, Mille de Noyers, who shared his feelings. Then, the jurist Raoul de Presles who, after rendering so many services to the Iron King, had had his goods confiscated, while his friend Enguerrand de Marigny had been hanged and he himself had been put to the question by water though no confession had been extracted from him; as a result, he suffered from permanent stomach-pains and bore the ex-Emperor of Constantinople a considerable grudge. He owed his safety and his return to favour to the Count of Poitiers.

Thus a sort of opposition party, which included the survivors among the great councillors of Philip the Fair, had formed about the Count of Poitiers. No one looked kindly on the ambitions of the Count of Valois or indeed wanted the Duke of Burgundy to meddle in the affairs of the Crown. They admired the speed with which the young Prince had acted and they placed their hopes in him.

Poitiers wrote to Eudes of Burgundy and to Charles of Valois, without mentioning their letters, indeed as if he had not received them, to inform them that he considered himself Regent by natural right, and that he would summon the Assembly of Peers to give him its sanction as soon as possible.

In the meantime he appointed commissaries to go to the principal cities of the kingdom and assume authority in his name. Thus that day saw the departure of several of his knights – who were later to become his 'Knights Pursuivant'[8] – such as Regnault de Lor, Thomas de Marfontaine and Guillaume

Courteheuse. He kept with him Anseau de Joinville, the son of the great Joinville, and Henry de Sully.

While the knell tolled from all the steeples, Philippe of Poitiers conferred for a long time with Gaucher de Châtillon. The Constable of France sat by right on every government assembly, the Chamber of Peers, the Grand Council and the Small Council. Philippe, therefore, asked Gaucher to go to Paris to represent him and oppose Charles of Valois's usurpation until his own arrival; moreover, the Constable would make sure that all the troops in the capital, particularly the Corps of Crossbowmen, were under his control.

For the new Regent, at first to the surprise, but then to the approbation, of his councillors, had determined to remain temporarily in Lyons.

'We cannot leave the tasks we have in hand,' he had declared; 'the most important thing for the kingdom is to have a Pope, and we shall be all the stronger when we have made him.'

He hurried on the signature of the contract of betrothal between his daughter and the Dauphiniet. At first sight this seemed to have no connection with the pontifical election, yet in Philippe's mind they were linked. The alliance with the Dauphin of Viennois, who ruled over all the territories south of Lyons and controlled the road to Italy, was a move in his game. If the Cardinals took it into their heads to slip through his fingers, they would not be able to take refuge in that direction. Furthermore, the betrothal consolidated his position as Regent; the Dauphin would be in his camp and would have sound reasons for not abandoning him.

Because of mourning the contract was signed during the following days without festivities.

At the same time Philippe of Poitiers negotiated with the most powerful baron of the region, the Count de Forez, who was also a brother-in-law of the Dauphin, and held the right bank of the Rhône.

Jean de Forez had fought in the campaign in Flanders, had several times represented Philip the Fair at the Papal Court, and had done very good work in getting Lyons ceded to the Crown. The Count of Poitiers knew that as soon as he resumed his father's policy he could count on him.

On the 16th of June the Count de Forez performed a highly spectacular gesture. He paid solemn homage to Philippe as the suzerain of all the suzerains of France, thus recognizing him as the holder of the royal authority.

The following day Count Bermond de la Voulte, whose fief of Pierregourde was in the seneschalship of Lyons, placed his hands between those of the Count of Poitiers and swore him a similar oath of loyalty.

Poitiers asked the Count de Forez to hold ready seven hundred men-at-arms in secret. The Cardinals would not now be able to escape from the town.

Nevertheless, there was still a long way to go before an election was achieved. Negotiations lagged. The Italians, feeling that the Regent was in haste to return to Paris, had hardened in their position. 'He'll tire first,' they said. Little they cared for the tragic state of anarchy in which the affairs of the Church were foundering.

Philippe of Poitiers had several interviews with Cardinal Duèze, who seemed to him much the most intelligent member of the Conclave, at once the most lucid and the most imaginative expert in religious matters, and the most desirable administrator for Christendom in these difficult times.

'Heresy is flourishing everywhere, Monseigneur,' said the Cardinal in his cracked, disquieting voice. 'And how could it be otherwise with the example we give? The Devil takes advantage of our discord to sow his tares. But it is above all in the diocese of Toulouse that they flourish the most vigorously. It is an old land of rebellion and nightmare! The next Pope should divide that too-extensive diocese, so difficult to govern, into five bishoprics, placed in firm hands.'

'Which would create a number of new benefices,' replied the Count of Poitiers, 'from which, of course, the Treasury of France would receive the annates. You see no objection to that?'

'None.'

The first year's revenues from new ecclesiastical benefices were called 'annates', which the King had a right to collect. The absence of a Pope prevented appointments being made to these benefices, which was a considerable loss to the Treasury, without taking into account the near-impossibility of collecting the arrears of taxes from the Church, while the clergy took advantage of the situation to raise every kind of difficulty which could not be resolved so long as the throne of Saint Peter was vacant. And indeed, when Philippe and Duèze considered the future, one as Regent, the other as eventual Pontiff, finance was the first concern of both.

Owing to the feudal rebellions, the revolt of the Flemings, the insurrection of the nobles of Artois and the brilliant inspirations of Charles of Valois, the royal Treasury was not only empty, but indebted for several years to come.

The papal Treasury, after two years of errant Conclave, was in no better state; and if the Cardinals sold themselves dearly to the princes of this world, it was because many of them no longer had any means of subsistence other than bartering their votes.

'Fines, Monseigneur, fines,' Duèze counselled the young Regent. 'Fine those who have misbehaved, and the richer they are, the more heavily. If someone should break the law who has a hundred *livres*, take twenty; if he has a thousand, take five hundred; and should he have a hundred thousand, take practically all that he has. You'll find that this policy has three advantages: in the first place, the yield will be the greater; in the second, deprived of his power, the malefactor will no longer be able to abuse it; and, finally, the poor, of whom there are great numbers, will be on your side and place confidence in your justice.'

Philippe of Poitiers smiled.

'What you so wisely suggest, Monseigneur, may be most suitable to royal justice which is a secular arm,' he replied, 'but in order to restore the finances of the Church, I do not see . . .'

'Fines, fines,' repeated Duèze. 'Let us place a tax on sin; it will be an inexhaustible source of revenue. Man is sinful by nature, but more disposed to penitence of the heart than of the purse. He will regret his sins the more keenly, and be the more hesitant to relapse into error, if our absolutions are accompanied by a tax. Whoever wishes to reform must pay for the privilege.'

'Is he joking?' thought Poitiers, who, as he saw more of Duèze, was discovering the Cardinal in Curia's liking for paradox and mystification.

'And what sins do you propose taxing, Monseigneur?' he asked, as if he were joining in the game.

'In the first place those committed by the clergy. We must

begin by reforming ourselves before we undertake to reform others. Our Holy Mother is too tolerant of shortcomings and abuses. Thus, neither holy orders nor priesthood may be given to men who are mutilated or deformed. And yet, the other day, I saw a certain Abbé Pierre, who is with Cardinal Caetani, with two thumbs on his left hand.'

'A little hit at our old enemy,' thought Poitiers.

'I have made inquiries,' Duèze went on, 'and it appears that the halt, the maimed and the eunuchs who conceal their misfortune beneath a habit, and indeed are beneficed by the Church, are legion. Are we to cast them from our bosom rather than efface their fault, reduce them to penury and perhaps throw them into the arms of the heretics of Toulouse or similar religious confraternities? Let us permit them rather to redeem themselves; and to redeem is to pay.'

The old prelate was perfectly serious. His imagination, stimulated by his meeting with the Abbé Pierre, had created, during these last nights, a complete and precise system on which he intended writing a memorandum to be submitted, so he modestly said, to the next Pope.

It was to create a Holy Office of Penitentiary, which would bring in revenue to the Holy See from bulls of absolution of all kinds. Mutilated priests might obtain absolution at the rate of a few *livres* for a missing finger, twice as much for a lost eye, and the same for the absence of one or both testicles. A priest who had castrated himself would have to pay a higher price. From bodily infirmities Duèze passed to those of the soul. Bastards who had concealed their condition when receiving orders, priests who had taken the tonsure though married, priests who married secretly after ordination while it was still current, priests who lived unmarried with a woman, priests who were bigamists, or incestuous, or sodomites, would all be taxed proportionately to their sin. Nuns who had wantoned with several men, either within or without their convent, would be subject to particularly costly rehabilitation.[9]

'If the creation of this Penitentiary', declared Duèze, 'does not bring in two hundred thousand *livres* the first year, I'll be . . .'

He was going to say 'I'll be burnt', but stopped in time.

'At least,' thought Poitiers, 'if he's elected, I shall have no need to be concerned for the papal finances.'

But in spite of all Duèze's manoeuvres, and in spite of the support Poitiers gave him secretly, the Conclave still marked time.

Moreover, the news from Paris was far from good. Gaucher de Châtillon, making common front with the Count of Evreux and Mahaut of Artois, was doing his best to put a brake on Charles of Valois's ambitions. But Charles was living in the Palace of the Cité, where he had Queen Clémence at his mercy; he was running affairs as he pleased, and sending out to the provinces instructions contrary to those sent by Poitiers from Lyons. Moreover, the Duke of Burgundy had arrived in Paris, on the 16th of June, to establish his rights; he knew that he had the support of the vassals of his huge duchy. France, therefore, had three regents. This situation could not continue for long, and Gaucher asked Philippe to return to Paris.

On the 27th of June, after a restricted council meeting, attended by the Count de Forez and the Count de la Voulte, the young Prince decided to set out as soon as possible, and ordered his escort's baggage-train to be assembled. At the same time, learning that no solemn mass had yet been held for the repose of his brother's soul, he ordered masses to be said on the following day, before his departure, in every parish in the town. All the high and low clergy were expected to attend to join their prayers with the Regent's.

The Cardinals, particularly the Italians, were delighted. Philippe of Poitiers was being compelled to leave Lyons without having made them give way.

'He is concealing his flight under the pomp of mourning,' said Caetani, 'but let him go all the same, that accursed young man. He thought he held us in the hollow of his hand. I assure you that we shall be back in Rome before the month is out.'

5

The Gates of the Conclave

CARDINALS ARE IMPORTANT PEOPLE who must not be mixed with the small fry of the clergy. The Count of Poitiers had ordered that the church of the monastery of the Predicant Friars, called the Church of the Jacobins,[10] the most beautiful, the largest, after the Primatial Saint-Jean, and also the best fortified, should be reserved to them for the service to the memory of Louis X. The Cardinals saw in this selection no more than normal respect for their dignity. None was absent from the ceremony.

They numbered but twenty-four and yet the church was full, for each Cardinal was escorted by his whole household – chaplain, secretary, treasurer, clerks, pages, valets, linkmen and trainbearers: nearly six hundred people in all were assembled between the massive white pillars.

Rarely had a funeral mass been followed with so little peaceful meditation. It was the first time for many months that the Cardinals, who had been living in cliques in separate residences, had found themselves all gathered together. Some had not seen each other for nearly two years. They watched each other, quizzed each other, commented on each other's actions and appearance.

'Did you see that?' someone would whisper. 'Orsini has greeted the younger Frédol. Stefaneschi has been talking for quite a while to Mandagout. Are they rallying to the Provençaux? But Duèze doesn't look at all well; he's grown much older.'

And, indeed, Jacques Duèze was making an effort to control his youthful lightness of foot, and walked in with slow step, replying to greetings vaguely, as if he were already detached from this world.

Guccio Baglioni, dressed as a page, formed part of his suite. He was supposed to speak nothing but Italian and to have come straight from Sienna.

'Perhaps I should have done better,' thought Guccio, 'to have put myself under the Count of Poitiers's protection, for I should certainly have gone back to Paris with him today and I should have been able to make inquiries about Marie, of whom I have had no news for so long. Instead of which, here I am, entirely dependent on this old fox, to whom I have promised my uncle's money, but who will do nothing for me till the money has arrived. And my uncle does not reply. They say that Paris is in turmoil. Marie, Marie, my beautiful Marie! She'll think I've abandoned her. Perhaps she even hates me now? What have they done with her?'

He imagined her shut up at Cressay by her brothers, or in some convent for Magdalens. 'Another week like this, and I shall go back to Paris.'

Duèze turned every now and then to look behind him with a curiously alert expression.

'Are you afraid of something, Monseigneur?' Guccio asked.

'No, no, I fear nothing,' replied the Cardinal, who began secretly observing his neighbours.

The redoubtable Cardinal Caetani, with his thin face divided by a long aquiline nose, and his hair which seemed to shoot out like white flames from the edge of his red skull-cap, made no attempt to conceal his triumph. The catafalque, symbol of Louis X's death, corresponded in his mind to the waxen doll, pierced with pins, with which he had cast a spell. The glances he exchanged with his following, the Abbé Pierre, Father Bost and the clerk Andrieu, his secretary, were those of victory. He wanted to say to all those present: 'This, Messeigneurs, is what happens when you attract the vengeance of the Caetani, who were already powerful at the time of Julius Caesar.'

The two brothers Colonna, each heavy chin divided by a vertical cleft, looked like warriors disguised as prelates.

The Count of Poitiers had not economized on the choir. There were a full hundred of them, their voices sounding above the organ, which had four men pumping at its bellows. A royal, reverberating music echoed among the vaults, saturated the air with vibrations, and enveloped the crowd. The junior clerks could gossip among themselves with impunity, and the pages laugh or mock their masters. It was impossible to hear what was being said three paces away, and still less what was taking place at the doors.

The service came to an end; the organ and the choir fell silent. Both wings of the great door stood open; but no daylight penetrated into the church.

Suddenly, the Cardinals understood; and an angry clamour broke out. A brand-new wall blocked the doorway. During the mass, the Regent had bricked up the exits. All occurred during the ceremony, obscuring the sun. The Cardinals were prisoners.

There was a fine panic; prelates, canons, priests and valets, all mingled together, ran to and fro like rats in a trap. The pages, climbing on each other's shoulders, hoisted themselves up to the windows, from where they shouted: 'The church is surrounded by armed men!'

'What are we going to do, what are we going to do?' groaned the Cardinals. 'The Regent has played a trick on us.'

'That's why he favoured us with such loud music!'

'It's an attack on the Church. What are we going to do?'

'We'll excommunicate him,' cried Caetani.

'But what if he starves us to death, or has us massacred?'

The two brothers Colonna and the people of their party had already armed themselves with heavy bronze candelabra, benches and processional maces, determined to sell their lives dearly. The Italians and the Gascons were already beginning to hurl reproaches at each other.

'All this is your fault,' cried the Italians. 'If you had only refused to come to Lyons. We knew some dastardly trick would be played on us.'

'If you had elected one of us, we should not be here now,' replied the Gascons.

'It's your fault, you bad Christians!'

They were almost on the point of coming to blows.

One door alone had not been entirely blocked; barely room for a man to pass through had been left, but the narrow opening was a hedge of pikes held in iron gauntlets. The pikes lifted and the Count de Forez, in armour, followed by

Bermond de la Voulte and a few more armed men, entered the church. They were received with a volley of threats and obscene insults.

His hands crossed on the hilt of his sword, the Count de Forez waited till the clamour died down. He was a strong, courageous man, unmoved by threats or entreaties, profoundly shocked by the example the Cardinals had given during the last two years, and prepared to go to any length to obey the Count of Poitiers's instructions. His rugged, wrinkled face appeared through his open visor.

When the Cardinals and their people had grown hoarse, his voice rang out over their heads, precise and emphatic, reaching to the end of the nave.

'Messeigneurs, I am here on the orders of the Regent of France to ask you to devote yourselves henceforth solely to electing a Pope, and to inform you that you will not leave here until that Pope is elected. Each Cardinal may keep with him only one chaplain and two pages or clerks of his choice to serve him. Everyone else will leave.'

The Gascons and the Provençaux were no less indignant than the Italians.

'It's a felony!' cried Cardinal de Pélagrue. 'The Count of Poitiers promised us that we should not even have to go into seclusion, and it was because of it that we agreed to meet him at Lyons.'

'The Count of Poitiers', replied Jean de Forez, 'was then speaking in the name of the King of France. But the King of France is dead, and it is in the name of the Regent that I am speaking to you today.'

There was unanimous indignation among his hearers. There were oaths in Italian, Provençal and French. Cardinal

Duèze had fallen prostrate in a confessional, his hand to his heart, as if his years could not bear the shock, and he pretended to join in the protests with inaudible murmurs. Arnaud d'Auch, the Cardinal Camerlingo, a corpulent and sanguine prelate, advanced on the Count de Forez and said menacingly: 'Messire, a Pope cannot be elected in such conditions, for you are violating the constitution of Gregory X, which obliges the Conclave to meet in the town in which the Pope died.'

'You were there, Monseigneur, two years ago, and you dispersed without having made a Pope, which is also a breach of the constitution. But if, by any chance, you should wish to be taken back to Carpentras, we will conduct you there under a good escort and in closed coaches.'

'We may not deliberate under the threat of force!'

'That is why there are seven hundred men outside, Monseigneur, to guard you. They have been provided by the authorities of the town to ensure your protection and your isolation, as the constitution prescribes. The Sire de la Voulte here, who is a native of Lyons, is in command of them. Messire the Regent also wishes you to know that if, by the third day, you have not agreed, you will receive but one dish in the twenty-four hours by way of food and, after the ninth day, there will be but bread and water, as is also prescribed in the constitution of Gregory. And finally, if enlightenment does not come to you through fasting, he will destroy the roof and expose you to the inclemency of the weather.'

Bérenger Frédol, the elder, intervened: 'Messire, you will be guilty of murder if you subject us to such treatment, for there are some among us who will not be able to support it. Look at Monseigneur Duèze, who has already collapsed and is in need of care.'

'Oh, yes, oh, most certainly,' Duèze complained feebly; 'I shall most certainly not be able to support it.'

'What's the use?' cried Caetani. 'Can't you see we have to do with savage and stinking beasts? But let me tell you, Messire, that instead of electing a Pope, we shall excommunicate you, you and your perjurer.'

'If you hold a meeting of excommunication, Monseigneur Caetani,' the Count de Forez replied calmly, 'the Regent might make known to the Conclave the name of certain sorcerers and casters of spells who should be put at the top of the list for roasting.'

'I really don't see,' said Caetani, beating a hasty retreat, 'I really don't see what sorcery has to do with the matter, since it's with the election of a Pope that we are concerned.'

'Ah, Monseigneur, I see we understand each other; please dismiss the people you do not need, because there will not be enough food to feed them all.'

The Cardinals realized that all resistance was vain and that this armed man, who was giving them the Count of Poitiers's orders in so firm a voice, was adamant. Already, behind Jean de Forez, the men-at-arms were beginning to enter one by one, pike in hand, and to deploy at the end of the church.

'Since we cannot use force, we shall use cunning,' said Caetani in a low voice to the Italians. 'Let us pretend to submit, because at the moment we can do no other.'

They each chose the three most faithful servants from among their following, those they thought might be the best advisers, the most cunning in intrigue, or the most apt at tending to their physical wants in the difficult material circumstances in which they would have to live. Caetani kept Father Bost, Andrieu and Pierre, the priest with the two thumbs, that is to say the men who had been implicated in casting the spell on Louis X; he preferred that they should be shut up with him, rather than risk their talking either for money or under torture. The Colonnas kept four pages who could fell an ox with their fists. Canons, clerks, linkmen and trainbearers began to leave, one by one, through the hedge of armed men. As they passed, their masters whispered:

'Let my brother the Bishop know . . . Write in my name to my cousin de Got . . . Leave at once for Rome . . .'

At the moment when Guccio Baglioni was preparing to leave, Jacques Duèze put out his thin hand from within the confessional, where he lay in a state of collapse, and seized the young Italian by his robe, murmuring: 'Stay with me, my boy. I am sure you will be a great help to me.'

Duèze knew from experience that the power of money was far from negligible within a Conclave; it was an unhoped-for piece of luck to have with him a representative of the Lombard banks.

An hour later there remained inside the Church of the Jacobins but ninety-six men, who were fated to stay there as long as twenty-four among them had not agreed on the election of one. Before leaving, the men-at-arms had carried in armfuls of straw to make beds, on the very stone itself, for the most powerful prelates of the world. A few basins had been brought, that they might wash themselves, and water, in great jars, had been placed at their disposal. Under the eye of the Count de Forez, the masons had walled up the last exit, merely leaving a little square opening halfway up, a window just wide enough to allow food to be passed in, but too narrow for a man to pass through. All round the church the soldiers had taken up their positions six yards apart and in two ranks: one rank with backs to the wall looked towards the town; the other faced the church and watched the windows.

Towards midday the Count of Poitiers set out for Paris. He took with him in his following the Dauphin of Viennois and the little Dauphiniet, who would henceforth live at his Court in order to get to know his five-year-old betrothed.

At the same hour the Cardinals received their first meal: since it was a fast day, they were given no meat.

6

From Neauphle to Saint-Marcel

ON A MORNING EARLY in July, well before dawn, Jean de Cressay entered his sister's room. The large young man carried a smoking candle; he had washed his beard and was wearing his best riding-cloak.

'Get up, Marie,' he said. 'You're leaving this morning. Pierre and I are going to take you.'

The girl sat up in bed.

'Leave? What do you mean? Have I got to leave this morning?'

Her mind was still hazy from sleep and she stared in incomprehension at her brother out of her huge dark blue eyes. She automatically shook back over her shoulders her long thick, silky hair, in which there were golden lights.

Jean de Cressay looked at his sister's beauty without pleasure, as if it were a sin.

'Pack up your clothes, for you won't be coming back for a long time.'

'But where are you taking me?' asked Marie.

'You'll see.'

'But why did you not say anything about it yesterday?'

'What, so that you might still have time to play another trick on us? Come on, hurry up; I want to get started before our serfs see us. You've brought us shame enough; there's no point in giving them more cause for gossip.'

Marie did not reply. For the last month her family had treated her like this and spoken to her in this tone of voice. She got up, feeling the weight of her five months' pregnancy which, though still light, always surprised her when she rose in the morning. By the light of the candle Jean had left her, she made ready, washed her face and neck and quickly tied up her hair; she noticed that her hands were trembling. Where were they taking her? To what convent? She placed about her neck the gold reliquary Guccio had given her, which had come, so he had said, from Queen Clémence. 'Up to now the relics have not been much protection,' she thought. 'Have I not prayed to them enough?' She packed an overdress, a few underdresses, a surcoat and some towels for washing.

'You'll wear your cloak with the big hood,' Jean said, as he looked into her room for a moment.

'But I shall die of heat!' said Marie. 'It's a winter cloak.'

'Your mother wishes you to travel with your face hidden. Do as you're told and hurry.'

In the courtyard the second brother, Pierre, was saddling the two horses himself.

Marie had known that this day was bound to come; in one way, however sad she felt at heart, she was not altogether sorry; at moments she had even looked forward to this departure. The most austere of convents would be more tolerable than the constant complaints and reproaches to which she had been subjected. At least she would be alone with her misfortune. She would no longer have to bear the anger of her mother, who had been bedridden from a stroke ever since the scandal had broken, and who cursed her daughter every time Marie brought her an infusion of herbs. They had had to summon urgently the surgeon-barber of Neauphle to draw a pint of dark blood from the stout lady of the manor. Dame Eliabel had been bled six times in less than a fortnight, but the treatment did not appear to be accelerating her return to health.

Marie was treated by her two brothers, particularly by Jean, as a criminal. Oh, rather the cloister a thousand times over! But would she ever be able to get news of Guccio in the convent? That was her obsession, her greatest fear at the fate awaiting her. Her wicked brothers had told her that Guccio had fled abroad.

'They don't want to admit it,' she thought, 'but they have had him put in prison. It's not possible, simply not possible, that he has deserted me! Or perhaps he has returned to the country to save me; and that is why they are in such a hurry to take me away; and then they'll kill him. Why did I not agree to go away with him? I refused to listen to him so as not to wound my mother and my brothers, and now the worst has befallen me as a result of trying to do right.'

Her imagination conjured up every possible form of disaster. There were moments when she even hoped that Guccio had really fled, leaving her to her fate. With no one from whom to ask advice or even compassion, she had no company but her unborn child; but that life was not yet of much help to her, except for the courage with which it inspired her.

At the moment of leaving, Marie de Cressay asked if she could say goodbye to her mother. Pierre went up to Dame Eliabel's room, but there issued from it such a shouting on the part of the widow, whose voice appeared but little affected by the bleedings, that Marie realized it was useless. Pierre came down again, his face sad, his hands spread wide in a gesture of impotence.

'She said that she no longer had a daughter,' he said.

And Marie thought once again: 'I should have done better to run away with Guccio. It's all my fault. I should have gone with him.'

The two brothers mounted their horses and Jean de Cressay took his sister up on the crupper, because his horse was the better of the two, or rather the less bad. Pierre was riding the broken-winded nag, whose nostrils made a roaring sound, and on which, the previous month, the two brothers had made so distinguished an entry into the capital.

Marie cast a final glance at the little manor she had never left since she was born and which now, in the half-light of the uncertain dawn, already seemed to be clothed in a grey mist of memory. Every moment of her life, since she had first opened her eyes, was contained within these walls and in this countryside: her childish games, the surprising daily discovery of herself and of the world, which every human being makes in his turn, the infinite diversity of plants in the fields, the strange shapes of flowers, the marvellous pollen in their hearts, the softness of the down on young ducks' breasts and the play of sunlight on dragonflies' wings. She was leaving all those hours she had spent in watching herself grow, listening to her dreams, every stage of her changing face that she had so often admired in the clear waters of the Mauldre, and also that great joy at being alive she had sometimes felt when she lay full length on her back in the middle of a field, looking for omens in the shapes of the clouds and imagining God in the depths of the sky. She passed by the chapel, where her father lay beneath a stone flag and where the Italian monk had married her secretly to Guccio.

'Lower your hood,' her brother Jean ordered.

As soon as they had crossed the river, he hastened his horse's pace, and Pierre's began roaring at once.

'Jean, aren't we going rather too fast?' said Pierre, indicating Marie with a jerk of the head.

'To hell with it! Bad seed's always solidly sown,' replied the elder, as if he hoped wickedly for an accident.

But his hopes were disappointed. Marie was a strong girl and made for motherhood. She rode the twenty-five miles from Neauphle to Paris without showing any signs of weakness. She was bruised and suffocating with heat, but did not complain. From under her hood she saw nothing of Paris but the surface of the streets, the bottoms of the houses and headless people. What legs! What shoes! She would have liked to raise her hood but dared not. What surprised her most was the noise, the immense rumbling of the city, the voices of the street-hawkers selling every kind of ware, the noises made by the various trades; in certain alleys the crowd was so dense that the horses could hardly force their way through. Passers-by jostled Marie's legs; but at length the horses came to a halt. She dismounted, feeling tired and dusty; she was allowed to raise her hood.

'Where are we?' she asked, gazing in surprise at the courtyard of a fine house.

'At your Lombard's uncle's house,' replied Jean de Cressay.

A few moments later Messer Tolomei, one eye shut and the other open, gazed at the three children of the late Sire de Cressay as they sat in a row before him, Jean bearded, Pierre clean-shaven, and their sister beside them, a little withdrawn, her head bowed.

'You understand, Messer Tolomei,' said Jean, 'that you made us a promise.'

'Of course, of course,' replied Tolomei, 'and I'm going to keep it, my friends, have no fear.'

'You understand that it must be kept quickly. You understand that after all the gossip there has been about her shame, our sister can no longer live with us. You understand that we no longer dare appear in our neighbours' houses, that even our serfs mock us as we go by, and that it will be worse still when our sister's sin becomes more apparent.'

Tolomei had a reply on the tip of his tongue: 'But, my lads, it's you who have caused all the scandal! No one compelled you to pursue Guccio like madmen, rousing the whole town of Neauphle and announcing the mishap more publicly than if it had been cried by the town-crier.'

'And our mother is not recovering from our misfortune; she has cursed her daughter, and seeing Marie near renews her anger until we fear she may die of it. You understand . . .'

'This idiot, like everyone who asks you to understand, can't have much sense in his head. When he has had his say he'll stop. But what I do very well understand,' the banker said to himself, 'is why Guccio is mad about this pretty girl. Till now I thought he was wrong, but I've changed my opinion since she came into the room; and if my age would still let me, I've no doubt that I should behave more foolishly than he has done. Beautiful eyes, beautiful hair, beautiful skin – a true spring flower. And how bravely she bears her misfortunes; really, they both make such a fuss you might think it was they who had been ravished. But, poor child, her suffering is greater than theirs. She must surely have a nice nature. What bad luck to have been born under the same roof as these two oafs, and how I should like Guccio to be able to marry her openly so she could live here and rejoice my old age with the sight of her.'

He did not stop looking at her. Marie raised her eyes to him, lowered them at once, then raised them again, troubled at what he might be thinking of her and by his insistent gaze.

'You understand, Messer, that your nephew . . .'

'Oh, I disown him, I've disinherited him! If he had not fled to Italy, I think I'd have killed him with my own hands. If I could only find out where he's hiding . . .' said Tolomei, taking his forehead in his hands with an air of dejection.

But through the little chink between his hands, allowing no one but the girl to see, he twice raised the heavy eyelid which normally he kept closed. Marie realized that she had an ally and could not restrain a sigh. Guccio was alive, Guccio was in a safe place, and Tolomei knew where. What did the cloister matter to her now!

She was no longer listening to what her brother Jean was saying. She knew it all by heart. Even Pierre de Cressay sat silent, looking vaguely weary. Without daring to say so, he blamed himself for having also given way to anger. He was leaving it to his brother to convince himself that he had acted properly; he left it to Jean to speak of the honour of their blood and the laws of chivalry, so as to justify their immense folly.

When the Cressay brothers came from their poor little

ramshackle manor, from their courtyard which stank of the dunghill all the year round, and saw Tolomei's princely residence, the brocades, the silver bowls, when they felt beneath their fingers the delicate carving on the chairs and became aware of that atmosphere of wealth and abundance which permeated the whole house, they were forced to recognize that their sister would not have been so badly off if they left her to her own inclination. The younger one sincerely regretted it. 'At least one of us would have been well provided for, and we should all have benefited,' he thought. But the bearded one, with his stubborn nature, merely felt the more spite as well as a base jealousy. 'Why should her sins give her a right to so much wealth through sinning, while we live so poorly?'

Nor was Marie insensible to the luxury around her; it dazzled her, and merely increased her regrets.

'If only Guccio had been even a little noble,' she thought, 'or if we had not been noble at all! What does chivalry matter? Can it be a good thing, when it makes one suffer so much? And is not wealth a sort of nobility in itself? What is the difference between making serfs labour and making money work?'

'You need have no concern, my friends,' said Tolomei at last; 'leave everything to me. It's the duty of uncles to repair the faults committed by their wicked nephews. Thanks to my influential friends, I have succeeded in getting your sister accepted by the Royal Convent of the Daughters of Saint-Marcel. Does that satisfy you?'

The two Cressay brothers looked at each other and nodded their heads in approval. The Convent of the Clarisses in the Faubourg Saint-Marcel enjoyed the highest reputation among female religious establishments. It was almost entirely confined to the daughters of the nobility. And it was there that the royal family's bastards were occasionally concealed behind the veil. Jean de Cressay's ill-temper vanished at once, appeased by the vanity of caste. And, to show that the Cressays were not unworthy of what was being done for their sister in her sin, he added hastily: 'Excellent, excellent; besides, I think the Abbess is some sort of a relation of ours; our mother has often quoted her to us as an example.'

'Then everything is for the best,' continued Tolomei. 'I shall take your sister to Messire Hugues de Bouville, the ex-Grand Chamberlain . . .'

The two brothers bowed slightly in their chairs to show their respect.

'. . . from whom I obtained this favour,' Tolomei went on; 'and tonight, I promise you, she shall be inside the convent. You can therefore go home reassured; I will keep you informed.'

The two brothers asked no better. They were getting rid of their sister, and thought that they had done enough by handing her over to the care of others. The silence of the cloister would close over the scandal which, at Cressay, need from now on be mentioned only in whispers, or not even be mentioned at all.

'May God keep you and inspire you with repentance,' said Jean to his sister by way of goodbye.

He put much more warmth into his farewell to Tolomei and thanked him for the trouble he was taking. He very nearly reproached Marie for the grief she was causing this excellent man.

'God keep you, Marie,' said Pierre with emotion.

He wanted to kiss his sister, but dared not do so under the severe eye of his elder brother. And Marie found herself alone with the fat banker with the dark complexion, the fleshy mouth and the closed eye, who, strange as it might seem, was her uncle.

The two horses left the courtyard and the roaring of the broken-winded nag could be heard growing fainter; it was the last sound of Cressay moving out of Marie's ken.

'And now, let us eat, my child. And while we dine, we don't weep,' said Tolomei.

He helped the girl take off the cloak which was suffocating her; Marie looked surprised and grateful, for it was the first mark of attention, or even of simple courtesy, she had been shown for many weeks.

'Ah, some of my cloth,' thought Tolomei when he saw the dress she was wearing.

The Lombard was an Oriental spice-merchant, as well as a banker; the stews into which he elegantly plunged his fingers, the little pieces of meat he removed so delicately from the bone, were impregnated with exotic, appetizing flavours. But Marie showed little appetite and barely helped herself to the dishes of the first course.

'He's at Lyons,' said Tolomei, raising his left eyelid. 'He cannot leave there for the moment, but he is thinking of you all the time and is completely faithful to you.'

'He's not in prison?' asked Marie.

'No, not exactly. He's shut up, but it has nothing to do with you, and he is sharing his captivity with such important people that we have no cause to fear for his safety; everything inclines me to believe that he will come out of the church, where he now is, more important than when he entered it.'

'The church?' asked Marie.

'I cannot tell you more.'

Marie did not press him. The idea of Guccio being shut up in a church with people who were so important that their names could not be mentioned was a mystery that was quite beyond her. But there had already been in Guccio's life many mysterious circumstances, indeed they were part of the admiration she felt for him. The first time she had seen him, had he not just returned from England on Queen Isabella's service? Had he not since then been twice long absent so as to travel to Naples in the service of Queen Clémence, who had given him the relic of Saint John the Baptist she wore about her neck? 'I shall call our child Jean or Jeanne and people will think it's because of my elder brother.' If Guccio were shut up at the present moment, it must again be in the service of some queen. Marie was astonished that, mingling with so many powerful princesses, he should continue to prefer herself, a poor country girl. Guccio was alive, Guccio loved her; no more was needed to restore her pleasure in life, and she began to eat with all the appetite of a girl of eighteen who had been travelling since dawn.

Tolomei, who knew how to talk easily to the mightiest barons, to peers of the realm, to jurists and archbishops, had for long been unaccustomed to conversing with women, particularly one so young. They did not say much to each other. The banker gazed with delight on this niece who had fallen to him from the sky and who pleased him more each moment.

'What a pity,' he thought, 'to place her in a convent! If Guccio had not shut himself up in the Conclave, I would send this pretty child to Lyons; but what would she do all alone there and without protection? And, by the look of things, the

Cardinals, as far as one can see, show no signs of yielding. Or should I keep her here to await my nephew's return? That's what I should like to do. But no, I can't; I asked Bouville to do something for her; what sort of figure would I cut if I took no account of the trouble he has taken? And, moreover, if the Abbess is a cousin of the Cressays, and the fools should take it into their heads to ask her for news? No, we must not lose our head too. She will go to the convent . . .'

'. . . but not for all your life,' he said, continuing aloud. 'There's no question of making you take the veil. You must accept these months of seclusion without too much complaint; I promise you that, when your child is born, I shall arrange things so that you can live happily with my nephew.'

Marie seized his hand and carried it to her lips; he was embarrassed; kindness was not natural to him, and his profession had not accustomed him to expressions of gratitude.

'I must now place you in the care of the Count de Bouville,' he said.

From the Street of the Lombards to the Palace of the Cité was no great distance. Marie walked beside Tolomei in wondering surprise. She had never seen so great a city; the movement of the crowds beneath the July sun, the beauty of the buildings, the quantity of shops, the glittering goldsmiths' stalls, the whole spectacle transported her into a sort of fairyland. 'How wonderful,' she thought, 'to live here, and what a nice man Guccio's uncle is, and what a blessing that he is prepared to protect us. Oh yes, I shall certainly put up with my time in the convent without complaint!' They crossed the Pont-au-Change and entered the Mercers' Gallery, which was cluttered with baskets of goods.

For the pleasure of hearing Marie thank him once again

and of seeing a smile reveal her pretty teeth, Tolomei could not help buying her a purse for her belt, embroidered with little pearls.

'This is on Guccio's behalf. I must take his place!' he said, calculating that, if he had gone to a wholesale merchant, he could have bought it for half the price.

They started up the grand staircase of the Palace. Thus, for having been seduced by a young Lombard, Marie de Cressay entered the royal dwelling, which her father and her brothers, for all their three hundred years of chivalry and the services they had rendered the King in battle, would never have dreamt of being able to do.

Within the Palace a certain disorder reigned, the result of everyone trying to show his own authority, the peculiar state of turmoil which became immediately evident wherever the Count of Valois happened to be. Having crossed galleries, corridors and suites of rooms, which, as they progressed, made Marie de Cressay feel smaller and smaller, they reached a secluded part of the Palace, behind the Sainte-Chapelle, giving on to the Seine and the Island of Jews. A guard of gentlemen-at-arms, dressed in coats of mail, barred their way. No one might enter Queen Clémence's apartments without the Curators' authority. Tolomei and Marie waited by a window, while someone went in search of the Count de Bouville.

'Do you see? That's where they burnt the Templars,' said Tolomei, pointing out the island.

Fat Bouville arrived, still dressed in armour, his paunch rolling under his coat of mail, his step as decisive as if he were about to command an assault. He made the guard move aside. Tolomei and Marie crossed a room in which the

Sire de Joinville was sleeping, sitting in an armchair. His two equerries were silently playing chess beside him. Then the visitors entered the Count de Bouville's lodging.

'Is Madame Clémence any better?' Tolomei asked Bouville.

'She weeps less,' replied the Curator, 'or rather she shows her tears less, as if they were flowing straight into her throat. But she is still suffering badly from shock. Moreover, the heat here is doing her no good in her condition; she suffers from exhaustion and often has fainting-fits.'

'So the Queen of France is nearby,' thought Marie, intensely curious. 'Perhaps I shall be presented to her? How shall I dare speak to her of Guccio?'

She then had to listen to a long conversation, of which she understood little, between the banker and the former Grand Chamberlain. When they mentioned certain names, they lowered their voices, or moved a little aside, and Marie tried hard not to listen to the whisperings.

The Count of Poitiers's arrival from Lyons was announced for the morrow. Bouville, who had so much desired his return, no longer knew whether it was a good thing or not. For Monseigneur of Valois had decided to leave immediately to meet Philippe, accompanied by the Count de La Marche; and Bouville pointed out to Tolomei, by a window giving on to the courtyard, the preparations for departure. The Duke of Burgundy, for his part, had taken up his residence in Paris and had mounted a guard of his own gentlemen about his niece, the little Jeanne of Navarre. The Treasury was empty. There was a sinister wind of rebellion blowing through the city, and this rivalry of regents could but end in the greatest calamities. In Bouville's opinion, Queen Clémence should have been made Regent and surrounded by a Council of the Crown composed of Valois, Poitiers and the Duke of Burgundy.

Interested though he was in these events, Tolomei several times endeavoured to bring Bouville back to the subject in hand.

'Of course, of course, we shall look after this young lady,' replied Bouville, who immediately returned to his political pre-occupations.

Had Tolomei any news from Lyons? The Curator had taken the banker familiarly by the shoulder and was practically talking cheek to cheek. What? Guccio was shut in the Conclave with Duèze? Oh, what a clever boy! Did Tolomei think he could communicate with his nephew? If he should receive any news from him, or was in a position to send him a message, would he let him know? It might be a very valuable channel. As for Marie . . .

'Yes, yes, of course,' said the Curator. 'My wife, who is an intelligent and extremely competent woman, has done all that is necessary. Don't worry.'

Madame de Bouville was summoned. She was a thin, authoritative little woman, her face seamed with vertical wrinkles, and her withered hands were never still for an instant. Marie, who had until then felt safe with the fat Tolomei and the equally fat Bouville, at once had a sensation of unease and anxiety.

'Oh, so it's you whose sin has to be concealed!' said Madame de Bouville, examining her with eyes that lacked all kindliness. 'You are expected at the Convent of the Clarisses. The Abbess showed very little eagerness, and less still when she heard your name, for it appears that, by I know not what link, she is related to your family, and your conduct is most displeasing to her. However, the interest which Messire

Hugues, my husband, enjoys carried weight. When I had insisted a little, she agreed to shelter you. I will take you there before nightfall.'

She talked quickly and it was difficult to interrupt her. When she stopped to take breath, Marie replied with great deference, but also with considerable dignity: 'Madame, I am not in a state of sin, for I was married to my husband before God.'

'Now, now,' replied Madame de Bouville, 'don't make us regret the kindness we're showing you. Give thanks to those who are taking the trouble to help you, instead of putting on airs.'

Tolomei thanked them on Marie's behalf. When she saw the banker about to leave, she felt so sad, lonely and distressed that she threw herself into his arms as if he had been her father.

'Let me know what happens to Guccio,' she whispered in his ear, 'and let him know that I long for him.'

Tolomei left and the Bouvilles also disappeared. Marie remained all the afternoon in their antechamber, not daring to leave it and with nothing to do but sit in the embrasure of the open window and watch the departure of Monseigneur of Valois and his escort. For a moment the spectacle distracted her from her sorrow. She had never seen such beautiful horses, harness and clothes, or in such great number. She thought of the peasants of Cressay dressed in their rags, their legs bound in strips of cloth, and thought how strange it was that human beings, who all had a head and two arms and were all created by God in His image, should be of such different races, if one were to judge by their clothing.

Two young equerries, seeing the beautiful girl gazing

down at them, smiled at her and blew her kisses. Suddenly they gathered about a figure, dressed in silver-embroidered clothes, who seemed to have a commanding presence and looked like a sovereign; then the cavalcade set off, and the heat of the afternoon lay over the courtyards and the gardens of the Palace.

Towards the end of the day Madame de Bouville came in search of Marie. Accompanied by several footmen, and mounted on mules harnessed with a sort of pack-saddle on which one sat to one side with one's feet on a bar, the two women crossed Paris.

There were riotous groups and shouting at the tavern doors; a brawl had broken out between the partisans of the Count of Valois and the people of the Duke of Burgundy, who had but recently arrived and were getting very drunk. The watch was restoring order with its maces.

'The city is in a state of excitement,' said Madame de Bouville. 'I should not be at all surprised if there were not a rising tomorrow.'

They left Paris by Mont Sainte-Geneviève and the Porte Saint-Marcel. Dusk was falling over the suburbs.

'When I was young,' said Madame de Bouville, 'there were only twenty houses to be seen here. But people can no longer find anywhere to live in the city and are constantly building in the fields.'

The Convent of the Clarisses was surrounded by a high, white wall, which enclosed the buildings, gardens and orchards. In the wall was a low door and, next to the door, a turning-box constructed in the thickness of the stone. A woman came walking along the wall, her head covered with a hood, went to the turning-box and quickly placed in it a package which she took from beneath her cloak; cries came from the package; the woman turned the wooden drum, pulled the bell and, seeing that someone was coming, ran away.

'What was she doing?' Marie asked.

'She has abandoned a fatherless child,' said Madame de Bouville, looking at Marie with an expression of severity. 'That is how they are received. Come along, hurry up.'

Marie urged on her mule. She was thinking that she might herself have been compelled one day soon to deposit her child in a turning-box, and she thought that her lot was by comparison enviable.

'I thank you, Madame, for taking such great care of me,' she murmured, tears in her eyes.

'Ah, at last, a grateful word,' replied Madame de Bouville.

A few moments later the door opened before them, and Marie disappeared into the silence of the convent.

7
The Gates of the Palace

THAT SAME EVENING THE Count of Poitiers was at the Château of Fontainebleau, where he was to sleep; it was the last stage on his journey to Paris. He was finishing supper in company with the Dauphin of Viennois, the Count of Savoy, and the members of his numerous suite, when the arrival was announced of his uncle the Count of Valois, his brother the Count de La Marche, and their cousin Saint-Pol.

'Show them in, show them in at once,' said Philippe of Poitiers.

But he did not go forward to greet his uncle. And when he appeared, walking with martial step, his chin held high and his clothes dusty, Philippe merely rose and waited for him, making not the slightest movement towards him. Valois, somewhat put out of countenance, stood for a few seconds on the threshold of the door, gazed round at the assembled company and, since Philippe obstinately refused to come to greet him, had at last to make up his mind to go forward himself. Everyone fell silent, watching them. When Valois had approached near enough, the Count of Poitiers took him by the shoulders and kissed him on both cheeks, which could be interpreted as the gesture of a loving nephew but, coming from a man who had held his ground, was more that of a king.

This behaviour annoyed Charles de La Marche, who thought: 'Have we come all this way to be welcomed like this? After all, I am equal with my brother; why should he treat us so haughtily?'

A bitter and jealous expression clouded the regular but unintelligent features of his handsome face.

Philippe extended his arms to him; La Marche had to exchange a brief embrace with his brother but, to give himself importance and try to assert his own authority, he indicated Valois and said:

'Philippe, here is our uncle, the eldest of the royal family. We congratulate you on agreeing with him that he should have the government of the kingdom. For the kingdom would be in too great peril if it were reduced to waiting for a child still unborn, who could not govern it, and would in any case be a foreigner through his mother.'

The speech was ambiguous and ill-conceived. It might have signified that the Count de La Marche wished to see his uncle regent until the birth of Louis X's posthumous child, or until the child's majority if it were a son; but it might also be taken to betray greater ambitions on the part of Valois. La Marche must have been misquoting words with which his uncle had primed him. Some of the phrases in this speech made Philippe frown. So Valois was trying to seize the crown, was he?

'Our cousin of Saint-Pol is with us,' went on Charles de

La Marche, 'to inform you that this is also the opinion of the barons.'

Philippe looked at him in some contempt.

'I am grateful to you, Brother, for your counsel,' he replied coldly, 'and for having come so far to give it me. I imagine that you must be tired as I am, and sound decisions are not taken in fatigue. I propose therefore that we go and sleep, and decide these matters tomorrow with fresh minds and in private council. Good night, Messeigneurs. Raoul, Anseau, Adam, accompany me, I pray you.'

And he left the room, without offering his visitors food or showing concern as to where they would sleep.

Followed by Adam Héron, Raoul de Presles and Anseau de Joinville, he went to the royal chamber. The bed, which had not been occupied since the Iron King had died in it, was made, the sheets spread. Philippe thought it most important that he should occupy this room; it was even more important that no one else should do so.

Adam Héron made ready to undress him.

'I think I shall not undress tonight,' said Philippe of Poitiers. 'Adam, you will send one of my bachelors to Messire Gaucher de Châtillon to inform him that I shall be at the Porte d'Enfer tomorrow morning. And then send me a barber later on, because I wish to arrive there freshly shaven. And have twenty horses made ready for midnight, but only after my uncle has gone to bed. As for you, Anseau,' he added, turning to the son of the Seneschal de Joinville, who was already middle-aged, 'I charge you to warn the Count of Savoy and the Dauphin that they may not be surprised or think that I distrust them. Stay here until morning, and when my uncle realizes that I have gone, ride close about him and delay him. Make him lose time on the road.'

Alone with Raoul de Presles, he seemed to sink into silent meditation, which the jurist took good care not to interrupt.

'Raoul,' he said at last, 'you worked day after day with my father, and knew him better than I did myself. What would he have done in these circumstances?'

'He would have done as you are doing, Monseigneur, I warrant, and I do not say so in order to flatter you, but because I really believe it. I loved our Lord Philip too much, and have suffered too much since his death, to serve you today if you did not remind me of him in all things.'

'Alas, alas, Raoul, I am but little beside him. He could follow his hawk in the air without losing sight of it, and I am short-sighted. He could twist a horse's shoe in his hands without difficulty. He has not bequeathed me his strength in arms, nor that majesty which let everyone know that he was King.'

As he spoke, he gazed fixedly at the bed.

At Lyons he had felt himself to be Regent with complete certainty. But, as he drew nearer the capital, this assurance, though he gave no sign of it, was diminishing a little. Raoul de Presles, as if he were replying to an unspoken question, said:

'There is no precedent for the situation in which we find ourselves, Monseigneur. We have discussed it enough these last days. In the present weak state of the kingdom, power will go to him who has the authority to seize it. If you succeed, France will not suffer for it.'

Soon he withdrew; and Philippe lay down on the bed, his eyes fixed on the little lamp suspended between the hangings. The Count of Poitiers felt no embarrassment, no uneasiness, at lying on that bed whose last occupant had been a corpse. On the contrary, he drew strength from it; he had the impression of being moulded to his father's shape, of taking his place, of occupying once more the same dimensions on the earth. 'Father, come back to me,' he prayed: and he lay still, his hands crossed on his breast, offering his body to the reincarnation of a soul which had fled twenty months before.

He heard steps in the corridor, voices, and his chamberlain answering, no doubt to some member of the Count of Valois's suite, that the Count of Poitiers was asleep. Silence fell over the Château. A little later the barber arrived with his basin, razors and hot towels. While he was being shaved, Philippe of Poitiers recalled his father's last instructions, given in this very room before the whole Court assembled, to Louis, who had paid but little heed to them: 'Weigh well, Louis, what it is to be the King of France. Learn as early as you can the state of your kingdom.'

Towards midnight Adam Héron came to tell him that the horses were ready. When the Count of Poitiers left the room, he felt that twenty months had been blotted out, and that he was taking affairs in hand from the point they had reached at his father's death, as if he were the direct successor.

A fair moon lit the road. The starry July night was like the Holy Virgin's cloak. The forest gave off a scent of moss, earth and fern; it was alive with the secret rustlings of wild-life. Philippe of Poitiers was riding an excellent horse and took delight in its strength. The fresh air fanned his cheeks, sensitive from the barber's ministrations.

'It would be a pity', he thought, 'to leave so fine a country in bad hands.'

The little cavalcade emerged from the forest, galloped through Ponthierry and stopped, as day broke, in the hollow of Essonnes, to breathe the horses and break their fast. Philippe ate his food sitting on a milestone. He seemed happy. He was but twenty-three, his expedition had some small air of success about it, and he talked happily to the companions of his adventure. His gaiety, so rare for him, confirmed their determination to support him.

Between prime and tierce he reached the gates of Paris while the harsh bells of the neighbouring convents rang out. He found Louis of Evreux and Gaucher de Châtillon waiting for him. The Constable looked depressed. He asked the Count of Poitiers to go at once to the Louvre.

'But why should I not go straight to the Palace of the Cité?' asked Philippe.

'Because our Seigneurs of Valois and de La Marche have occupied the Palace with their men-at-arms. At the Louvre you will have the royal troops who are all under my orders, that is to say loyal to you, with the crossbowmen of Messire de Galard. But you must act quickly and resolutely,' added the Constable, 'so as to forestall the return of our two Charleses. If you give me the order, Monseigneur, I will take the Palace by storm.'

Philippe knew that minutes were precious. Nevertheless, he calculated that he had a start of six or seven hours over Valois.

'I do not wish to undertake anything until I know whether it will be approved by the burgesses and the people of the city,' he replied.

And as soon as he reached the Louvre, he sent to summon to the Aldermen's Council room Master Coquatrix, Master

Gentien and some other important notables such as Provost Guillaume de La Madeleine, who had succeeded Provost Ployebouche in March.

Philippe told them in a few words of the importance he attached to the burgesses of Paris and to the men who directed the arts of manufacture and trade. The burgesses felt honoured and above all reassured. They had not heard words of this nature since the death of Philip the Fair, of whom they had often complained while he ruled them but whom they now never ceased regretting. It was Geoffroy Coquatrix, commissary for forged coinage, collector of subventions and subsidies, treasurer for the wars, purveyor to garrisons, visitor to the ports and thoroughfares of the kingdom and a master of the Chamber of Audits, who replied. He held these posts from Philip the Fair, who had even endowed him with a hereditary income, as was done for the great servants of the Crown, and he had never rendered accounts of his administration.[11] He feared that Charles of Valois, always hostile to the appointment of burgesses to great positions – he had sufficiently proved it in Marigny's case – would dismiss him from his posts so as to despoil him of the enormous fortune he had garnered in them. Coquatrix assured the Count of Poitiers, calling him 'Messire Regent' at least a dozen times, of the devotion of the population of Paris. His adherence was valuable, for he was all-powerful in the Aldermen's Council and rich enough, if need be, to bribe every beggar in the city to revolt.

The news of Philippe of Poitiers's return had spread rapidly. The barons and knights who supported him hastened to the Louvre, Mahaut of Artois, who had been personally informed, in the lead.

'How is my dearest Jeanne?' Philippe asked his mother-in-law as he embraced her.

'We are expecting her to be brought to bed at any moment.'

'I'll go and see her as soon as I have completed my business.'

Then he discussed plans with his uncle Louis and the Constable.

'You can now advance on the Palace, Gaucher. Try and finish the business, if you can, by midday. But do everything possible to avoid shedding blood. Conquer by fear rather than by violence. I would rather not have to enter the Palace over dead bodies.'

Gaucher went and placed himself at the head of the companies of men-at-arms he had gathered at the Louvre, and set out for the Cité. At the same time he sent the Provost to the Temple district in search of the best carpenters and locksmiths.

The Palace gates were shut. Gaucher, with the Grand Master of the Crossbowmen beside him, demanded entrance. The Officer of the Guard, appearing at a window above the main gate, replied that he could not open without the authorization of the Count of Valois or the Count de La Marche.

'You must open all the same,' replied the Constable, 'for I wish to enter and put the Palace in a fit state to receive the Regent, who is on his way.'

'We cannot.'

Gaucher de Châtillon sat more firmly in his saddle.

'Very well, we shall open the gates ourselves,' he said.

And he signalled Pierre of the Temple, the royal carpenter, to approach with his workmen, carrying saws, pincers and big iron levers. At the same time the crossbowmen put their feet in a sort of stirrup at the top of their bows, bent their weapons, nocked their quarrels, and took up positions covering the battlements and embrasures. The archers and pikemen joined their shields in a huge testudo above and around the carpenters. In the neighbouring streets loungers and urchins had gathered at a respectful distance to watch the siege. They were being offered a splendid entertainment, which would be matter for conversation for many days to come.

'I was there as sure as I'm standing here . . . I saw the Constable draw his great sword . . . There were more than two thousand of them, for sure, more than two thousand they were!'

Finally Gaucher, in the voice he used for giving orders on the field of battle, shouted, through the raised visor of his helmet: 'Messires inside there, here is the master carpenter and the master locksmith, who are going to break down the gates. Here, too, are the crossbowmen of Messire de Galard surrounding the Palace at all points. No one can escape. I summon you for the last time to open the gates, for if you do not surrender at discretion, you will all lose your heads, however noble you may be. The Regent will give no quarter.'

Then he lowered his visor as a sign that he was prepared to argue no further.

There must have been a fine panic inside the Palace for, at the very moment that the workmen were putting their levers under the gates, they opened of their own accord. The Count of Valois's garrison was surrendering.

'It was time you took the wise course,' said the Constable,

as he took possession of the Palace. 'Go back to your homes and to the houses of your masters; if you do not assemble, no harm will come to you.'

An hour later Philippe of Poitiers was in occupation of the royal apartments. He immediately took measures for his safety. The courtyard of the Palace, normally open to the public, was closed, a military guard placed on it, and all visitors were carefully checked. The mercers, who had the privilege of trading in the Great Gallery, were asked to close their stalls temporarily.

When the Counts of Valois and de La Marche arrived in Paris, they realized that the game was lost.

'Philippe has played a dirty trick on us,' they said.

And they hastened to the Palace to negotiate their submission, having no longer any alternative. About the Count of Poitiers was a large number of lords, burgesses and ecclesiastics, among whom was the Archbishop Jean de Marigny, always prompt to join the winning side.

'He won't last. He must be very uncertain of himself if he feels obliged to seek the support of the commonalty,' Valois whispered to Charles de La Marche when he saw with some vexation that Coquatrix, Gentien and other notables were present.

Nevertheless, he assumed his best manner when advancing towards his nephew and presenting his excuses for the morning's incident.

'My equerries of the guard knew no better. They had received definite orders because of Queen Clémence . . .'

He expected a harsh rebuff and almost hoped for it so that he might have a pretext for opposing Philippe openly. But his nephew gave him no opportunity for a quarrel and replied in the same tone: 'I had to act as I did, and with the greatest regret, Uncle, to forestall the plans of the Duke of Burgundy, who had a free hand in your absence. I received the news during the night at Fontainebleau, but did not wish to disturb you.'

Valois, to minimize his defeat, pretended to credit the explanation, and even brought himself to be polite to the Constable, whom he believed to be the author of the whole plot.

Charles de La Marche, who was less clever at dissimulation, clenched his teeth.

The Count of Evreux then made the proposal which had been previously agreed with Philippe. While the Count of Poitiers pretended to be engaged in military questions with the Constable and Mille de Noyers, in a corner of the room, Louis of Evreux said: 'My noble Lords, and you too, Messires, I counsel, for the good of the kingdom and so as to avoid dangerous disturbances, that our well-beloved nephew, Philippe, take possession of the government, we all consenting, and that he should fulfil the royal duties in the name of his unborn nephew, if God so wishes that Queen Clémence should give birth to a son. I counsel also that an assembly of all the chief men of the kingdom be held as soon as it can be convoked, with the peers and the barons, in order to approve our decision and swear fealty to the Regent.'

It was a precise counterstroke to the declaration Charles de La Marche had made the evening before on his arrival at Fontainebleau. But this act had been prepared by better artists. Led by those who were loyal to the Count of Poitiers, everyone present approved with acclamation. Then Louis of Evreux, repeating the gesture the Count de Forez had made at Lyons, went and placed his hands between those of Philippe.

'I swear fealty to you, Nephew,' he said, falling upon his knees.

Philippe raised him and, embracing him, whispered in his ear: 'Everything is going splendidly; thank you, Uncle.'

Charles de La Marche, furiously angry at Philippe's success, muttered: 'He thinks he's the King.'

But Louis of Evreux had already turned to Charles of Valois and was saying: 'I am sorry, Brother, to have taken precedence of you, my elder.'

There was nothing Valois could do but obey. He went forward with his hands outstretched; the Count of Poitiers left them in the air.

'I shall be grateful to you, Uncle,' he said, 'if you will sit on my Council.'

Valois turned pale. Only the day before he had been signing ordinances and sealing them with his seal. Today he was being offered, as if it were a great honour, a place on a council to which he belonged by right.

'You will also hand over to us the keys of the Treasury,' Philippe added, lowering his voice. 'I know that there is nothing in it but air. But I don't want any more to blow away.'

Valois retreated. He was being asked to give up everything.

'Nephew, I cannot,' he replied. 'I must have the accounts drawn up.'

'Are you really so anxious to put the accounts in order, Uncle?' said Philippe, with scarcely perceptible irony. 'For we should then be compelled to look into them, and to examine also the administration of the sums confiscated from

Enguerrand de Marigny. Give us the keys, and we will hold you exempt.'

Valois understood the threat.

'Very well, Nephew; the keys will be brought you within the hour.'

Philippe extended his hands to receive the homage of his most powerful rival.

The Constable of France then came forward in his turn.

'Now, Gaucher,' Philippe whispered to him, 'we must deal with the Burgundian.'

8

The Count of Poitiers's Visits

THE COUNT OF POITIERS had no illusions. He had just had a first, quick and spectacular success; but he knew that his adversaries were not to be disarmed so easily.

As soon as he had received the meaningless oath of loyalty from Monseigneur of Valois, Philippe crossed the Palace to pay his respects to his sister-in-law, Clémence. He was accompanied by Anseau de Joinville and the Countess Mahaut. Hugues de Bouville, as soon as he saw Philippe, burst into tears and fell on his knees, kissing his hands. The ex-Chamberlain, though he was a member of the Council of Peers, had not put in an appearance at the afternoon's meeting; he had not left his post nor sheathed his sword during all these last hours. The assault on the Palace by the Constable and the panic and departure of the Count of Valois's men had subjected his nerves to too harsh an ordeal.

'Forgive me, Monseigneur, forgive my weakness; it is from joy of seeing you back . . .' he said, wetting the Regent's hands with his tears.

'It's all right, my friend, it's all right,' replied Philippe.

The old Joinville did not recognize the Count of Poitiers. Nor did he recognize his own son and, when he had been told three times that they stood before him, he mistook one for the other and bowed ceremoniously to Anseau.

Bouville opened the door of the Queen's room. But, as Mahaut made to follow Philippe, the Curator, recovering his energy, cried: 'You alone, Monseigneur, you alone!'

And he shut the door in the Countess's face.

Queen Clémence was pale and weak and clearly did not share the preoccupations that excited the Court and the people of Paris. As she saw the Count of Poitiers come towards her, his hands outstretched, she could not help thinking: 'If I had been married to him, I should not be a widow today. Why should it have been Louis? Why was it not Philippe?' She forbade herself questions of this nature, which seemed to her reproaches to Almighty God. But nothing, even piety, could prevent a widow of twenty-three from wondering why other young men, other husbands, were alive.

Philippe told her that he had assumed the regency and assured her of his utter devotion.

'Oh, yes, Brother, oh yes,' she murmured, 'help me!'

She wanted to say, without knowing how to express herself: 'Help me to live, help me against despair, help me to put into the world this new life which from now on is my only task on earth.' She went on: 'Why did our uncle Valois make me leave my house at Vincennes almost by force? Louis gave it to me with his last breath.'

'Do you wish to return there?' Poitiers asked.

'It is my only desire, Brother! I shall feel better there. And my child will be born as near as possible to his father's spirit, in the place where he left this world.'

Philippe took no decisions, even lesser ones, lightly. He turned his eyes away from the white veils which framed Clémence's face and looked out of the window at the spire of the Sainte-Chapelle, whose outline seemed uncertain and misty to his short-sighted eyes, like a great gold-and-stone stalk, on the summit of which seemed to blossom the royal lily.

'If I grant her this wish,' he thought, 'she will be grateful to me, will look on me as her defender and will obey my decisions in all things. On the other hand, my adversaries will have less easy access to her at Vincennes than here, and will have less chance of using her against me. Besides, in her present state of grief, she is of no use to anyone.'

'I want to do everything you wish, Sister,' he replied; 'as soon as the Assembly of Notables has confirmed me in my position, my first care will be to take you back to Vincennes. Today is Monday; the assembly, which I am hastening on, will doubtless take place on Friday. I think you will be able to hear mass in your own house next Sunday.'

'I knew you were a kind brother, Philippe. Your return is the first relief God has granted me.'

When he came out of the Queen's apartment, Philippe found his mother-in-law waiting for him. She had been disputing with Bouville and was walking alone, with long mannish strides, up and down the flagstones of the gallery beneath the wary eyes of the equerries of the guard.

'Well, how is she?' she asked Philippe.

'Pious and resigned, and well worthy of giving France a king,' replied the Count of Poitiers, loud enough to be heard by all those present.

Then, in a low voice, he added: 'I think, in the state of health in which I found her, that she will lose her child before her time.'

'It would be the best present she could give us, and would make everything much easier,' replied Mahaut in a whisper; 'and then we should have done with all this mistrust and armed men about her. Since when have the peers of the realm been forbidden access to the Queen? I've been widowed too, devil take it, and people could always come and see me on affairs of state!'

Poisoner though she was, she was genuinely indignant that the general security measures should apply to her.

Philippe, who had not yet seen his wife since his return, went with Mahaut to the Hôtel d'Artois.

'Your absence has seemed very long to my daughter,' said Mahaut. 'But you will find her wonderfully well. No one would think that she was on the point of being brought to bed. I was just the same in my pregnancies, active till the last day.'

The meeting between the Count of Poitiers and his wife was moving but there were no tears. Jeanne, though she was heavy and moved with difficulty, showed every sign of health and happiness. Night had fallen, and the glow of the candles, so becoming to the complexion, blurred any signs on the young woman's face of her condition. She was wearing a number of necklaces of red coral, well known to have a beneficent effect on childbirth.

It was in Jeanne's presence that Philippe became truly

aware of the successes he had already achieved, and allowed himself some self-satisfaction. Taking his wife in his arms, he said: 'I really think, my darling, that I can now call you Madame la Régente.'

'Pray God, my dear Lord, that I may give you a son,' she replied, clinging to her husband's strong, spare body.

'God will put the crown on His mercies,' Philippe whispered to her, 'if He does not allow the child to be born till after Friday.'

An argument soon arose between Mahaut and Philippe. The Countess of Artois thought that her daughter should be moved to the Palace at once, to share her husband's apartments. Philippe took the opposite view and wished Jeanne to remain in the Hôtel d'Artois. He put forward several arguments, sound in themselves, though they did not reveal the whole of his thought and failed to convince Mahaut. The Palace, during the next few days, might be the scene of violent assemblies and considerable turmoil, dangerous to a woman in labour; besides, Philippe thought it more fitting to await Clémence's departure for Vincennes before installing Jeanne in the royal Palace.

'But look at her, Philippe!' cried Mahaut. 'Tomorrow she may no longer be able to be moved. Don't you want your child to be born in the Palace?'

'That is precisely what I do not want.'

'Well, really, I don't understand you, my son,' said Mahaut, shrugging her powerful shoulders.

The argument wearied Philippe; he had not slept for thirty-six hours, had ridden thirty-seven miles the previous night, and had followed it with the busiest and most difficult day of his life. He felt the stubble on his chin and, at moments, his eyes seemed to close of their own accord. But he had made up his mind not to give way. 'Bed,' he thought; 'let them obey me, so that I can go to bed!'

'Let us ask Jeanne's opinion. What do you wish, my dear?' he said, certain of his wife's submissiveness.

Mahaut had a man's intelligence and strength of will, as well as a constant determination to assert the prestige of her family. Jeanne, whose nature was quite other, had become accustomed through fate to never being at the summit of events. Betrothed first to the Hutin, merely to have been given later, by a sort of exchange, to the second son of Philip the Fair, she had missed both the Crown of Navarre and the Crown of France. In the affair of the Tower of Nesle, if she had been compromised in the loves of her sisters-in-law, she had skirted adultery without committing it; and in her punishment, imprisonment for life had been avoided. She had been implicated in every drama, but had never taken the leading part. Out of a sort of delicacy, rather than from any moral consideration, she disliked all excess; the years she had spent in the Fortress of Dourdan had reinforced her prudence. She was shrewd, sensible, intelligent and knew how to make use of that entirely feminine weapon: submission.

Guessing that Philippe's insistence was based on strong reasons, she suppressed a slight feeling of legitimate vanity and said: 'I should like to have my child here, Mother. I should be more comfortable.'

She did not care overmuch whether her fourth child was born in the Palace or elsewhere. Philippe thanked her with a smile. Sitting in a great, upright chair, his crossed legs extended, he asked the names of the matrons and midwives who were to attend Jeanne, wishing to know where each came from, and whether she could be completely relied upon. He recommended that they should be made to take an oath, a precaution which was normally taken only at the birth of the King's children.

'What a good husband I have, and what care he takes of me!' Jeanne thought, as she listened to him.

Philippe ordered also that, from the moment the Countess of Poitiers's pains began, the gates of the Hôtel d'Artois should be closed. No one was to leave it, except for one person who would bring him news of the birth.

'You,' he said, indicating the beautiful Béatrice d'Hirson, who was present at the conversation. 'Orders will be given to my chamberlain that you may come to me at any hour, even if I am in council. And if there are people about me, you will give me the news in a whisper, and tell it to no one else, if it is a son. I trust you, because I remember that you have already rendered me good service.'

'And greater indeed than you know of, Monseigneur,' replied Béatrice, making a slight bow.

Mahaut threw Béatrice a furious glance. The wench, with her meek expression, her false ingenuousness and her sly audacities, made her tremble. Béatrice continued to smile. These facial expressions did not escape Jeanne, who nevertheless asked no questions. Between her mother and the lady-in-waiting there were dark secrets of which she preferred to know nothing.

She looked anxiously at her husband, but he had noticed nothing. With his head against the back of the chair, he had suddenly dropped off, overcome with the sleep of victory. On his angular face, normally so severe, was an expression of sweet concern in which could be traced the child he once had been. Jeanne, much moved, went to him silently and kissed him lightly on the forehead.

9

Friday's Child

On the following day the Count of Poitiers began to make preparations for the Assembly to be held on Friday. If he emerged from it the victor, no one for many long years would be able to contest his power.

He sent messengers and couriers to summon, as had been arranged, all the great men in the kingdom – all those, that is, who lived no further away than two days' journey on horseback, thus allowing him to prevent the situation from getting out of hand and to eliminate certain great vassals, whose enmity Philippe had reason to fear, such as the Count of Flanders and the King of England.

At the same time he entrusted to Gaucher de Châtillon, to Mille de Noyers and to Raoul de Presles the task of preparing the act of regency that would be submitted to the Assembly. The following principles, based on the decisions already made, were incorporated: the Count of Poitiers was to administer both kingdoms with the provisional title of Regent, Governor and Guardian, and would receive all the royal revenues.

If Queen Clémence bore a son, the latter would naturally be King, and Philippe would hold the regency until his nephew's majority. But if Clémence bore a daughter . . . This was where all the difficulties began. For, in all justice, in these circumstances the crown should go to the little Jeanne of Navarre, the Hutin's elder daughter. But was she really his daughter? That was the question which the Court, indeed the whole kingdom, was asking. Without the love affair of the Tower of Nesle, without the scandal and the sentence pronounced at Pontoise, the rights of this child would have been unquestioned and, in the absence of a male heir, she would have had to be made Queen of France. But there hung over her a grave suspicion to which Charles of Valois, in particular, had given weight when arranging Louis X's second marriage, and of which Philippe, in the circumstances, did not fail to take advantage. The dates of the beginning of Marguerite's guilty love affair and the birth of Jeanne corresponded suspiciously. It was also suspicious that Louis had always shown a dislike for this child, and had always kept her at a distance. There was, therefore, some reason for people to whisper: 'She is the daughter of Philippe d'Aunay.'

Thus the affair of the Tower of Nesle, which popular imagination through the ages turned into a sort of mythical fable of legendary love, vice, crime and horror, though it was in fact a fairly simple case of adultery, created, two years after the event, a grave dynastic problem altering the natural succession of the French monarchy.

Someone suggested that it should be decided at once that the crown should definitely go to Clèmence's child, whether it were a boy or a girl.

Philippe of Poitiers did not welcome the suggestion, and

found good arguments for putting it aside. Certainly the suspicions about Jeanne of Navarre were strongly based, but there was no formal proof. Neither Marguerite's mother, old Agnès, dowager Duchess of Burgundy, nor her son, Eudes IV, the present Duke, could subscribe to this harsh barring of their niece. All the enemies of the Crown, beginning with the Count of Flanders, would not fail to use it to serve their personal interests. There was a risk of giving France over to an immediate civil war, the War of the Two Queens.

'In that case,' said Gaucher de Châtillon, 'let us decree here and now that girls are unable to inherit the crown. There must be some precedent to support it.'

'Alas, Brother-in-law,' replied Mille de Noyers, 'I have already had search made, for your idea also occurred to me, but nothing has been found.'

'Further search must be made! Put your friends, the Masters of the University and of Parliament, on to the research. Those people can always find precedents for everything, if they take the trouble. They go back to Clovis in order to prove that you ought to have your head cut off, be burnt at the stake or quartered.'

'It's true', said Mille, 'that I haven't had the researches carried as far back as that. I was thinking only of royal precedents since the great Hugues. We must look earlier than that. But I don't think we shall find anything between now and Friday.'

The Constable was a misogynist like all good soldiers, and he jutted his square chin and screwed up his saurian eyes. 'It would be madness to allow a girl to ascend the throne,' he went on. 'Can you see a woman or a wench commanding the armies, unclean every month, pregnant every year? Can you see them dealing with the vassals when they cannot even control their own bodies' heat? No, I don't see it, and I should put up my sword at once. Messeigneurs, I tell you France is too noble a country to fall to the distaff and be handed over to a woman. Lilies do not spin!'

This last suggestion was not adopted on the spot, but it made a strong impression, and was put to good use later.[12]

Philippe of Poitiers gave his assent to a somewhat tortuous document; it postponed all these decisions for a long time to come.

'Draft it in such a way that the difficulties are apparent, but without our proposing solutions,' he said. 'Confuse the issues a little so that everyone may believe he finds in it something to his own advantage.'

Thus, if Queen Clémence gave birth to a daughter, Philippe would keep the regency until the majority of his eldest niece, Jeanne. And only then would the devolution of the crown be decided, either to the advantage of the two Princesses, who would then share between them France and Navarre, or to the advantage of one of them, who would preserve the unity of both kingdoms, or again to the advantage of neither should they renounce their rights or if the Assembly of Peers, summoned to debate the issue, decided that a woman could not rule over the kingdom of France; in this last case, the crown would go to the nearest male relative of the late King, which was to say, Philippe. In this way his candidature was officially put forward for the first time, but subject to so many conditions that it looked as if the eventual solution must be made by compromise or arbitration.

This law, submitted individually to the chief barons who favoured Philippe, received their acquiescence.

Only Mahaut seemed strangely to have reservations about an act which, in fact, was preparing the accession of her son-in-law and her daughter to the throne of France. Something in the draft upset her.

'Could you not', she asked, 'declare simply: "If the two daughters renounce their rights . . ." without talking of submitting the question of whether women may reign or not to the Assembly of Peers?'

'Well, Mother,' Philippe replied, 'in that case they would not renounce their rights at all. The peers, of whom you are one, are the only court of appeal. Originally they were electors of the King, as the Cardinals are of the Pope or the Palatines of the Emperor, and it was thus that they chose Hugues, our ancestor, who was Duke of France. If they no longer elect, it's because for three centuries our kings have always had a son to ascend the throne.'[13]

'It's a purely chance custom!' replied Mahaut. 'Your new law is precisely calculated to serve the pretensions of my nephew Robert. You'll see that he will not fail to use it to try and take my county back from me.'

She was thinking only of the quarrel over the succession of Artois, and not of the whole of France.

'The custom of the kingdom is not necessarily the custom of a fief, Mother. And you'll be more likely to keep your county with your son-in-law as King, than by the arguments of jurists.'

Mahaut surrendered without being convinced.

'There's the gratitude of sons-in-law for you,' she said a little later to Béatrice d'Hirson. 'You poison a king so that they may take his place, and then they do exactly as they please without consideration for anyone!'

'The fact is, Madame, he doesn't know what he owes you, nor how our Lord Louis came to die.'

'And, Lord, he must never know!' cried Mahaut, quickly putting her hands to her dress and feeling for the relic of Saint Druon, as she always did when she spoke of her crimes. 'It was his brother, after all, and Philippe has strange ideas about justice. Hold your tongue, for God's sake, hold your tongue!'

During these days Charles of Valois, with the assistance of Charles de La Marche and Robert of Artois, was very active everywhere, spreading the view that it was lunacy to confirm the Count of Poitiers in the regency, and still more so to consider him as heir-presumptive. Philippe and his mother-in-law had made too many enemies; and the death of Louis served their designs, now openly avowed, too well for this suspect death not to be their work. Valois was in a position to offer other guarantees and put himself forward as the only man who could find a solution for the kingdom's difficulties. He was on the best possible terms with the King of Naples, and declared that he could put a stop to any difficulties likely to be made by Queen Clémence. He was the only member of the royal family who, despite the wars, had preserved relations with the Count of Flanders. Having served the Roman Papacy, he had the confidence of the Italian Cardinals, without whom a Pope could not be elected, in spite of the infamous procedure of locking up the Conclave. The ex-Templars remembered that he had never approved the suppression of their Order, and on this account, too, he carried considerable weight.

When Philippe heard of this campaign, he ordered his friends to reply that it was very strange to see the King's uncle relying, for the purpose of seizing power, on his good relations with the enemies of the kingdom, and that if one wished to see the Pope in Rome, and France in the hands of the Angevins, the Flemings or the resuscitated Temple, the Count of Valois should immediately be offered the crown.

At last the decisive Friday, on which the Assembly was to be held, arrived. At dawn Béatrice d'Hirson came to the Palace and was immediately shown into the Count of Poitiers's room. The lady-in-waiting was somewhat out of breath from having run all the way from the Rue de Mauconseil. Philippe sat up among his pillows.

'A boy?' he asked.

'A boy, Monseigneur, and well-membered,' replied Béatrice, flashing her eyelashes. Philippe dressed hastily and hurried to the Hôtel d'Artois.

'The gates! The gates! Keep the gates shut!' he said as soon as he had entered. 'Have my orders been properly obeyed? No one, except Béatrice, has been allowed to leave? Let it remain so for the rest of the day.'

Then he dashed upstairs. He had lost the stiffness and solemnity which he normally forced himself to adopt.

The birth-chamber, as was the custom in princely families, had been sumptuously decorated. There were tall hangings depicting flowers and parrots, the fine tapestries from Arras of which the Countess Mahaut was so proud, entirely covering the walls. The ground was strewn with flowers, irises, roses and daisies, which got trampled under foot. The mother, pale, her eyes bright, and her face still showing signs of strain, was lying in a huge bed surrounded with silk curtains, under white sheets which stretched from the bed an ell across the floor. In the corners of the room were two small beds, one for the sworn midwife and the other for the nurse on duty.

The young Regent went straight to the ostentatious cradle, and bent low to take a good look at the son who had been born to him. Ugly and yet touching, as are all babies in their first hours, red, wrinkled, its eyelids stuck together and its lips dribbling, with a small wisp of fair hair sticking up from its bald head, the child was still sleeping its embryonic sleep, and looked, in the swaddling clothes which covered it to the shoulders, like a tiny mummy.

'So here's my little Philippe,[14] whom I so longed for and who has arrived so well named and at the right moment,' said the Count of Poitiers.

Only then did he go to his wife, kiss her on both cheeks, and say in a tone of profound gratitude: 'Thank you, darling, thank you. You have given me great joy, and this wipes out for ever our disagreements of the past.'

Jeanne took her husband's long hand, carried it to her lips and stroked her face with it.

'God has blessed us, Philippe; God has blessed our reunion of last autumn,' she murmured. She was still wearing her coral necklaces.

The Countess Mahaut, her sleeves rolled up over her forearms, which were covered with thick hair, was a triumphant witness of the scene. She tapped her stomach with a lively gesture.

'Well, my son!' she cried. 'Didn't I tell you so? We have good wombs, we of Artois and Burgundy.'

She spoke as if discussing the merits of brood mares.

Philippe went back to the cradle.

'Can he not be unwrapped so that I may see him better?' he asked.

'Monseigneur,' replied the midwife, 'it is not advisable.

A child's limbs are very soft and must remain swaddled as long as possible, that they may become strong and be prevented from growing crooked. But have no fear, Monseigneur, we have rubbed him well with salt and honey and have enveloped him in crushed roses to remove the viscous humour, and he has had his mouth cleaned with a finger dipped in honey, to give him sweetness and appetite. You may be sure that he is well cared for.'

'And your Jeanne too,' added Mahaut; 'I have had her anointed with a good unguent mixed with hare's droppings to contract her, according to the receipt of Master Arnaud of Villeneuve.'

She wished to reassure her son-in-law as to the quality of his future pleasures.

'But, Mother,' said Jeanne, 'I thought it was a receipt for a barren woman.'

'Nonsense! Hare's droppings are good for everything.'

Philippe went on gazing at his heir.

'Don't you think he looks very like my father, the great King?' he asked. 'He's got his forehead, and his chin.'

'A little perhaps,' replied Mahaut. 'To tell you the truth, when I looked at him a little while ago, I thought I discerned the features of my late good Othon. May he have the strength of mind and body of them both, that is what I hope.'

'He looks more like you than anyone, Philippe,' said Jeanne softly.

The Count of Poitiers straightened himself up with some pride.

'I think', he said, 'that you now understand my orders better, Mother, and why I asked you to keep your gates closed. No one must know yet that I have a son. For it would be said that I have drawn up the law of succession expressly to assure him the throne after me, if Clémence does not have a male child; and I know many, my brother Charles to begin with, who would give trouble if they knew that their hopes had been so soon destroyed. Therefore, if you wish this child one day to have a chance of becoming King, don't say a word to anybody during the Assembly today.'

'Of course, there's the Assembly! That young gallant made me forget all about it,' cried Mahaut pointing to the cradle. 'It's high time I went and dressed, and had a morsel to eat so as to be fit and strong for it. I feel hollow inside from having got up so early. Philippe, you'll join me. Béatrice, Béatrice!'

She clapped her hands, and ordered a pike pie, boiled eggs, a white spiced cheese, pickled walnuts, peaches and white wine from Château-Chalon.

'It's Friday; we must fast,' she said.

The sun, rising over the roofs of the city, bathed the happy family in its light.

'Have a little something to eat. Pike pie won't lie heavy on your stomach,' said Mahaut to her daughter.

Philippe soon left to see to the last preparations for the Assembly, the hour for which was drawing near.

'My dear, no one will come to pay you their respects today,' he said to Jeanne, indicating the cushions for visitors arranged in a semicircle round the bed. 'But you will have a crowd of people tomorrow.'

As he was leaving, Mahaut caught him by the sleeve.

'My son, think of Blanche a little; she is still in Château-Gaillard. She is your wife's sister.'

'I'll think about it, I'll think about it. I'll see what can be done to improve her lot.'

And he went, carrying away on the sole of his boot one of the irises from the birth-chamber.

Mahaut closed the gates.

'Well, nurses,' she cried, 'why don't you sing a lullaby!'

10

The Assembly of the Three Dynasties

SECLUDED IN HER APARTMENTS, Queen Clémence became aware that the lords and great men were arriving for the Assembly, and heard the tumult of voices in the courtyards and under the vaulted roofs.

Her forty days' seclusion, imposed on the Queen by mourning, had come to an end the day before, and Clémence had thought ingenuously that the date of the meeting had been chosen expressly that she might be able to preside at it. She had prepared herself for this solemn reappearance with interest, curiosity and even impatience; and it had seemed to her that she had begun to take pleasure in life again these last days. But, at the last minute, a council of sages and doctors, among whom were the Count of Poitiers's and the Countess Mahaut's personal physicians, had forbidden her to attend on the ground that the fatigue might be dangerous in her condition.

Everyone approved this decision, for indeed no one wished to put forward Clémence's rights to the regency nor even her right to be associated with it. And yet, since so determined a search had been made into the history of the kingdom for possible precedents, they had naturally not failed to be reminded of Anne of Russia, widow of Henri I, who had shared the government with her brother-in-law Beaudoin of Flanders 'owing to the ineffaceable quality conferred on her by her coronation', or again of Queen Blanche of Castile, who was very present to their memories.[15]

But the Dauphin of Viennois, Clémence's brother-in-law, who was therefore in the best position to defend her prerogative, had gone completely over to Philippe since the contract of marriage between their two children had been signed.

Charles of Valois, who gave himself out as his niece's great protector, made no more effort in her favour than the others; he had enough to do standing up for himself.

As for Duke Eudes of Burgundy, who was there, as he had been saying for the last month, to support the rights of his sister Marguerite, and avenge her death, he could not but be utterly hostile to Clémence.

As she had been on the throne for too short a time to become known to and acquire an ascendancy over the great barons, they looked on her merely as the survivor of a brief and troubled reign which had been calamitous in more ways than one.

'She has not brought the kingdom luck,' they said of her.

And if she still existed as an expectant mother, she had ceased to exist as Queen.

Shut up in a wing of the Palace, she heard the sound of voices diminish as the Assembly began its session in the Grand Council Hall and the doors were closed.

'My God,' she thought, 'why did I not remain in Naples!'

And she began to weep as she thought of her childhood, the blue sea, and the swarming, noisy, generous people, who were compassionate towards sorrow, *her* people who knew so well how to love.

And now Mille de Noyers was reading the Act of Succession.

The Count of Poitiers had taken care not to surround himself with any of the trappings of royal majesty; his faldstool was placed in the middle of a dais, but he had refused to have it surmounted by a canopy. He was dressed in sombre clothes without ornament, though the official mourning had come to an end. He seemed to be saying: 'Messeigneurs, we are here in council to do business.' The only outward show was provided by the three mace-bearers who preceded him at his entry and now stood behind his chair. It was clearly he who exercised sovereignty, but without any of its trappings. All the same, he had carefully arranged the room and had everyone shown to his place by his chamberlain, inaugurating an arbitrary and inflexible ceremonial which impressed those present, for they recognized in it the touch of Philip the Fair.

On his right Philippe had placed Charles of Valois and, immediately beyond him, Gaucher de Châtillon, so as to keep the ex-Emperor of Constantinople under control and isolate him from his clan. Philippe of Valois was placed six places away from his father. On his left the Regent had placed his uncle, Louis of Evreux, and only beyond him his brother, Charles de La Marche; he was endeavouring to prevent the two Charleses from concerting together during the course of the meeting and going back on their oath of four days before.

But the Count of Poitiers's attention was mostly concentrated on his cousin, the Duke of Burgundy, whom he watched in his place at the end of the dais, where he was flanked by the Countess Mahaut and the Dauphin of Viennois.

Philippe knew that the Duke was going to speak in the name of his mother, the Duchess Agnès, on whom the fact that she was the last daughter of Louis IX conferred, even in her absence, great prestige among the barons. Anyone who awakened a memory of the canonized King, the defender of Christendom, the hero of Tunis, anyone whom his hand had caressed, was an object of veneration; indeed, anyone still living who had seen him, had been spoken to by him or been the object of his affection, was endued with an almost sacred quality.

In order to move the hearts of his hearers, Eudes of Burgundy had only to say: 'My mother, the daughter of Monsieur Saint Louis, who blessed her before going to die in a heathen land . . .'

So to check this manoeuvre, Philippe had another and most unexpected card up his sleeve: Robert of Clermont, the other survivor of the Saint's eleven children, the sixth and last son. Since they desired the blessing of Saint Louis, they should have it.

The presence of Robert, Count of Clermont, seemed something of a miracle, since the last of his rare appearances at Court had been more than five years ago; his very existence was almost forgotten, and when he was remembered no one dared speak of him save in a whisper.

Indeed, Great-uncle Robert had been mad since the age of twenty-four, when he had been hit on the head with a mace. His madness was violent but intermittent, with long calm periods which had allowed Philip the Fair to make use of him from time to time for purely ornamental missions. He was not dangerous because of what he said; indeed he hardly spoke. He was dangerous because of what he did; for there were no preliminary signs of an attack, and he might hurl himself, sword in hand, on friends for whom he felt a sudden and murderous hatred.[16] It was a shocking sight to see a lord of so noble a race and so handsome an appearance – for at sixty he had still a majestic air – hack the furniture to pieces, slash the tapestries and pursue the female servants, believing them to be adversaries in a tournament.

The Count of Poitiers had placed him on the other wing of the dais, opposite the Duke of Burgundy and close to a door. Two enormous equerries stood nearby, their duty being to take hold of him at the first signs of a seizure. He gazed round in a bored, scornful, absent way, his eyes coming suddenly to rest on a face here or there in a sort of agonized anxiety of irrecoverable recollection, only to pass on. Everyone stared at him and his presence caused a certain uneasiness.

Next to the madman sat his son, Louis I of Bourbon, who was lame, which had always prevented him from distinguishing himself in battle, but had in no way impaired his ability to run away, as had indeed been evident at the battle of Courtrai. Gawky, deformed and a coward, Bourbon had in contrast to his father a clear brain, which he had shown by joining Philippe of Poitiers's party.

From these splendid origins, crippled in both head and limb, was to descend the long line of the Bourbons.

Thus, here in this Assembly of 16 July 1316 were gathered the three Capet branches who were to reign over France for five more centuries. The three dynasties might therefore look on both an end and a beginning: the direct Capet line which was soon to become extinct in Philippe of Poitiers and Charles de La Marche; that of Valois which, with Charles's son, was to hold the succession for thirteen reigns; and, finally, that of the Bourbons, who were to come to the throne when the Valois were extinct and it became necessary to return once more to the descendants of Saint Louis to find a king. Each change of dynasty was to be accompanied by exhausting and disastrous wars.

By that invariably surprising combination of men's actions and the unexpected twists of fate, the history of the French monarchy, in all its grandeur and tragedy, was to flow from the Act of Succession which Messire Mille, the jurist, was at this moment reading.

Sitting on benches or leaning against the walls, the barons, the prelates, the masters of Parliament and the delegates of the burgesses of Paris listened attentively.

'I've got a son: I've got a son, and they won't hear of it till tomorrow,' thought the Count of Poitiers, who supposed that his actions were merely for his own benefit and that of his son. And he prepared to meet the Duke of Burgundy's inevitable attack. But the attack came from another quarter.

There was one man present at the Assembly over whom no one had an ascendancy; he forgot the money with which he had been bought; noble blood failed to impress him, for his was of the best; he was not subject to force, for he could overturn a horse with his own hands; no party had a hold over him, except those he created himself; and even the spectacle of madness left him indifferent. This was Robert of Artois. And it was he who, as soon as Mille de Noyers had finished reading, rose to his feet to join battle alone.

As everyone was that day making a display of his family,

Robert of Artois had brought his mother, Blanche of Brittany, a tiny little woman with a thin face, white hair and fragile limbs, who seemed in a state of constant surprise at having given birth to so wonderful a giant.

Standing firmly planted in his red boots, his thumbs in his silver belt, Robert of Artois said: 'I am astonished, Messeigneurs, that a new Act of Regency should have been drawn up and laid before us, when there already exists the statement of our last King.'

All eyes turned to the Count of Poitiers and some of those present wondered anxiously whether there was a will of Louis X's which had been stolen.

'I do not know, Cousin,' said Philippe of Poitiers, 'of what statement you are speaking. You were a witness of my brother's last moments, with many other lords here present, and no one has ever told me that he expressed his will on the subject.'

'When I spoke, Cousin,' replied Robert, with a somewhat cunning expression, 'of "our last King", I was not talking of your brother, Louis X – whom God keep! – but of your father, our well-beloved Lord Philip, whom may God keep also! And King Philip decided, had it written down and made his peers swear it, that if he should die before his son were old enough to hold the reins of government, the royal office and the position of regent should fall to his brother, Monseigneur Charles, Count of Valois. So, Cousin, since no act has been made since then, it should, so it seems to me, be that one which must be put into force.'

Little Blanche of Brittany nodded her head, showed her toothless gums in a smile, and glanced round the room with her live bright eyes, inviting her neighbours to approve her son's speech. There was no word this brawler uttered, no argument this trickster put forward, no violence, escapade or rape this blackguard committed which she did not approve and admire as a sign that he was a prodigy. She received the Count of Valois's silent thanks, indicated by the flicker of an eyelid.

Philippe of Poitiers, leaning on the arm of his faldstool, slowly waved his hand. 'I am delighted, Robert, quite delighted,' he said, 'to see you so earnestly in favour of my father's wishes today, when you were so little obedient to his will while he was alive. No doubt a proper feeling comes with age, Cousin! You may be reassured. It is precisely my father's wishes we are doing our best to respect. Is that not so, Uncle?' he added, turning to Louis of Evreux.

Lord of Evreux, who had been exasperated for the last six weeks by the manoeuvres of his half-brother Valois and his brother-in-law Artois, did not deny himself the pleasure of putting them in their place.

'The rule on which you are taking your stand, Robert, is valid for the principle, but not indefinitely for the person. For if, in fifty or a hundred years, a similar accident should once more overtake the Crown, it would not be my brother Charles who would be made regent of the kingdom, though I wish him a long life. For indeed,' he cried in a loud voice, unusual in this quiet man, 'the Lord God has not made Charles eternal that he may make an attempt on the throne every time it becomes vacant. If it is to the elder brother that the regency should go, it must be Philippe who is indicated, and that is why we paid him homage the other day. Do not therefore reopen a matter which is already decided.'

It seemed to be checkmate. But they did not know Robert.

He took two paces forward, inclined his head a little, so that the sun shone through the windows on his bull-neck, while his shadow lay like a menace across the flagstones reaching to the feet of the Count of Poitiers.

'The will of King Philip', he went on, 'contained nothing about the royal girls, nor that they must renounce their rights, nor that the Assembly of Peers was to decide whether they should reign.'

There was a sign of approval among the Burgundian lords, and Duke Eudes cried out: 'Well said, Cousin; it is exactly the point I was going to make myself!'

Blanche of Brittany looked brightly round again. The Constable was beginning to fidget in his chair. He could be heard muttering, and those who knew him well foresaw an outburst.

'Since when', went on the Duke of Burgundy, rising, 'has this new departure been introduced into the customs of the Crown? Only since yesterday, I believe! Since when have daughters, if there are no sons, been deprived of the possessions and crowns of their fathers?'

The Constable rose in his turn.

'Since, Messire Duke,' he said with calculated deliberation, 'a certain daughter cannot be guaranteed to the kingdom as having been born of the father whose heir you wish to make her. Indeed, you must know what is generally said and what my cousin of Valois has so often himself mentioned in the Small Council. France is too great and splendid a country, Messire Duke, for its crown to be handed, without the matter having been deliberated by the peers, to a Princess of whom one cannot tell whether she is the daughter of the King or the daughter of an equerry.'

A horrified silence fell over the Assembly. Eudes of Burgundy turned pale. His councillor, Guillaume de Mello, whom Duchess Agnès had sent with him, was whispering into his ear but he could not hear what he was saying. It looked as if he were about to hurl himself on Gaucher de Châtillon, who was waiting for him, ready poised, his body inclined forward, his fists clenched. Even though the Constable was thirty years older than his adversary and shorter by half a head, he appeared to have no fear of a contest and, indeed, one might have expected him to win it. But the Duke of Burgundy's anger was spent in words against Charles of Valois.

'So it is you, Charles,' he cried, 'you, who sought my other sister's hand in marriage for your elder son, whom I see here present, it is you who have been dishonouring the dead?'

'Well, my friend,' said Valois, 'if it be a question of dishonour, Queen Marguerite – may God forgive her her sins! – had but little need of my assistance.'

And he said in an undertone to Gaucher de Châtillon: 'What did you want to bring me into this for?'

'And you, Brother-in-law,' continued Eudes, now attacking Philippe of Valois, 'do you approve these slanders?'

But Philippe of Valois, who was standing awkwardly, because of his great height, a few paces away, was seeking vainly for counsel from his father with his eyes; he merely raised his arms in a gesture of impotence and said: 'You must admit, Brother, that the scandal was considerable.'

There was a stir in the Assembly. From the back of the hall came sounds of argument; some lords were arguing Jeanne's bastardy, others her legitimacy. Charles de La Marche, ill-at-ease and pale, lowered his head to avoid other people's eyes as he did whenever the unfortunate business was mentioned. 'Marguerite is dead; Louis is dead,' he thought; 'but my wife, Blanche, is still living and I still bear my dishonour for all to see.'

At this moment the Count of Clermont, to whom nobody was paying any attention, began to show signs of agitation: 'I challenge you, Messires, I challenge you all!' cried Saint Louis's last surviving son, rising to his feet.

'Later, Father, later, when we go to the tournament,' Louis of Bourbon said and signalled the two huge equerries to draw near and stand ready.

Robert of Artois watched the disturbance he had caused, delighted with himself.

The Duke of Burgundy, in spite of the efforts Guillaume de Mello was making to allay his anger, was still shouting at Charles of Valois: 'I hope too, Charles, that God will pardon my sister her sins, if she committed any! But I am not so concerned that he should forgive her assassin!'

'Those are lies you have heard, Eudes,' replied Valois, 'and you know well that your sister died in prison of remorse.'

And he glanced at Robert to make sure that he had not flinched.

Now that the Count of Valois and the Duke of Burgundy were wholeheartedly quarrelling, and there was no chance of their uniting in their demands for a long time to come, Philippe of Poitiers stretched out his hand in a gesture of pacification.

But Eudes did not want peace. He had not come there to make it; on the contrary.

'I have heard Burgundy outraged enough for one day,

Cousin,' he said. 'I declare to you that I do not recognize you as Regent, and that I maintain before everyone the rights of my niece, Jeanne.'

Then, making a sign to the Burgundian lords to follow him, he left the hall.

'Messeigneurs, Messires,' said the Count of Poitiers, 'this is precisely what our jurists have endeavoured to avoid by postponing the necessity, should it indeed ever arise, of the Council of Peers having to decide this question of the girls. For should Queen Clémence present the kingdom with a male heir, this whole dispute is pointless.'

Robert of Artois was still standing in front of the dais, his hands on his hips.

'I gather therefore, Cousin,' he said, 'that from henceforth it is the custom in France for a woman's right of succession to be contested. I demand, therefore, that my county of Artois, which was wrongly given to my aunt Mahaut, who is well known to have a female body, the which, I believe, a number of lords can testify, should be returned to me. And as long as you have not done justice by me, I shall not appear at your Council.'

Thereupon he went towards the side door, followed by his mother, who trotted behind him, proud both of him and of herself.

The Countess Mahaut waved her hand towards Philippe in a gesture which meant: 'There! Didn't I tell you so!'

Before going out of the door, Robert, passing behind the Count of Clermont, whispered wickedly in his ear: 'To your lance, Cousin, to your lance!'

'Cut the cords! Cry battle!'[17] shouted Clermont, rising to his feet.

'Swine, devil take your guts!' cried Louis of Bourbon to Robert.

Then he said to his father: 'Stay with us. The trumpets have not sounded.'

'Oh, they haven't sounded yet, haven't they? Well, let them sound. It's getting late,' said Clermont.

He was waiting, his stare vacant, his arms outstretched.

Louis of Bourbon limped over to the Count of Poitiers and told him in a low voice that he must hurry. Philippe agreed with a nod of the head.

Bourbon returned to the madman, took him by the hand, and said: 'Homage, Father; you must give homage now.'

'Oh, yes, of course, homage!'

The lame man leading the madman, they crossed the dais.

'Messeigneurs,' said Louis of Bourbon, 'here is my father, the eldest of the blood of Saint Louis, who approves the Act on all points, recognizes Messire Philippe as Regent and swears fealty to him.'

'Yes, Messires, yes . . .' said Robert of Clermont.

Philippe trembled to think what the other might say. 'He'll call me Madame and ask for my scarf.'

But Clermont continued in a loud voice: 'I recognize you, Philippe, because you have the best right and are the most wise. May my father's saintly soul watch over you from heaven to help you keep the peace in the kingdom and defend our holy faith.'

The Assembly stirred in happy surprise. What went on in that man's head that he could pass without transition from madness to reason, from the absurd to the sublime?

Slowly and with great dignity, he knelt before his great-nephew and held out his hands; when he rose and turned about, having received the embrace, his great blue eyes were drowned in tears.

The whole Assembly rose to its feet and gave the two Princes a long ovation.

Philippe was thus recognized as Regent by the whole kingdom, with the exception of one province, Burgundy, and one man, Robert of Artois.

II

The Betrothed Play Tag

THE GREAT BARONIAL ASSEMBLIES were, in one respect at least, similar to modern international conferences. The member who noisily left the council chamber to protest against a decision would, if he were pressed a little, still accept an invitation to dine afterwards at the same table as his adversaries. And this was what the Duke of Burgundy did when Philippe sent him a messenger to express his regret at the morning's incident, assure him of his affection, and remind him that he was counting on his company.

The dinner was to be held in the Château of Vincennes; the Regent wished to see what state it was in before he handed it back to Clémence, and had had the necessary furnishings for a banquet taken there. The whole Court went; they sat down at trestle-tables, covered with immense white cloths, between high and low vespers, about five o'clock in the afternoon.

The presence of the Duke of Burgundy made Robert of Artois's absence all the more conspicuous.

'My son fainted as he came out of the Palace, he was

so upset by what had happened,' said Blanche of Brittany.

'Robert fainted! Really!' said Philippe of Poitiers. 'I hope he did not hurt himself falling from so great a height? I feel reassured to see that you are not over-anxious.'

On the other hand, no one was surprised at the absence of the Count of Clermont, whom his son had hastily taken home immediately he had paid homage. The Duke of Bourbon was congratulated on the splendid impression his father had created, while it was deplored that his illness – a noble illness, moreover, since it had occurred in an accident of arms – did not allow him to take part in the affairs of the realm more often.

The meal thus opened in comparatively good humour. The Constable had been placed some distance from the Duke of Burgundy, and they took care not to meet each other's eyes. Valois held forth on his own account.

The most surprising aspect of this dinner was the number of children present; for Eudes of Burgundy, having made it a condition of his own attendance that his niece, Jeanne of Navarre, should be present as some reparation for the outrage done her at the Assembly, the Count of Poitiers had decided to bring his three girls, the Count of Valois his latest offspring by his third marriage, the Count of Evreux his son and daughter, who were still of an age to play with dolls, the Dauphin of Viennois his little Guigues, the betrothed of the Regent's third daughter, and the Duke of Burgundy his three children. There was continual confusion over Christian names; Blanches, Isabelles, Charleses and Philippes abounded; when someone cried 'Jeanne!' six heads turned together.

These cousins were all destined to marry each other to serve the political strategy of their parents, who had themselves all been married in similar fashion: in the closest consanguinity. How many dispensations must be asked of the Pope that territorial interests might take precedence of the laws of religion and the most elementary considerations of health! How many cripples and madmen were there in prospect! The only difference between Adam's descendants and Capet's was that the latter had so far avoided incest between brothers and sisters.

The Dauphiniet and his betrothed, the little Isabelle of Poitiers, who would soon be called Isabelle of France, discovered a most touching friendship for each other. They ate out of the same dish; the Dauphiniet selecting the best morsels of eel stew for his future wife, searching diligently in the sauce, stuffing them into her mouth and smearing her face. The other children much envied them their betrothal, for they were to have their own little establishment in the Regent's house with their own groom, their own footman and their own housemaids.

Jeanne of Navarre ate nothing. It was known that her presence had been forced on the feast, and since children are quick at knowing their parents' feelings and exaggerating them, all the unhappy orphan's cousins turned their backs on her. Jeanne was the youngest; she was only five. But for the fact that she was fair, she was beginning to show a resemblance in many of her features, the jutting brow and high cheekbones, to her mother, Marguerite of Burgundy. A solitary child, who did not know how to play, living alone with servants in the sinister rooms of the Hôtel de Nesle, she had never seen so many people gathered in one room, nor heard so many voices, and she looked with a mixture of terror and admiration at the constant succession of dishes placed on the huge tables surrounded by hearty trenchermen. She knew very well that she was unloved; when she asked a question, no one answered her; young as she was, her intelligence was sufficiently developed, and her mind subtle enough, to repeat over and over again: 'My father was King, my mother was Queen; they are dead and no one speaks to me any more.' She was never to forget that dinner at Vincennes. As the voices rose and laughter spread, little Jeanne's sadness, her distress at this banquet of giants, weighed more heavily on her. Louis of Evreux who, from far off, saw her on the point of tears, said to his son: 'Philippe! Look after your cousin Jeanne.'[18]

Little Philippe wished to imitate the Dauphiniet and put a piece of sturgeon and orange sauce into her mouth but she did not like it and spat it out on to the cloth.

As the cupbearers ceremoniously served the wines to all the guests, it soon became apparent that this crowd of brats, dressed in brocade, were going to be ill and, before the sixth course, they were sent out into the courtyards. Thus these children of kings suffered the same fate as all children at banquets; they were deprived of the food they liked best, sweetmeats, puddings and dessert.

As soon as the feast was over, Philippe of Poitiers took the Duke of Burgundy by the arm and said that he wished to talk to him privately.

'Let us take our comfits away from the crowd, Cousin. Come with us, Uncle,' he added, turning to Louis of Evreux, 'and you too, Messire de Mello.'

He took the three men into a little neighbouring room, and while the sweet wine and spiced comfits were being handed round, he began explaining to the Duke of Burgundy how much he wished to come to an arrangement, and what the advantages of the Act of Regency were.

'I wished to postpone the final decisions until Jeanne's majority,' he said, 'because I know that people are over-excited at the moment. From now until then there will be some ten years, and you know as well as I do that in ten years opinions change, if only because the most violent now may well by then be dead. I thought I was serving you in acting thus, and I think you have misunderstood my designs. Since you and Valois cannot at present agree with one another why don't you both come to an agreement with me?'

The Duke of Burgundy frowned; he was not an intelligent man; he was always afraid of being tricked and, indeed, frequently was. Duchess Agnès, whose maternal love did not blind her, saw her son as he was, and had given him sound advice on his departure: 'Take care not to allow tricks to be played on you. Be careful not to speak before having thought, and if you have no thoughts, keep quiet and let Messire de Mello do the talking; he is more intelligent than you are.'

Eudes of Burgundy, at thirty-five, invested with the titles and powers of Duke, still lived in fear of his mother, and knew that he would have to justify his actions to her. He did not, therefore, dare reply to Philippe's overtures directly.

'My mother, the Duchess, sent you a letter, Cousin, in which she said . . . what did the letter say, Messire de Mello?'

'Madame Agnès asked that Madame Jeanne of Navarre should be placed in her charge, and she is surprised, Monseigneur, that you have not yet answered her.'

'But how could I, Cousin?' Philippe replied, still talking to Eudes as if Mello were merely an interpreter between them. 'It is a decision that could be taken only by the Regent. Only today am I in a position to grant her request. What makes you think, Cousin, that I intend to refuse? I expect you would like to take your niece back with you when you go.'

The Duke, surprised at meeting no resistance, looked at Mello, and his expression seemed to say: 'Here's a man one can come to terms with!'

'On condition, Cousin,' went on the Count of Poitiers, 'on condition, of course, that your niece is not married without my consent. That is an obvious measure; this matter is too important to the Crown for our advice to be neglected in giving a husband to the girl who may, one day, be Queen of France.'

The second part of the speech took away the sting of the first. Eudes really believed that it was Philippe's intention to have Jeanne crowned, if Queen Clémence did not bear a son.

'Of course, of course, Cousin,' he said; 'on that point we are in agreement.'

'In that case, there is no longer anything dividing us and we will sign an agreement,' said Philippe.

He sent immediately for Mille de Noyers, who was the best hand at drafting treaties of this kind.

'Messire Mille,' he said, when the jurist appeared, 'you will inscribe this on vellum: "We, Philippe, Peer and Count of Poitiers, Regent, by the Grace of God, of the two Kingdoms, and our well-beloved Cousin, the Magnificent and Puissant Lord Eudes IV, Peer and Duke of Burgundy, swear by Holy Writ to render each other good service and loyal friendship . . ." This is the broad outline I'm giving you, Messire Mille. "And by this friendship, which we mutually swear, have decided in common that Madame Jeanne of Navarre . . ."'

Guillaume de Mello took the Duke by the sleeve and

whispered in his ear, and the Duke grasped the fact that he was being made a fool of.

'Oh, but Cousin,' he cried, 'my mother did not authorize me to recognize you as Regent!'

They soon reached a deadlock. Philippe would grant the guardianship only if the Duke recognized his powers. He even went so far as to guarantee Jeanne her rights of possession over Navarre, Champagne and Brie. But the other grew obstinate. Without a formal agreement about the Crown, he refused to acknowledge the regency.

'If Mello, who is clever, were not here,' thought the Count of Poitiers, 'Eudes would already have capitulated.' He pretended to be tired, stretched out his long legs, crossed his feet one over the other and rubbed his chin.

Louis of Evreux watched him, wondering how his nephew was going to get out of the difficulty. 'I can see lances waving soon around Dijon,' that wise man thought. He was on the point of intervening to say: 'Very well, let us yield over the right to the Crown,' when Philippe suddenly asked the Burgundian: 'Let's see, Cousin, don't you want to get married?'

The other opened his eyes wide, thinking at first, since he was not very bright, that Philippe intended him to be affianced to Jeanne of Navarre.

'Since we have just sworn each other eternal friendship,' went on Philippe, as if the few half-finished lines had been ratified, 'and by that, my dear Cousin, you are giving me great support, I should like, on my side, to do something for you, and it would give me great pleasure to reinforce this link of affection with a closer relationship. Why don't you marry my eldest girl, Jeanne?'

Eudes IV looked at Mello, then at Louis of Evreux, then at Mille de Noyers, who was waiting, his pen poised.

'But how old is she, Cousin?' he asked.

'Eight years old, Cousin,' replied Philippe, falling silent for a moment; and then added, 'She can also have the county of Burgundy, which comes to us from her mother.'

Eudes raised his head like a horse smelling oats. To unite the two Burgundies, the duchy and the county, had been a dream of the hereditary Dukes since the time of Robert I, grandson of Hugues Capet. To amalgamate the Court of Dôle with that of Dijon, to unite the territories which stretched from Auxerre to Pontarlier and from Mâcon to Besançon, to have one foot in France and the other in the Holy Roman Empire, since the county was a Palatinate, all this was a mirage which suddenly assumed reality. No more was needed to make the Burgundians dream of rebuilding Charlemagne's empire for themselves.

Louis of Evreux could not but admire his nephew's audacity; in a game which had seemed lost this was a considerable counterstroke. But looked at more closely, Philippe's reasoning was easily discoverable; he was simply disposing of Mahaut's territories. She had been given Artois, at Robert's expense, to persuade her to surrender the county; while Philippe had been given the county as his wife's dowry that he might be a candidate at the Imperial election. But Philippe had now an eye on the Crown of France, or at least on a ten years' regency; the county was therefore of less interest to him, provided it went to a vassal, which would be the case.

'May I see Madame your daughter?' asked Eudes at once, and without even thinking of referring the matter to his mother.

'You saw her just now, Cousin, at the feast.'

'Of course, but I did not look at her closely. I mean I did not consider her with this in view.'

They sent to summon the Count of Poitiers's eldest daughter, who was playing tag with her sisters and the other children of the family.[19]

'What do they want me for? Why can't I go on playing?' said the little girl, who was pursuing the Dauphiniet by the stables.

'Monseigneur your father has sent for you,' they said.

She delayed to catch the little Guigues and, as she hit him in the back, cried: 'You're it!' Then, unhappily sulking, she went with the chamberlain, who led her by the hand.

Still out of breath, her cheeks damp, her hair across her face, and her figured dress dusty, she came into the presence of her cousin Eudes, who was twenty-seven years older than she was. She was neither ugly or pretty, still thin, and had no idea that at that moment her fate was mingled with that of France. There are children in whom one sees at an early age what they will look like when they are grown up; but with this child one could not tell. There was merely the aura of the county of Burgundy.

A province is a fine thing; but a wife must still not be deformed. 'If she has straight legs, I'll accept,' thought the Duke of Burgundy. He had reason to beware of a surprise of that nature, since his second sister, who was younger than Marguerite, and was married to Philippe of Valois, had legs of different lengths.[20] In the present animosity between the Valois and Burgundy, this lameness naturally played its part. The Duke asked therefore, without its seeming to surprise anyone, that the child's skirts should be raised that he might see the shape of her legs. The child had thin thighs and calves; she took after her father, but her bones were straight.

'You are quite right, Cousin,' said the Duke. 'It would be an admirable way of sealing our friendship.'

'There, you see!' said Poitiers. 'Is not this a far better solution than quarrelling with each other? From now on I want to be able to call you son-in-law.'

He opened his arms to embrace him; the son-in-law was twelve years older than the father-in-law.

'There, my girl, go and give your betrothed a kiss,' said Philippe to the child.

'Oh, he's my betrothed, is he?' said the little girl.

She drew herself up proudly.

'What's more,' she added, 'he's bigger than the Dauphiniet!'

'How lucky it was,' thought Philippe, 'that it was only my third daughter that I gave the Dauphin last month, and kept this one, who can inherit the county.'

The Duke of Burgundy raised his future wife in his arms so that she might implant a large wet kiss on his cheek. Then, when he had put her down again, she went off to the courtyard to announce proudly to the other children: 'I am betrothed!'

The games were interrupted.

'And not to a little fiancé like yours,' she said to her sister, indicating the Dauphiniet. 'Mine is as big as our father.'

Then, seeing the little Jeanne of Navarre who was sulking somewhat apart from the others, she cried: 'Now I shall be your aunt.'

'Why my aunt?' asked the orphan.

'Because I shall be the wife of your uncle Eudes.'

One of the younger daughters of the Count of Valois, who

was not yet seven years old, but had already been taught to repeat everything she heard, rushed to the Château, found her father plotting in company with Blanche of Brittany and a few lords of his party, and told him what she had just heard. Charles got up, overturning his chair, and departed, his head thrust forward, towards the room in which the Regent was.

'Ah, my dear Uncle, you've come just at the right moment!' cried Philippe of Poitiers; 'I was about to send for you in order that you may witness our agreement.'

And he handed him the document which Mille de Noyers had just finished drawing up: '. . . for signing here with all our family the convention we have made with our good Cousin of Burgundy, and by which we agree to the whole.'

It was a bitter week for the ex-Emperor of Constantinople, who could do no other than sign. After him followed Louis of Evreux, Mahaut of Artois, the Dauphin of Viennois, Aimé of Savoy, Charles de La Marche, Louis of Bourbon, Blanche of Brittany, Guy de Saint-Pol, Henry de Sully, Guillaume d'Harcourt, Anseau de Joinville and the Constable Gaucher de Châtillon, all of whom put their signatures to the agreement.

The late dusk of July was falling over Vincennes. The earth and the trees were still impregnated with the heat of the day. Most of the guests had left.

The Regent went for a stroll under the oaks, in company with his most devoted intimates, those who had followed him from Lyons and had assured his triumph. He joked a bit about Saint Louis's tree, which they could not find. Suddenly the Regent said: 'Messeigneurs, there is joy in my heart; my dear wife has this day borne a son.'

He breathed deeply with happiness and delight, as if the

air of the kingdom of France really belonged to him. He sat down on the moss, his back against the trunk of a tree, and was gazing up at the patterns of the leaves against the rose-coloured sky, when Gaucher de Châtillon came hurrying up. The Constable was looking grave.

'I have come to give you bad news, Monseigneur,' he said.

'Already?' said the Regent.

'Count Robert set out a little while ago for Artois.'

PART TWO

ARTOIS AND THE CONCLAVE

I

The Arrival of Count Robert

A DOZEN HORSEMEN, coming from Doullens and led by a giant in a blood-red surcoat, galloped through the village of Bouquemaison and stopped on the highest point of the road. From there they had a view over a vast plateau of cornfields, intersected by valleys and beech-groves, and descending in terraces towards a crescent-shaped horizon of distant forests.

'This is where Artois begins, Monseigneur,' said one of the horsemen, the Sire Jean de Varennes, addressing the leader of the cavalcade.

'My county! My county at last!' said the giant. 'Here is my own good earth that I have not trodden for fourteen years!'

The silence of midday lay over the sunlit fields. There was no sound but the breathing of the horses after their gallop and the murmur of bumble-bees drunken with heat.

Robert of Artois jumped briskly from his horse, throwing the reins to his valet Lormet, climbed the bank, treading down the grass, and entered the nearest field. His companions remained still, respecting the privacy of his joy. Robert strode hugely forward through the corn, whose heavy golden ears waved about his thighs. He caressed them with his hands as if they were the coat of some quiet horse or the fair hair of a mistress.

'My earth, my corn!' he repeated.

Suddenly he threw himself to the ground, stretched himself out, rolled wallowing wildly among the corn as if he wished to merge with it; he crammed ears of corn into his mouth, chewing them to find that milky flavour at the heart which they have a month before harvest; he did not notice that his lips were scratched with the beards of the wheat. He was drunk with the blue sky, the dry earth and the scent of crushed stalks, doing as much damage by himself as a herd of wild pig. He rose to his feet, superb and rumpled. As he returned to his companions, he was brandishing a handful of corn.

'Lormet,' he said to his valet, 'unclasp my surcoat, unlace my hauberk.'[21]

When this had been done, he slipped the corn beneath his shirt against his skin.

'I swear to God, Messeigneurs,' he said in a great voice, 'that these ears of corn shall not leave my breast till I have reconquered my county to the last field, to the last tree. Now, forward into battle!'

He remounted his horse, dug in his heels, and set it into a gallop.

'Do you not think, Lormet,' he shouted into the wind of their passage, 'that the earth here has a better sound beneath our horses' hooves?'

'Yes indeed, Monseigneur,' replied that tender-hearted killer, who shared all his master's opinions and waited on him like a wet-nurse. 'But your surcoat is loose in the wind; slow down a little so that I can do it up for you.'

They rode on thus for a moment. Then the plateau fell quickly away, and Robert saw a great mass of armed men awaiting him; they were drawn up in a field and glistened in the sun, an army of eighteen hundred knights come to greet him. He could never have believed that his partisans would come in such numbers to the meeting-place.

'Well done, Varennes! You've done good work, my friend,' cried Robert in astonishment.

When the knights of Artois recognized him there were shouts of acclamation from their ranks.

'Welcome to our Count Robert! Long life to our sweet Lord!'

And the most eager set their horses towards him, their steel knee-pieces jostling, their lances waving like another field of corn.

'Ah, here's Caumont! Here's Souastre! I know you by your shields, my friends,' said Robert.

The knights' faces showed through the raised visors of their helms, running with sweat, but gay with their ardour for war. Many of them were but little country lords, wearing ancient, old-fashioned armour, inherited from father or great-uncle, and which they had themselves altered to their measure: work done in the manor house. Before night they would be galled by the joints and their bodies covered with bleeding sores; indeed they all carried with them in the baggage of their valets of arms a pot of unguent prepared by their wives and strips of linen for bandages.

Before Robert's eyes was every pattern of military fashion for the last century: every shape of helm and bascinet; some of the hauberks and great swords had been on the Crusade. The provincial dandies had adorned their helmets with feathers of cocks, pheasants or peacocks; golden dragons decorated others, and a naked woman was bolted to one of them, which attracted much attention.

They had all freshly painted their short shields, which carried their armorial bearings in brilliant colours; their coats-of-arms were simple or complex according to their degree of nobility and the age of their house, the more simple designs being naturally those of the oldest families.

'This is Saint-Venant, this is Longvillers, this is Nédonchel,' said Jean de Varennes, presenting the knights to Robert.

'Your *féal*, Monseigneur, your *féal*,' each one said as his name was called.

'*Féal*, Nédonchel . . . *féal*, Bailiencourt . . . *féal*, Picquigny . . .' replied Robert, as he passed in front of each in turn.

To some of the young men, sitting upright on their horses and proud to be wearing the harness of war for the first time, Robert promised that he would arm them knights himself if they behaved well in the imminent engagements.

He then decided to appoint two marshals at once, as was done for the royal army. He chose first the Sire de Hautponlieu, who had been very active in gathering these unruly lords.

'And then I'll have, let's see, you, Beauval!' Robert announced. 'The Regent has a Beaumont for a marshal; I shall have a Beauval.'

The little lords, who were partial to a pun or a play on words, laughingly acclaimed Jean de Beauval who had been thus selected because of his name.

'And now, Monseigneur Robert,' said Jean de Varennes,

'which road do you wish to take? Do we go first to Saint-Pol, or straight to Arras? Artois is all yours, you have but to choose.'

'Which road leads to Hesdin?'

'The one you're on, Monseigneur, which goes by Frévent.'

'Very well, I wish to go first to the castle of my fathers.'

The knights looked a little uneasy. It was most unfortunate that the Count of Artois should wish to go to Hesdin immediately on his arrival.

'The fact is, Monseigneur,' said Souastre, the knight who was wearing the naked woman on his helmet, 'the fact is that the castle is in no fit state to receive you.'

'What's that? Is it still occupied by the Sire de Brosse, whom my cousin the Hutin installed there?'

'No, no; we put Jean de Brosse to flight; but we also sacked the castle a little in the process.'

'Sacked it?' said Robert. 'You have not burnt it down, I trust?'

'No, Monseigneur, no; the walls are perfectly sound.'

'But you've done a bit of pillaging, eh, my pretty gentlemen? Well, if that's all, you did well. All that belongs to that sow Mahaut, that slut Mahaut, that bitch Mahaut, is yours, Messeigneurs, and I make you a gift of it.'

How could they not love so generous a lord! Once again they roared long life to their noble Count Robert, and the army of the rebellion set out for Hesdin.

Towards the end of the afternoon they reached the fortified town of the Counts of Artois, with its fourteen towers, where the castle alone occupied the enormous expanse of some twelve acres.

What taxes, what labour and what sweat this fabulous

building had cost the common people of the neighbourhood, though they had been told it was to protect them against the disasters of war! Wars had succeeded each other, but the protection seemed far from effective, and since armies were always fighting for the castle, the population preferred to go to ground in their cob-built houses, praying God that the avalanche might pass to one side.

There were few people in the streets to cheer their Seigneur Robert; the inhabitants, who had suffered enough during the sack the day before, were in hiding. A few of the more craven had come out to shout a little, but their acclamations were thin.

The approaches to the castle were not a pleasant sight; the royal garrison, hanged from the battlements, were beginning to stink a little of carrion. At the great gate, called the Porte des Poulets, the drawbridge had been lowered. Inside was a scene of desolation: in the cellars wine was running from the broken vats; dead chickens were lying all over the place; from the stables came the sad lowing of unmilked cows; and on the bricks, which paved the interior courtyards, a rare luxury at the period, the story of the recent massacre could be read in great patches of dried blood.

The buildings that housed the apartments of the family of Artois consisted of fifty rooms, and none of them had been spared by Robert's good friends. Everything which had not been taken away to adorn the neighbouring manors had been smashed on the spot.

From the chapel the great silver-gilt Cross and the bust of Saint Louis, containing a fragment of the King's bone and a few of his hairs, had disappeared. So had the gold chalice which Ferry de Picquigny had purloined. Later he sold it and it was discovered in a Paris shop. The twelve volumes of the library and the chessmen of jasper and chalcedony had been stolen. With Mahaut's dresses, dressing-gowns and linen, the little lords had provided handsome presents for their lady loves and had inexpensively prepared for themselves warm nights of gratitude. Even the kitchen stores of pepper, ginger, saffron and cinnamon had been looted.[22]

They walked over broken dishes and torn brocades; everywhere bed-curtains had been torn down, furniture hacked to pieces and tapestries destroyed. The leaders of the rebellion were somewhat abashed as they followed Robert on his tour; but at every new discovery the giant burst out into such loud and sincere laughter that they soon felt cheered again.

In the hall of escutcheons Mahaut had arranged along the walls stone statues of the Counts and Countesses of Artois from their beginnings to herself. The faces were all a little alike, but the total effect was one of grandeur.

'Here, Monseigneur,' declared Picquigny, who had something of a bad conscience, 'we wished to touch nothing.'

'And you were wrong, my friend,' replied Robert, 'for I see among these statues at least one head which displeases me. Lormet! A mace!'

Taking the heavy mace from his valet, he whirled it three times round his head and brought it down with all his strength on Mahaut's face. The statue reeled on its base and the head, broken at the neck, was shivered on the flagstones.

'May the living head suffer the same fate when all the allies of Artois have well pissed on it!' cried Robert.

If you like breaking things, it's just a matter of making a start; the mace seemed to have a friendly weight in the scarlet-clothed giant's hand.

'Ah, my sow of an aunt, you robbed me of Artois because he who begot me . . .'

And he sent the head flying from the statue of his father, Count Philippe.

'. . . was foolish enough to die before this one . . .'

And he decapitated his grandfather, Count Robert II.

'. . . and I shall perhaps live among these statues which you ordered, to do yourself an honour to which you had no right! Down with my ancestors! We shall begin all over again and not with stolen wealth.'

The walls trembled; the stone lay scattered about the floor. The barons of Artois had fallen silent, breathless at the spectacle of the monumental fury of this man who far surpassed them in the art of violence. How could they not give such a leader their passionate devotion!

When he had finished decapitating his family, Count Robert III threw his mace through a window-pane, and said, stretching himself: 'Now we are ready to talk. Messires, my friends, my trusty companions, I desire that in each town, provostship and castellany which we deliver from the yoke of Mahaut and those damned Hirsons, all complaints against her should be noted down, and the register of her wickedness precisely kept, so that an exact tally of it may be sent to her son-in-law, Messire of the Closed Gates – for wherever he appears, that man, he encloses everything, towns, conclaves, the Treasury – to Messire Short-of-Sight, our good Lord Philippe the Myope,[23] who calls himself Regent and for whose benefit we were deprived, fourteen years ago, of this county, in order that he might grow fat with Burgundy! May the beast die of it, his throat strangled with his own guts!'

Little Gérard Kiérez, who was clever in all the chicanery of legal proceedings, and who had pleaded before the King the cause of the barons against Mahaut, then said: 'There is a grave matter, Monseigneur, which is of interest not only to Artois, but to the whole kingdom, and perhaps the Regent might not be indifferent to knowing how his brother, Louis X, died.'

'By the living devil, Gérard, do you believe what I believe myself? Have you any proof that my aunt had an evil hand in that affair too?'

'Proof, proof, Monseigneur, it's easy enough to talk of proof; but a strong suspicion certainly, which can be supported by evidence. I know a woman at Arras who calls herself Isabelle de Fériennes and her son, Jean, both sellers of magic potions, who supplied a certain Demoiselle d'Hirson, Béatrice . . .'

'One day I'll make you a present of that one,' said Robert. 'I know her and, judging from her looks, she'd be a treat in bed!'

'The Fériennes gave her a good poison to kill deer for Madame Mahaut, not more than two weeks before the King died. What can serve for deer can serve also for a king.'

The barons' chuckles showed that they understood and appreciated this allusion.

'In any case it was a poison for the wearers of horns,' said Robert, outdoing him. 'God keep my cuckold of a cousin's soul!'

The laughter grew louder.

'And it seems all the more likely, Messire Robert,' went on Kiérez, 'because the Dame de Fériennes was boasting last year that she compounded the philtre which reconciled

Messire Philippe, whom you call the Myope, and Madame Jeanne, Mahaut's daughter . . .'

'She's a bitch like her mother, and you did wrong, my Barons, not to have strangled her like a viper when you had her at your mercy here last autumn,' said Robert. 'I want this woman Fériennes and I want her son. See that they are captured as soon as we reach Arras. And now we shall eat: the day has given me a great appetite. Kill the biggest ox in the stable and have it roasted whole; empty the pond of Mahaut's carp; and bring us such wine as you have not already drunk.'

Two hours later, when night had fallen, all the fine company was roaring drunk. Robert sent Lormet, who carried the mixture of wines pretty well, with a good escort, to round up as many women as the gallant humour of the barons demanded. As they pulled them from their beds, they did not look too closely to see whether they were maids or mothers of families. Lormet drove a flock of them in their nightshirts, bleating with terror, to the castle. There was a fine sabbath in Mahaut's pillaged rooms. The women's screams lent ardour to the knights, who went to the assault as if they were charging the infidel, rivalling each other in their prowess in pleasure, and hurling themselves three at a time on the same prize. Robert seized by the hair the choicest morsels for himself, stripping them roughly enough. As he weighed over two hundred pounds, his conquests had not even breath enough to scream. Meanwhile Souastre, who had mislaid his splendid helmet, was doubled up, his hands to his stomach, vomiting like a gargoyle in a thunderstorm.

Then, one by one, these valiant gentlemen began to snore. A single man would have had no trouble in cutting the throats of all the nobility of Artois that night.

The next day an unsteady army, tongues furred and minds foggy, set out for Arras where Robert had decided to set up his headquarters. He himself seemed as fresh as a pike straight from the river, which once and for all earned him the admiration of his troops. The journey was broken with halts, for Mahaut possessed several other castles in the neighbourhood, the sight of which reawakened the barons' courage.

But when, on Saint Magdalene's Day, Robert reached Arras, the Dame de Fériennes had disappeared.

2

The Pope's Lombard

At Lyons the Cardinals were still shut up. They had thought to weary the Regent; their seclusion had lasted for more than a month. The seven hundred men-at-arms of the Count de Forez continued to mount guard round the church and monastery of the Predicant Friars; and if, from respect for precedent, Count Savelli, Marshal of the Conclave, carried the keys permanently on his person, they were of little use, since the doors they opened had all been walled up.

The Cardinals daily transgressed the Constitution of Gregory, but their consciences were quiet, for they had been compelled to meet by force. Nor did they fail to point this out daily to the Count de Forez, when he put his helmeted head in through the narrow opening which served to pass in their food. To which the Count de Forez daily replied that he had been given orders to see that the law of the Conclave should be respected. They could each go on talking to deaf ears indefinitely.

The Cardinals had ceased living together, as was prescribed, for, though the nave of the Jacobins was large, a hundred people living there, with straw for bedding, had soon become intolerable. The stench created during the first nights was hardly encouraging to the election of a Pope. The prelates had therefore taken possession of the monastery which abutted on the church and was within the precincts. Turning out the monks, they had organized themselves three to a cell, which was not much more comfortable. The pages had forcibly occupied a dormitory, and the chaplains the hospice, which no longer received travellers.

The rule of diminishing rations of food had not been applied either; had it been, they would by now have been an assembly of skeletons. The Cardinals, therefore, had sent in from outside certain luxuries which were supposed to be for the Abbot. The secrecy of the deliberations was constantly being violated; every day letters either came in to the Conclave or went out from it, hidden in bread or in empty dishes. Meal-time had become the hour for the post, and the correspondence which claimed to rule the fate of Christendom was sadly stained with grease.

The Count of Forez had informed the Regent of all these inobservances, but the latter had replied to let things be. 'The more faults and inobservances they commit,' declared Philippe of Poitiers, 'the better position we shall be in to treat them with rigour when we decide to do so. As for the letters, pretend to let them go on their way, but open them as often as you can, and let me know their contents.'

Thus it was known that there had been four candidatures which failed almost as soon as they were put forward: in the first place that of Arnaud Nouvel, ex-Abbot of Fontfroide, concerning whom the Count of Poitiers let it be known through Jean de Forez 'that he did not consider this Cardinal friendly enough to the kingdom of France', then the candidatures of Guillaume de Mandagout, Cardinal of Prenestre, Arnaud de Pélagrue and Bérenger Frédol the elder. Gascons and Provençaux held each other in check. It was also learned that the redoubtable Caetani was beginning to disgust some of the Italians, including even his own cousin Stefaneschi, by the baseness of his intrigues and the frenzied excesses of his calumnies.

Had he not suggested as a joke – but it was known what his jokes were like! – that they should raise the Devil and place the selection of a Pope in his hands, since God seemed to have decided not to make a choice?

To which Duèze, in his whispering voice, had replied: 'It would not be the first time, Francesco, that Satan sat among us.'

When Caetani asked for a candle, it was murmured that it was not to give himself light, but to use the wax for casting a spell.

Until they had been shut up, the Cardinals had opposed each other from motives of doctrine, prestige or interest. But, having lived together for a month cramped in a limited space, they had begun to hate each other for personal reasons, physical reasons almost. Some neglected their appearance, had not shaved for four weeks, and were dirty in their habits. It was no longer by promises of money or ecclesiastical benefices that a candidate sought to acquire votes, but by sharing his rations with the gluttons, an action which was strictly prohibited. Denunciations went the rounds: 'The Camerlingo has again eaten three of his party's dinners,' it was murmured.

These extras kept their stomachs more or less satisfied; it was not the same for their chastity, to which certain Cardinals were little used to submit, and which began to sour some of their characters unpleasantly. There was a joke going the rounds among the Provençaux:

'Monseigneur d'Auch', they said, 'suffers from abstemiousness in flesh while Messeigneurs Colonna suffer both from abstemiousness and the flesh.'

For the two Colonna brothers, physically athletic and better suited to the coat of mail than the soutane, lay in wait for pages in the passages of the monastery, promising them good absolution.

They never stopped throwing old grievances at each other's heads.

'If you had not canonized Célestin . . . If you had not denied Boniface . . . If you had not agreed to leave Rome . . . If you had not condemned the Templars . . .'

They mutually accused each other of weakness in defence of the Church, ambition and venality. To hear the Cardinals talk of each other, one might have thought that not one among them deserved so much as a country cure.

Monseigneur Duèze alone seemed unaware of the discomfort, the intrigues and the back-biting. For two years he had so embroiled his colleagues that he now had no need to interfere, and could leave the perversities he had implanted in their minds to do their work on their own. Having very little appetite, the meagre allowance of food in no way inconvenienced him. He had chosen to share his cell with the two Norman Cardinals who had joined the Provençal party, Nicolas de Fréauville, once confessor to Philip the Fair, and Michel du Bec, whom no one was proposing as candidates.

They were too weak to form a party of their own. No one feared them, and their living with Duèze could not take on the appearance of a conspiracy. Besides, Duèze saw but little of his two companions. At a given hour he strolled in the monastery cloisters, generally leaning on the arm of Guccio, who was continually warning him: 'Monseigneur, don't walk so quickly! Look, I can hardly keep up with you, my leg is still so stiff from my accident in Marseilles when I fell from Queen Clémence's ship. You know well that your chances, if I can trust what I hear, will be better the more people think that you are weak.'

'It's true, it's true, you're quite right,' replied the Cardinal, who then did his best to stoop, totter at the knees and discipline his seventy-two years.

He spent the rest of the time reading or writing. He had managed to procure what was more necessary to him than anything else in the world: books, candle and paper. When he was summoned to a meeting in the choir of the church, he pretended only to be able to tear himself with difficulty from his work, dragged himself to his stall, and there, thoroughly enjoying hearing his colleagues insult and betray each other, he contented himself with whispering: 'I pray, my brothers; I pray that God will inspire us to make a worthy choice.'

Those who knew him well found him altered. He seemed steeped in Christian virtues, much given to mortifications of the flesh, and set an example of kindliness and charity. When someone remarked on it, he would reply simply with a murmur and a gesture of disillusion: 'The approach of death . . . it is high time I prepared myself . . .'

He hardly touched his bowl at meal-times and had it carried

to one or another of his colleagues, excusing himself for breaking the rule for reasons of health. Thus Guccio would go, his hands laden, to the Camerlingo, who was prospering like a fatted ox, and say to him: 'Monseigneur Duèze is sending you this. He thought you were looking thin this morning.'

Of the ninety-six prisoners, Guccio could communicate the most easily with the outside world; he had indeed quickly been able to establish contact with the agent of the Tolomei bank at Lyons. Through this agency passed not only the letters Guccio wrote his uncle, but also the most secret correspondence between Duèze and the Regent. These letters were spared the disgrace of journeying in greasy dishes; they were transmitted inside the books which were so indispensable to the Cardinal's pious studies.

Indeed, Duèze had no other confidant but the young Lombard, whose cunning was more use to him each day. Their fate was closely linked, for if one wished to leave the monastery, which was overheated by the summer weather, as Pope, the other wished to depart as soon as possible, and with powerful protection, to rescue his beloved. Guccio was, however, somewhat reassured about Marie since Tolomei had written that he was watching over her like a true uncle.

At the beginning of the last week of July, when Duèze saw that his colleagues were extremely weary, exhausted by the heat, and irrevocably at daggers drawn with each other, he decided to act the farce he had long been considering and had carefully rehearsed with Guccio.

'Have I tottered enough? Have I fasted enough? Do I look sick enough?' he asked his temporary page. 'And are my fellow-Cardinals so disgusted with each other that they will come to a decision through sheer weariness?'

'I think so, Monseigneur, I think they're ripe for it.'

'Then, my young friend, go and set your tongue to work; as for me, I think I shall go and lie down, probably never to get up again.'

Guccio began mixing with the servants of the other Cardinals, saying that Monseigneur Duèze was much exhausted, that he showed signs of being ill, and that it was to be feared, taking his great age into consideration, that he would not quit the Conclave alive.

The next day Duèze did not appear at the daily meeting, and the Cardinals murmured among themselves, each one repeating, as if of his own knowledge, the rumours Guccio had spread.

The following day Cardinal Orsini, who had just had a violent altercation with the Colonnas, met Guccio and asked him whether it were true that Monseigneur Duèze was so very weak.

'Oh, yes, Monseigneur, and you see me sick at heart,' replied Guccio. 'Do you know that my good master has even given up reading? It is as much as to say that his life is drawing to a close.'

Then, with that ingenuously audacious air which he knew so well how to make use of at the right moment, he added: 'If I were in your place, Monseigneur, I know what I should do. I should elect Monseigneur Duèze. You would thus be able to leave this Conclave at last, and hold another under your own auspices as soon as he is dead, which, I repeat, cannot now be long. In a week's time you may well have lost the opportunity.'

That very evening Guccio saw Napoléon Orsini in council with Stefaneschi, who was an Orsini through his mother,

Albertini de Prato and Guillaume de Longis, that is to say all the Italians who favoured Duèze. The following day the same group met again as if by accident in the cloisters, but with the addition of the Spaniard Luca Flisco, half-brother to Jaime II of Aragon, and Arnaud de Pélagrue, the leader of the Gascon party; and Guccio, passing close by, heard one of them say: 'And if he does not die?'

'A pity, but if he dies tomorrow, we shall doubtless be here for another six months.'

Guccio immediately sent a letter to his uncle in which he advised him to buy up from the Bardi company all the debts Jacques Duèze owed that bank. 'You should be able to acquire them without difficulty at half their value, for the debtor is given out as dying, and the lender will think you mad. Buy them even at eighty *livres* for the hundred, I assure you that it will be good business or I am no longer your nephew.'

He also advised Tolomei to come to Lyons himself as soon as he could.

On the 29th of July the Count de Forez had an official letter handed to the Cardinal Camerlingo from the Regent. In order to hear it read, Jacques Duèze consented to leave his pallet; he was practically carried to the meeting.

The Count of Poitiers's letter was harsh. It detailed all the lapses from the rule of Gregory. It recalled his threat to demolish the roof of the church. It took the Cardinals to task for their discord, and suggested that, if they could reach no conclusion, the tiara should be conferred on the oldest among them. And the oldest was Jacques Duèze.

When the old Cardinal heard these words, he waved his arms in a sort of dying gesture and said in a hardly audible voice: 'The most worthy, Brothers, the most worthy! What would you do with a pastor who has not even the strength to carry himself, and whose place is in Heaven, if the Lord will receive me there, rather than here below?'

He had himself carried back to his cell, lay down on his pallet and turned his face to the wall. It was only because Guccio knew him well that he realized that his shoulders were shaking with laughter and that he was not gasping like a dying man.

The following day Duèze seemed to have recovered a little strength; a too consistent weakness would have aroused suspicion. But, when there arrived a recommendation from the King of Naples supporting that of the Count of Poitiers, the old man began coughing in the most pitiful way; he must have been in very poor health to have caught cold in such hot weather.

Bargaining still went on, for not all the Cardinals' hopes had yet been extinguished. Of the twenty-four Cardinals there was doubtless not a single one, however ill-placed, who had not at one moment or another said to himself: 'Why not I?'

Among the public who had gathered in Lyons, attracted by the expectation of an early decision, the opinion began to grow that there were no perfect institutions, that they were all as bad as each other, equally vitiated by human ambition; the elective system designed to fill the throne of Saint Peter was proving no better than the hereditary system was for the throne of France.

But the Count de Forez was beginning to prove still harsher. He was now having the food openly searched, reducing it to one course a day, and he confiscated the correspondence or threw it back into the monastery.

By the 5th of August Napoléon Orsini had succeeded in

bringing over to the supporters of Duèze the terrible Caetani himself, as well as several members of the Gascon party. The Provençaux were beginning to scent victory.

It became evident, on the 6th of August, that Monseigneur Duèze could count on eighteen votes, that is to say on two votes more than the absolute majority that no one had been able to muster in two years and three months. The last dissidents, seeing that the election was about to take place in their despite, and fearing that they might suffer for their obstinacy, proceeded to take credit for recognizing the high Christian virtues of Monseigneur Duèze, and declared themselves ready to give him their suffrage.

The following day, 7 August 1316, it was decided to vote.[24] Four tellers were appointed. Duèze appeared, carried by Guccio and his second page.

'He weighs very light,' Guccio murmured to the Cardinals who watched them go by and made way with a deference which was already significant of the choice they were about to make.

'Since you wish it so, Lord, since you wish it so . . .' Duèze whispered to the paper on which he was about to record his vote.

A few minutes later he was unanimously proclaimed Pope and his twenty-three rivals gave him an ovation.

He was to lead them a terrible life during the next eighteen years!

Guccio moved forward to help to his feet the pathetic old man, who had become the supreme authority of the world.

'No, my son, no,' said Duèze. 'I shall endeavour to walk on my own. May God sustain my steps.'

A few idiots then thought that they were witnessing a miracle, but others realized they had been made fools of.

But the Camerlingo had already burnt the voting-papers in the fireplace and the white smoke announced to the world that there was a new Pope. The sound of picks began echoing against the brickwork which walled up the great door. But the Count de Forez was a prudent man; as soon as space enough had been made, he entered the opening himself.

'Yes, yes, my son, it is I,' said Duèze, who had trotted to the door.

Then the masons finished breaking down the walls; the two leaves of the door were opened and the sun, for the first time for forty days, shone into the church of the Jacobins.

There was a great crowd about the steps outside: commoners, burgesses of Lyons, consuls, lords and observers from foreign courts; the whole crowd knelt. A fat man with an olive complexion and one eye closed pushed forward by the Count de Forez. He seized the hem of the Pope's robe and carried it to his lips; it was on his grey head that there fell the first blessing of him who was henceforward to be called John XXII.

'Uncle Spinello,' cried Guccio, when he saw the fat man kneeling.

'Ah, so you are his uncle! I like your nephew well, my son,' said Duèze to the banker, motioning him to rise; 'he has served me faithfully, and I wish to keep him by me. Embrace him, embrace him!'

Guccio fell into Tolomei's arms.

'I bought it all up as you told me, and at six for ten,' Tolomei immediately whispered, while Duèze continued blessing the crowd. 'That Pope now owes us several thousands of *livres*.

Bel lavoro, figlio mio. You are a true nephew of my own blood.'

There was a man standing behind them with a face as long as those of the Cardinals; it was Signor Boccaccio, the principal traveller for the Bardi.

'Ah, so you were inside, were you, rascal?' he said to Guccio. 'If I had known that, I should not have sold.'

'And Marie? Where is Marie?' Guccio asked his uncle anxiously.

'Your Marie is well. She's as beautiful as you are cunning, and if the little Lombard she is carrying takes after you both, he'll get on in the world. But go quickly, go, my boy! Can't you see that the Holy Father wants you?'

3

The Wages of Sin

THE REGENT PHILIPPE WAS determined to attend the coronation of the Pope he had made, and thus establish himself as the Protector of Christendom.

'It gave me enough trouble,' he said. 'It is only right that he should now help me to establish my government. I wish to be at Lyons for his coronation.'

But the news from Artois continued disquieting. Robert had taken Arras, Avesnes and Thérouanne without difficulty, and went on conquering the countryside. In Paris Charles of Valois was secretly helping him.

Faithful to the tactics of encirclement, which were natural to his character, the Regent began by working on the border regions of Artois in order to prevent the rebellion from spreading. He wrote to the barons of Picardy to remind them of their loyalty to the Crown of France, courteously intimating that he would tolerate no lapse from their duty; and a large contingent of troops and sergeants-at-arms was sent into the provostships to police the country. To the

Flemings, who, after the lapse of a year, were still making mock of the Hutin's ridiculous expedition in which he had lost his army in the mud, Philippe proposed a new treaty of peace which gave them very advantageous conditions.

'In the mess we have been left to clear up we must be prepared to lose a little so as to save the whole,' the Regent explained to his councillors.

Even though his son-in-law, Jean de Fiennes, was one of Robert's chief lieutenants, the Count of Flanders felt that such a good opportunity for making a treaty was unlikely to arise again. He agreed to negotiations and so remained neutral in the affairs of the neighbouring county.

Philippe had thus to all intents and purposes shut the gates on Artois. He then sent Gaucher de Châtillon to negotiate directly with the leaders of the rebellion, and to assure them of the Countess Mahaut's good intentions.

'Listen well, Gaucher; you must not negotiate with Robert,' he warned the Constable, 'because that would be recognizing the rights he claims. We still consider he has forfeited Artois in accordance with my father's judgment. You are going there only to negotiate the differences between the Countess and her vassals, which, in our view, have nothing to do with Robert. Pretend to ignore him.'

'Monseigneur,' said the Constable, 'do you mean to make your mother-in-law triumph everywhere?'

'Not at all, Gaucher; particularly if she has frequently abused her rights, as I think she has. The fact is that Dame Mahaut is an extremely imperious woman, and she believes that everyone was born expressly to serve her to the last farthing and the last drop of sweat! I want peace,' the Regent continued, 'and to achieve it there must be an equitable settlement. We know that the townsfolk support the Countess because they are always wrangling with the nobles, while the nobles have taken up Robert's cause so as to get their wrongs righted. Find out if their demands are justified and try to satisfy them without impairing the prerogatives of the Crown; try to detach the barons from our turbulent cousin by pointing out to them that they can obtain more from us through justice than they can from him through violence.'

'You're a clever man, Monseigneur; you're certainly a clever man,' said the Constable. 'I did not believe that in my latter years it would be given me to serve with such pleasure so wise a prince, who is not a third of my age.'

Meanwhile the Regent, through the Count de Forez, was asking the Pope to postpone his coronation a little. Duèze, though properly anxious to see his election quickly confirmed by coronation, agreed most politely to a delay of a fortnight.

But when the fortnight had elapsed the affairs of Artois were still far from settled; and the agreement with the Flemings could not be ratified before the 1st of September. Philippe therefore asked Duèze, this time through the Dauphin of Viennois, to postpone the ceremony once more, but Duèze, to the Regent's surprise, showed firmness, almost obstinacy, by fixing the date of his coronation irrevocably for the 5th of September.

He wished to hold it on that date for imperative reasons which he kept secret and which indeed would not have been apparent to all. The fact was that he had been consecrated Bishop of Fréjus on the 5th of September, in the year 1300; his protector, King Robert of Naples, had been crowned in the first week of September 1309; and, though it had been by forging a royal letter, it was on the 4th of September 1310 that the trick had succeeded in obtaining for him the episcopal see of Avignon.

The new Pope's relations with the stars were excellent, and he knew how to suit the stages of his own ascension to that of the sun.

'If Monseigneur the Regent of France and Navarre, whom we love so well,' he replied, 'is prevented by the duties of the realm from being at our side on that solemn day, we shall regret it much, but we shall then no longer fear causing him so long a journey, and shall go and don the tiara in the town of Avignon.'

Philippe of Poitiers signed the treaty with the Flemings on the morning of the 1st of September. On the 5th, at dawn, he reached Lyons, accompanied by the Count of Valois and the Count de La Marche, whom he did not wish to leave in Paris out of his sight, as well as Louis of Evreux.

'You've made us ride as fast as a courier, Nephew,' said Valois as he dismounted.

They barely had time to put on the clothes specially prepared for the ceremony, which had been ordered by the Bursar, Geoffroy de Fleury. The Regent wore an open robe the colour of peach blossom, lined with two hundred skins of miniver.[25] Charles of Valois, Louis of Evreux, Charles de La Marche and Philippe of Valois, who was also present at the ceremony, had each received as a present a robe of *camocas* lined in the same manner.

In Lyons, which was all decked with flags, a huge crowd gathered to watch the procession.

Jacques Duèze, preceded by the Regent of France, rode to the primatial church of Saint-Jean on horseback through a huge kneeling crowd. All the bells of the town were pealing. The reins of the Pontiff's horse were held on one side by the Count of Evreux and on the other by the Count de La Marche. The papacy was closely framed by the French monarchy. The Cardinals followed, wearing their red hats, fastened under the chin by knotted strings above their copes. The bishops' mitres sparkled in the sun. It was Cardinal Orsini, a descendant of Roman patricians, who placed the tiara on the head of Jacques Duèze, the son of a burgess of Cahors.

Guccio, from a good place in the cathedral, was lost in admiration of his master. The little old man, with his thin chin and narrow shoulders who, four weeks earlier, had been thought to be dying, bore without difficulty the heavy sacerdotal emblems with which he was laden. The Pharaonic rites of the interminable ceremony, which raised him so much above his fellows, making of him a symbol of divinity, seemed to leave their imprint on his personality almost without his knowing it, lending his features an unexpected and impressive majesty, which became more evident as the liturgy unfolded. He could not, however, restrain a slight smile when he donned the pontifical sandals.

'Scarpinelli! They called me Scarpinelli, Cardinal Little Shoes,' he thought. 'They said I was the son of a cobbler. But now I'm wearing the little shoes! Lord, I have nothing further to wish for. I have but to rule well.'

That very day he got the Regent to confer a patent of nobility on his brother Pierre Duèze, before proceeding, during the course of the next two years, to make five of his own nephews cardinals.

If the patent of nobility which Philippe of Poitiers dictated himself after the ceremony was intended to honour the Holy

Father through his brother, it nevertheless showed an astonishing aspect of the young Prince's mind. 'It is not family wealth,' he wrote, 'nor individual wealth, nor the other favours of fortune, which carry weight in the combination of moral qualities and meritorious actions. These are things which blind chance bestows on the deserving as on the undeserving, and which may happen equally to the worthy as to the unworthy . . . On the other hand, every man establishes himself as the inheritor of his own actions and his own merits, while it is of no importance whence we come, if indeed we even know from whom we come . . .'

But the Regent had not journeyed so far or given the new Pope such marks of his esteem to obtain nothing in return. Between these two men, separated in age by half a century – 'You are the rising sun, Monseigneur, and I am the setting sun,' Duèze was accustomed to say to Philippe – there existed, since their first meeting, a secret affinity and an enduring understanding. John XXII did not forget the promises of Jacques Duèze, nor the Regent those of the Count of Poitiers. Hardly had the Regent broached the subject of the ecclesiastical benefices, whose first year's income was to be paid to the Treasury, than the new Pope told him that the documents were ready for signing. But, before the seals were affixed, Philippe had a private conversation with Charles of Valois.

'Uncle,' he said, 'have you anything to complain of in me?'

'Most assuredly not, Nephew,' said the ex-Emperor of Constantinople.

How can one tell someone to his face that the only complaint one has against him is the fact that he exists!

'Then, Uncle, if you have no complaint against me, why do you work against me? I assured you, when you handed over to me the keys of the Treasury, that you would not be asked to render an account, and I have kept my word. You have sworn me homage and loyalty, but you have not kept faith, Uncle, for you are supporting Robert of Artois's cause.'

Valois made a gesture of denial.

'You are making a bad bet, Uncle,' Philippe went on, 'for Robert will cost you dear. He has no money; he has no other resources than the income paid him by the Treasury, which I have just cut off. It is, therefore, to you that he will turn for subsidies. Where will you find them, since you no longer control the finances of the kingdom? Now, don't be angry, don't go scarlet in the face, or give way to insults which you will later regret, for I want nothing but your good. Give me your word not to help Robert, and I, on my side, will ask the Holy Father that the annates of Valois and Maine be paid direct to you, rather than to the Treasury.'

For a moment the Count of Valois was torn between hatred and cupidity.

'How much do the annates amount to?' he asked.

'From ten to thirteen thousand *livres* a year, Uncle, for the sums which were not collected during the last years of my father's and the whole of Louis's reign must be included.'

For Valois, who was always in debt and yet lived regally, who had promised huge dowries to his daughters so as to marry them the better, ten or thirteen thousand *livres* a year presented, if not permanent salvation, at least a temporary one.

'You are a good nephew who understands my needs,' he replied.

The news from Gaucher de Châtillon being satisfactory, Philippe returned home by short stages, attending to a variety of business on the way, and making a last stop at Vincennes, to bring Clémence the blessing of the new Pope.

'I am glad', said the Queen, 'that our dear Duèze has taken the name of Jean, because it is the one I have chosen for my child, in accordance with the vow I took, during the storm, in the ship which brought me to France.'

She seemed still as much a stranger as ever to the problems of power and concerned solely with the memories of her married life and the anxieties of motherhood. Living at Vincennes seemed to suit her health; she had regained her looks and, seven months gone as she was, seemed to be enjoying that respite which occurs sometimes towards the end of a difficult pregnancy.

'Jean is no name for a King of France,' said the Regent. 'We have never had a Jean.'

'Brother, I tell you it was an oath I made.'

'In that case we shall respect it. If it's a boy, he will be called Jean I.'

In the Palace of the Cité Philippe found his wife perfectly happy, dandling the little Louis-Philippe who was bawling with all the strength of his eight weeks.

But the Countess Mahaut, when she heard that her son-in-law had returned, arrived like a fury from the Hôtel d'Artois with her sleeves rolled up.

'I've been betrayed, my son, since you've been away! Do you know what your fool of a Gaucher has been doing in Artois?'

'Gaucher is the Constable, Mother, and but a little while ago you did not think him foolish at all. What has he done to you?'

'He has declared me wrong!' cried Mahaut. 'He has

condemned me on all points. Your envoys are hand in glove with my vassals; they have taken it on themselves to order that I may not go into Artois! You hear what I say, that I, Mahaut, am to be forbidden to go into my own county, until I have sealed this wicked peace which I refused to Louis last December? And they order me to make restitution of I don't know what amount of taxes that, so they say, I have received wrongfully!'

'I have no doubt this is all perfectly just. My envoys have faithfully carried out my orders,' Philippe replied calmly.

For a moment Mahaut was taken aback with surprise. She stood there with her mouth open and her eyes staring. Then she went on, shouting louder than ever, 'Just, to pillage my castles, hang my sergeants-at-arms, ravage my harvest! And it's on your orders, is it, that my enemies are supported? Your orders! That's a fine way to pay me back for all I have done for you!'

A thick purple vein swelled on her forehead and Philippe thought that she would need to be bled that night.

'Except for giving me your daughter,' he replied, 'I do not see that you have done so much for me that I should let injury be done to my subjects and compromise the whole peace of the realm for your advantage.'

For a second Mahaut hesitated between prudence and anger. But the phrase her son-in-law had used, 'my subjects', a king's phrase, won the day.

Advancing towards him, she cried, 'Is to have killed your brother nothing?'

Ten weeks of deeply preserved secrecy had come to an end at a single blow.

Philippe neither started nor exclaimed, he simply rushed to

the doors to make sure with his shortsighted eyes that there was no one near who could have overheard. He locked the doors, removed the keys and put them in his belt. Mahaut was suddenly afraid, and still more so when she saw his expression as he returned towards her.

'So it was you,' he said in a low voice, 'and what has been whispered throughout the kingdom is true.'

Mahaut stood up to him since it was natural to her to attack.

'And who else should it be, Son-in-law? To whom else do you think you owe it that you are Regent and possibly, one day, may seize the Crown? Don't pretend to be so ingenuous. Your brother confiscated Artois from me; Valois was turning it against me; and you were in Lyons busy with the papacy. The papacy is always linked to my affairs as March to Lent! Don't be so sanctimonious as to tell me that you blame me! You had no love for Louis, and you're delighted that I've made it possible for you to take his place by putting a little seasoning in his sweets; but I did not expect to find that you were worse than he was.'

Philippe sat down, crossed his legs, and considered.

'This was bound to happen one day or another,' thought Mahaut. 'In one sense it may be just as well; I have a hold over him now.'

'Does Jeanne know?' Philippe asked suddenly.

'She knows nothing. These are not women's matters.'

'Who knows besides yourself?'

'Béatrice, my lady-in-waiting.'

'Too many,' said Philippe.

'Oh, don't you touch her!' cried Mahaut. 'She has a powerful family!'

'Indeed yes, a family who have made you greatly beloved in Artois! And besides Béatrice? Who furnished you with the seasoning, as you call it?'

'A witch of Arras, whom I have never seen, but whom Béatrice knows. I pretended to want to rid myself of the deer which infested my park and I took care to kill a number of them.'

'This woman must be found,' said Philippe.

'Do you now understand', went on Mahaut, 'that you cannot abandon me? If it is thought that you are no longer supporting me, my enemies will take courage, libels will spread . . .'

'Slanders, Mother, slanders,' Philippe corrected.

'And if I am accused, the weight of the accusation will fall on you, for it will be said that I did it for your advantage, if not on your orders even.'

'I know, Mother, I know. I've already thought of all that.'

'You must remember, Philippe, that I have risked the salvation of my soul in this action. Do not be ungrateful.'

This was one of the very rare occasions in Philippe's life when he lost his temper.

'Really, it's going too far, Mother! You'll be asking me next to kiss your feet because you've poisoned my brother! If I had known that this was the price of the regency, I would never, do you hear, never have accepted it! I reprobate this murder; there is never any need to kill in order to achieve one's ends; it's a bad political method, and I order you, as long as I am your suzerain, never to use it again.'

For a moment he was tempted to take the honest course: summon the Council of Peers, denounce the crime and demand punishment. Mahaut, who guessed how his mind was working, had some unpleasant moments. But Philippe never gave way to impulse, even when it was a virtuous one. To act thus would be to bring discredit on his wife and on himself. And what accusations might Mahaut not make to defend herself or bring him down with her for not having defended her? It would be a splendid opportunity for reopening the question of the regency and the succession. Philippe had already done too much for the kingdom, and thought too much about what he was going to do, to run the risk of being deprived of power. His brother Louis, all in all, had been a bad king, and a murderer into the bargain. Perhaps it was the intention of Providence to punish the assassin by assassination, and to place France in better hands.

'God will judge you, Mother, God will judge you,' he said. 'I should merely like to prevent the flames of Hell beginning to lick us all while we are still alive because of you. I must therefore pay the wages of your sin, and as I cannot put you in prison, I am compelled to support you. Your plan was well thought out. Messire Gaucher will receive new instructions the day after tomorrow. I won't conceal from you the fact that it weighs on me.'

Mahaut tried to embrace him. He pushed her away.

'But mark well', he continued, 'that from now on the dishes set before me will be tasted three times and that, at the first stomach-pain that causes me distress, your hours will be numbered. You had better pray for my health.'

Mahaut inclined her head.

'I will serve you so well, my son,' she said, 'that you will end by giving me back your love.'

4
We Must Go to War

NO ONE UNDERSTOOD, and Gaucher de Châtillon least of all, what had caused Philippe's change of mind concerning the affairs of Artois. The Regent, suddenly disavowing his envoys, declared that the agreement they had made was unacceptable and demanded that they draw up a new one more favourable to Mahaut. The results were immediate. The negotiations were broken off and those who were conducting them on the Artois side, representing the moderate elements among the nobility, at once rejoined the party of the extremists. They were very indignant; the Constable had deceived and betrayed them; from now on force was the only resource.

Count Robert was triumphant.

'Haven't I told you often enough that you can't deal with those traitors?' he told them.

He marched once more on Arras at the head of his whole army.

Gaucher, who was in the town with only a small escort,

had just time to escape by the Porte de Péronne while Robert was entering by the Porte Saint-Omer with flags flying and trumpets sounding. A quarter of an hour earlier and the Constable of France would have been a prisoner. This event occurred on the 22nd of September. On the same day Robert wrote his aunt the following letter:

'To the most high and noble Dame Mahaut of Artois, Countess of Burgundy, from Robert of Artois, Knight. As you have wrongly obstructed my right to the County of Artois, which much angers me and weighs on me every day, which thing I will no longer continue to suffer, by this I make known to you that I will put this affair in order and recover my property as soon as I can.'

Robert was not a great letter-writer; fine shades of meaning were not his forte, and he was delighted with this epistle, because it expressed so well what it was meant to say.

The Constable, when he reached Paris, did not cut a very good figure, nor did he mince his words when he met the Count of Poitiers. He was not intimidated by the Regent's person; he had seen the young man born and wet his clothes; he told him forthrightly that it was ill-using a good servant and a loyal relation, who had commanded the armies of the kingdom for twenty years, to send him to negotiate on assurances which were later disavowed.

'Until this day, Monseigneur, I have always been considered a true man whose word of honour could not be doubted. You have made me play the part of a traitor and a dastard. When I supported your rights to the regency I thought to find in you something of my King, your father, whom until now you have shown signs of resembling. I see that I have been cruelly mistaken. Have you fallen so completely under a woman's tutelage that you change your policy as you might your coat?'

Philippe did his best to calm the Constable, accusing himself of having ill-judged the affair in the first place, and of having issued mistaken instructions. There was no point in dealing with the nobility of Artois so long as Robert was undefeated. Robert was a danger to the kingdom and a peril to the honour of the royal family. Was he not the instigator of this campaign of slander which pointed to Mahaut as the poisoner of Louis X?

Gaucher shrugged his shoulders.

'And who believes that nonsense?' he cried.

'Not you, Gaucher, not you,' said Philippe, 'but others listen to it, only too happy to be able to injure us thereby; and tomorrow they'll be saying that I, and you, were implicated in this death they wish people to believe was suspect. But Robert has just made the mistake I was awaiting. Look at what he has written to Mahaut.'

And he handed the Constable the letter of the 22nd of September.

'By this letter,' went on the Regent, 'he rejects the judgment given by my father and Parliament in 1309. Until now he has done no more than support the Countess's enemies; but by this he enters into rebellion against the law of the realm. You will return to Artois.'

'Oh, no, Monseigneur!' cried Gaucher. 'I have cut too poor a figure there. I had to fly from Arras like an old boar from the hounds, without even time to piss. Do me the favour of choosing someone else to handle this business.'

Philippe put his hand to his mouth. 'If you knew, Gaucher,' he thought, 'if you only knew how painful it is to me to deceive you! But if I told you the truth, you would despise me still more!' He went on obstinately: 'You will go back to Artois, Gaucher, for love of me, and because I ask you to do so. You will take with you your brother-in-law, Messire Mille, and this time a good band of knights and also some of the commonalty, enlisting reinforcements in Picardy; and you will summon Robert to appear before Parliament to render an account of his conduct. At the same time you will supply money and men-at-arms to the burgesses of the towns which have remained loyal. And if Robert will not submit, I will take other steps to make him. A prince is like anyone else, Gaucher,' Philippe went on, taking the Constable by the shoulders, 'he may make an error at the start, but it would be a still greater error to continue in it. The royal trade has to be learned like any other, and I have still much to learn. Forgive me for forcing you to appear in such a bad light.'

Nothing moves an older man more than a confession of inexperience from a younger, particularly if the latter be his social superior. Beneath their saurian lids Gaucher's eyes dimmed a little.

'Oh, I forgot,' went on Philippe. 'I have decided that you shall be tutor to the future child of Madame Clémence – our King, if God so wills that it be a boy – and his second godfather, immediately after myself.'[26]

'Monseigneur, Monseigneur Philippe ...' said the Constable, much moved.

And he embraced the Regent, as if it had been he who had been at fault.

'As for godmother,' said Philippe, 'we have decided with Madame Clémence that it shall be the Countess Mahaut, so as to still the gossip.'

Eight days later the Constable set out once more.

Robert of Artois, as might have been foreseen, refused to submit to the summons and continued to rage at the head of his horde of knights. But the month of October was not a lucky one for him. If he was a valiant warrior, he was not a great strategist; he sent out forays without plan, one day to the north, the next to the south, at the mere whim of the moment. A *Reiter* before *Reiter*, a *condottiere* before *condottieri*, he was more suited to taking service with others as a great fighting man – as he was indeed to do, fifteen years later, in the service of England – than to command on his own behalf. In this county, which he considered his own, he behaved as if he were in enemy territory, leading the wild, dangerous and exciting life he loved. He rejoiced in the terror created by his approach, but did not see the hate he left in his wake. His passage was marked by too many bodies hanging from the branches of trees, too many headless corpses, too many victims buried alive amid gusts of cruel laughter, too many women raped, their flesh bearing the marks of mailed coats, and too many acts of arson. Mothers threatened their naughty children with calling Monseigneur Robert; but if he was said to be in the neighbourhood they hid their brats in their skirts and ran for the nearest forest.

The towns barricaded themselves; artisans, following the example of the Flemish towns, sharpened their knives, and the aldermen kept contact with Gaucher's emissaries. Robert liked open warfare; he hated a war of siege. The burgesses of Saint-Omer or of Calais would shut their gates in his face; he would shrug his shoulders and say: 'I'll come back another day and kill the lot of you!'

And he would go off to frolic elsewhere.

But money was beginning to run short. Valois no longer answered his demands, and his rare messages contained only good advice and exhortations to wisdom. Tolomei, his dear banker Tolomei, also turned a deaf ear. He was away; his clerks had no orders. The Pope himself took a hand in the affair; he wrote personally to Robert and to several of the Artois barons to recall them to their duty.

Then, one morning towards the end of October, the Regent, as he sat in council, declared with that extraordinary calm which was the accompaniment to his decisions: 'Our cousin Robert has too long made mock of our power. Since we must resolve to go to war, we will take the oriflamme at Saint-Denis against him on the last day of this month and, since Messire Gaucher is absent, the army, which I shall lead myself, will be under the command of our uncle . . .'

Everyone looked at Charles of Valois, but Philippe went on, '. . . our uncle, Monseigneur of Evreux. We would willingly have confided this duty to Monseigneur of Valois, who has given proof of being a great leader in war, if he had not to go to his territories of Maine in order to receive the annates of the Church.'

'I thank you, Nephew,' replied Valois, 'for you know that I dearly love Robert, and that, though I disapprove his rebellion, which is a piece of pig-headed foolishness, I should not like to take up arms against him.'

The army which the Regent gathered to go into Artois bore no resemblance to the enormous host his brother, sixteen months earlier, had engulfed in the mud of Flanders. The army for Artois consisted of permanent troops and levies made in the royal domain. Its pay was high: thirty *sols* a day for a knight banneret, fifteen *sols* for a knight, three *sols* for a foot-soldier. Not only were nobles called up, but also commoners. The two marshals, Jean de Corbeil and Jean de Beaumont, called the Déramé, Lord of Clichy, assembled the banners. Pierre de Galard's crossbowmen were already in commission. Geoffroy Coquatrix had secretly received instructions a fortnight earlier to organize transport and supplies.

On the 30th of October Philippe of Poitiers took the oriflamme at Saint-Denis. On the 4th of November he was at Amiens, whence he immediately sent his second chamberlain, Robert de Gamaches, escorted by a few equerries, to carry a last summons to the Count of Artois.

5

The Regent's Army Takes a Prisoner

THE STUBBLE FROM THE already distant harvest was grey and rotting in the bare muddy fields. Heavy dark clouds were moving across the autumn sky and one might have thought that the world ended at the edge of the plateau. The sharp wind, blowing in short gusts, carried with it an underlying smell of smoke.

Near the village of Bouquemaison, at the very place where, three months before, Count Robert had entered Artois, the Regent's army was drawn up in battle array, pennants flying at lance-heads along more than a mile of front.

Philippe of Poitiers, surrounded by his principal officers, was at the centre, a few yards from the road. He had crossed his gauntleted hands on the pommel of his saddle; his head was bare. Behind him an equerry was carrying his helm.

'It was here he told you that he would come and surrender?' the Regent asked Robert de Gamaches, who had returned from his mission that morning.

'Yes, here, Monseigneur,' replied the second chamberlain.

'He chose the place. "In the field by the stone with a cross on it," he said. And he assured me that he would be here at the hour of tierce.'

'Are you sure that there is no other stone surmounted by a cross in the neighbourhood? For he would be quite capable of playing us a trick on that account, go elsewhere and then say that I was not at the meeting-place. Do you really think he will come?'

'I think so, Monseigneur, for he seemed very perturbed. I told him the size of your army, and I also informed him that Monseigneur the Constable was holding the Flanders borders and the towns to the north, that he would thus be taken between pincers, and would not even be able to escape by the gates. Then I gave him Monseigneur of Valois's letter and advised him to surrender without fighting, since he could not but be defeated, and I informed him that you were so incensed against him that he might well fear the loss of his head if you took him in arms. This seemed to depress him greatly.'

The Regent bent his long body forward over his horse's neck. He decidedly disliked wearing armour; the twenty pounds of steel weighed on his shoulders and prevented him from stretching himself.

'He then went into council with his barons,' went on Gamaches, 'and I don't know what they said to each other. But I gathered that some among them were refusing to support him further while others were beseeching him not to abandon them. Finally he came out to me and gave me the answer I have brought you, assuring me that he has too great a respect for Monseigneur the Regent to disobey him in anything.'

Philippe of Poitiers was incredulous. He suspected this

too-easy surrender, and feared a trap. Screwing up his eyes, he gazed over the melancholy countryside.

'It would be a good enough place to turn our flank and fall on us from behind while we stand here waiting. Corbeil! Le Déramé!' he called to his two marshals. 'Send a few bannerets to reconnoitre both our flanks, search the valleys, and make sure that there are no troops concealed in them or making their way along the roads behind us. And if, when tierce has rung from the steeple behind us, Robert has not come,' he added to Louis of Evreux, 'we shall advance.' But soon there were shouts from the ranks of the banners.

'Here he is! Here he is!'

The Regent screwed up his eyes again but could see nothing.

'Straight to the front, Monseigneur,' someone said, 'just to the right of your horse's head, on the ridge!'

Robert of Artois was riding towards them; he had no companions, no equerries, not even a servant. He was advancing at a walk, sitting erect on his huge horse, and appeared, in his solitariness, even bigger than he in fact was. His tall figure stood out red against the murky sky, and the point of his lance seemed to be pricking the clouds.

'It's another way of defying you, Monseigneur, coming to you like this.'

'Well, let him defy me, let him!' replied Philippe of Poitiers.

The knights who had been sent to reconnoitre returned at a gallop and reported that the neighbourhood was completely quiet.

'I should have thought him more implacable in despair,' said the Regent.

Another man would have wished to display panache

and would doubtless have ridden forward alone to meet the solitary figure. But Philippe of Poitiers had a different conception of his dignity; it was no knightly gesture he needed to make, but that of a king. He therefore waited, making no move, till Robert of Artois, all mudstained and steaming, came to a halt in front of him.

The whole army seemed to hold its breath; there was nothing to be heard but the chink of bits in the horses' mouths.

The giant threw his lance to the ground; the Regent looked down at the lance lying in the stubble and said nothing.

Robert unfastened his helm and his great two-handed sword from the saddle and threw them to join the lance.

The Regent still kept silence; instead of raising his eyes to Robert, he stared at the arms, as if he were awaiting something more.

Robert of Artois decided to dismount. He took two paces forward. Quivering with anger, he went down on one knee so as to meet the Regent's eyes.

'My noble Cousin . . .' he cried, spreading wide his arms. But Philippe cut him short.

'Are you not hungry, Cousin?' he said.

And the other, expecting a splendid scene and noble words, that he would be raised to his feet, embraced, pardoned, was left aghast.

Then Philippe added: 'Very well, mount your horse; we shall go to Amiens as quickly as we may, and I shall there dictate to you my terms for peace. You will ride beside me; we shall eat on the way. Héron! Gamaches! Pick up my cousin's arms.'

Robert of Artois paused before remounting and stared about him.

'Are you looking for something?' the Regent asked.

'No, Philippe. I'm merely gazing at this field that I may not forget it,' replied Artois.

And he put his hand to his breast where, through the hauberk, he could feel the velvet bag in which he had placed, together with relics, the ears of corn, now reduced to powder, which he had plucked in this very place one summer's day. His lips parted in an arrogant smile.

As he rode along by the Regent's side he began to recover his usual assurance.

'This is a splendid army you've gathered, Cousin, to take one prisoner,' he said banteringly.

'The capture of twenty banners, Cousin,' replied Philippe in the same tone, 'would give me less pleasure today than your company. But tell me, what persuaded you to surrender so soon, for though I have numbers on my side, I know well that you do not lack courage!'

'I thought that, if we went to war, too many poor people would suffer.'

'How sensitive you have suddenly become, Robert,' said Philippe of Poitiers. 'I had not heard that you have given much proof of charity in recent times.'

'Our Holy Father, the Pope, was kind enough to write to me and recall me to my duty.'

'Ah, pious too!' cried the Regent.

'I long meditated the good Pope's letter. He was elected without difficulty, I'm told. And indeed, since it was couched in much the same terms as your summons, I determined to show myself both a loyal subject and a good Christian.'

'Kindliness, religion, loyalty: you have much changed, Cousin!'

Meanwhile, Philippe, looking sideways at the giant's jutting chin, was thinking: 'You may mock, you may well mock; but you'll be a little less merry later on, when you know the terms of the peace I shall dictate to you.'

But face to face with the Council, which met as soon as they reached Amiens, Robert adopted the same attitude. He agreed to everything that was asked of him, without cavil or objection, almost as if he had not been listening to the treaty as it was read out to him.

He agreed to surrender 'all castles, fortresses, manors and all else that he had taken or occupied'. He guaranteed the restitution of all the places seized by his partisans. He made a truce with Mahaut until the following Easter; between now and then the Countess would make her claims, and the Court of Peers would judge between the rights of both parties. For the moment the Regent would govern Artois direct and would install such guardians, officers and commanders of castles as he thought fit. Finally, until the peers had given their decision, the revenues of the county would be received by the Count of Evreux and by the Count of Valois.

When he heard this last clause, Robert realized the price of his principal ally's defection. But he did not hesitate even then, and signed every clause.

This extraordinary humility began to worry the Regent. 'What card has he up his sleeve?' Philippe wondered.

As he was in haste to return to Paris for the Queen's lying-in, he left his two marshals, with some of the regular troops, to relieve the Constable in Artois and see for themselves that the treaty was carried out. Robert smiled as he watched the marshals set off.

His plan was a simple one. In coming to surrender alone he

had averted the destruction of his army. Fiennes, Souastre, Picquigny and the others would continue a limited, harassing war of attrition. The Regent could not organize an expedition of this size once a fortnight; the Treasury could not afford it. Robert had therefore several months of peace before him. At the moment he preferred to return to Paris, and found the occasion given him of doing so opportune enough. For it was quite possible that in the near future there would be no longer either a Regent or a Mahaut.

In fact – and it was the real reason for his smile – Robert had discovered the Dame de Fériennes, who provided the Countess of Artois with poisons. He had found her by having two of the Regent's spies, who were also in search of her, followed. Isabelle de Fériennes and her son had been arrested as they were selling the necessary materials for casting spells. Robert's people had killed the Regent's spies, and now the witch, having dictated an admirably complete confession, was sequestered in an Artois castle.

'You'll cut a pretty figure, Cousin,' he thought, as he looked at Philippe, 'when I tell Jean de Varennes to bring me this woman and I produce her before the Council of Peers and let her tell them how you had your brother murdered! Your dear Pope himself won't be able to do anything about it then.'

The Regent kept Robert at his side throughout the whole journey; at the halts they ate at the same table; at night, in the monasteries or royal castles, they slept in adjacent rooms; and the Regent's numerous servants kept Robert under strict surveillance. But when you drink, dine and sleep beside your enemy, you cannot help developing a certain human feeling for him; the two cousins had never known each other so intimately before. The Regent appeared to bear Robert no particular grudge for the trouble and expense he had occasioned; he even seemed to be quite amused by the giant's gross jokes and his air of specious frankness.

'But a little more, and he really will like me, the idiot!' Robert thought. 'What a fool I'm making of him, what a proper fool!'

On the morning of the 11th of November, as they approached the gates of Paris, Philippe suddenly stopped his horse.

'My good Cousin, the other day, at Amiens, you guaranteed that all the castles would be handed over to my marshals. But I am now sorry to hear that several of your friends are disobeying the treaty and refusing to surrender them.'

Robert smiled and spread his hands in a gesture of helplessness.

'But you guaranteed it,' repeated Philippe.

'Yes, Cousin, I signed everything you wished. But as you have taken all power from me, it's up to your marshals to make you obeyed.'

The Regent thoughtfully stroked his horse's neck.

'Is it true, Robert,' he went on, 'that you often call me Philippe of the Closed Gates?'

'Yes it is, Cousin, yes indeed it is!' said the other, laughing. 'It seems that you use gates a good deal in governing.'

'Well, Cousin,' said the Regent, 'in that case you will be lodged in the prison of the Châtelet, and there you will remain until the last castle of Artois is handed over to me.'

For the first time since his surrender Robert paled a little. His whole plan had collapsed, and the Dame de Fériennes would be of little immediate use to him.

PART THREE

FROM MOURNING TO CORONATION

I

A Wet-nurse for the King

JEAN I, KING OF FRANCE, posthumous son of Louis X, the Hutin, and of Queen Clémence of Hungary, was born during the night of the 13th to 14th November 1316 in the Château of Vincennes.

The news was proclaimed at once and the lords put on their silken robes. In the taverns the idlers and drunkards, for whom every event was an opportunity for a drink, began getting drunk and brawling by midday. And the traders in rich and rare goods, goldsmiths, silk merchants, weavers of fine cloth and makers of lace, sellers of spices, rare fishes and produce from overseas, rubbed their hands as they calculated the money that would be spent on the rejoicings.

The streets were a gay scene. People shouted to each other: 'Well, my friend, so we've got a King!'

The people of Paris felt enlivened, and the prostitutes with their yellow hair had plenty of business that day, in spite of the cold north wind which blew through the sordid alleys behind Notre-Dame, to which an edict of Saint Louis had confined them.

In the hospice of the Convent of the Clarisses, Marie de Cressay had given birth four days earlier to a boy who weighed his full eight pounds, gave promise of being fair like his mother, and sucked, his eyes tight shut, like a voracious young puppy.

The novices, in their white hoods, were continually entering Marie's cell to watch her dress her baby, gaze at her radiant face as she fed him at her pink, abundant, expansive breast, while they who were destined to perpetual virginity admired the miracle of motherhood outside a painted figure in a window.

For if it sometimes happened that a nun sinned, this did not occur as frequently as the public rhymesters stated in their songs, and a newborn child in a convent of the Clarisses was not a very frequent occurrence.

There was great excitement on this particular day, for the Chaplain had announced the birth of a King; the joy of the town penetrated even to the cloister.

'The King is called Jean, like my baby,' said Marie.

In this she saw a good augury. A whole generation would be born to whom the King's Christian name would be given, and it was all the more striking because it was new to the monarchy. To all the little Philippes, to all the little Louis, would succeed an infinity of little Jeans throughout the kingdom. 'Mine is the first,' thought Marie.

The short twilight of autumn was beginning to fall when a young nun entered the cell.

'Dame Marie,' she said, 'the Mother Abbess is asking for you in the parlour. There is someone to see you.'

'Who is it?'

'I don't know, I didn't see. But I think you are going to leave us.'

The blood flowed to Marie's cheeks.

'It's Guccio. It's Guccio! It's his father,' she explained to the novices. 'It's my husband come to take us away, I'm sure.'

She closed the opening of her bodice, quickly did her hair, gazing into the window-pane which served her as a dull mirror, put her cloak about her shoulders, and then hesitated a moment before the cradle which lay on the ground. Should she take the child down with her and give Guccio this wonderful surprise at once?

'Look how he sleeps, the angel!' said the little novices. 'Don't wake him or let him catch cold! Run along; we'll watch over him.'

'Don't take him out of his cradle, don't touch him!' said Marie.

As she went downstairs she was already a prey to maternal anxiety. 'As long as they don't play with him and drop him!' But her feet flew on towards the visiting-room, and she was astonished to find herself feeling so light.

In the white room, whose only decoration was a huge Crucifix and two candles which duplicated the huge shadows, the Mother Abbess, her hands folded in her sleeves, was talking to Madame de Bouville.

When she saw the Curator's wife, Marie felt more than mere disappointment; she had an immediate certainty, inexplicable but absolute, that this dry woman with vertical wrinkles on her face was bringing her bad luck.

Anyone else but Marie would merely have thought that they did not like Madame de Bouville; but with Marie de

Cressay all feelings took on a sort of passionate quality, and she attributed to her likes and dislikes the importance of harbingers of fate. 'I'm sure she has come to do me harm,' she thought.

Madame de Bouville glanced at her sharply, looking her up and down without kindness.

'Only four days since you had your baby,' she cried, 'and here you are as fresh and pink as an eglantine! I compliment you, my girl; one might think you were ready to begin all over again. In truth God is very merciful towards those who despise His commandments and seems to reserve His trials for the most meritorious. For, would you believe it, Mother,' went on Madame de Bouville, turning to the Abbess, 'our poor Queen's pains lasted thirty hours? Her screams are still ringing in my ears. The King presented himself seat first and they had to use forceps. He was within an ace of dying, and the mother too. It's the Queen's sorrow at the death of her husband which is the cause of it all, and if you ask me, it's a miracle the child was born alive. But when fate takes a hand, you have to admit that everything goes wrong! There was Eudeline, the linen-maid – you know whom I mean?'

The Abbess discreetly nodded her head. She had, among the little novices in the convent, a child of eleven who was the natural daughter of the Hutin and Eudeline.

'... who was a great help to the Queen, and whom Madame Clémence liked to have continually at her bedside,' went on Madame de Bouville; 'well, Eudeline broke her arm falling off a step-ladder and had to be taken to the Hôtel-Dieu. And now, to crown all, here's the wet-nurse we engaged, who's been ready waiting for a week, with her milk suddenly dried up. Really, to do a thing like that to us at such a moment! For the Queen, of course, is in no condition to feed the King; she has the fever. My poor Hugues turns this way and that till he's utterly exhausted and has no idea what to do next, for these are not matters for a man; as for the Sire de Joinville, who no longer has a glimmering of sight or memory, all that we can hope for from him is that he should not take it into his head to expire in our arms! In other words, Mother, I am the only person capable of seeing to things.'

Marie de Cressay wondered why she was being allowed to hear of these royal tribulations, when Madame de Bouville, still cackling, went up to her and said: 'Luckily I've got my head screwed on, and I remembered that this girl I brought here was about to have a child. I am sure you feed it well and that your child is doing splendidly, isn't that so?'

She seemed to be reproaching the young mother with her good health.

'Let's have a closer look,' she went on.

And with a competent hand, as if she were selecting fruit in the market, she felt Marie's breasts. The girl took a step backwards with a feeling of revulsion.

'You can easily feed two,' went on Madame de Bouville. 'You will therefore come with me, my good girl, and give your milk to the King.'

'I cannot, Madame!' cried Marie, before she had even thought how she could justify her refusal.

'And why can you not? Because of your sin? You are, nevertheless, a daughter of the nobility; moreover, sin does not prevent your being rich in milk. It will be a means of redeeming yourself a little.'

'I have not sinned, Madame, I am married!'

'You're the only one who says so, my poor girl! In the first place, if you were married, you wouldn't be here. And in any case that's beside the point. We need a wet-nurse.'

'I cannot, because I am awaiting my husband, who is coming here to fetch me. He has let me know that he will come soon and the Pope has promised . . .'

'The Pope! The Pope!' screamed the Curator's wife. 'She's out of her mind, I swear it! She believes she's married, she believes the Pope's concerned about her . . . Stop talking nonsense, and don't blaspheme the name of the Holy Father! You will come to Vincennes at once!'

'No, Madame, I shall not,' replied Marie obstinately.

Little Madame de Bouville lost her temper and, taking Marie by the top of her dress, began shaking her.

'Here's an ungrateful creature for you! She sins and gets herself in the family way; we take care of her, save her from the law, put her in the best convent, and when we come to fetch her to be wet-nurse to the King of France, the hussy jibs. Here's a good subject of the King for you! Don't you realize that you are being offered an honour that the greatest ladies in the kingdom would fight for?'

'In that case, Madame,' said Marie resolutely, 'why don't you ask these great ladies who are more worthy than I?'

'Because they didn't sin at the right moment, the idiots! But what are you making me say? Enough talk, you're coming with me.'

If Uncle Tolomei, or the Count de Bouville himself, had come to make the same demand of Marie de Cressay, she would certainly have accepted. She had a generous heart, and would have offered to feed any child in distress; particularly the Queen's. Pride, and interest too, would have persuaded her to it as well as kindness of heart. Wet-nurse to the King, while Guccio was page to the Pope, should smooth away all their difficulties and make their fortune. But the Curator's wife had not approached her in the right way. Because she was treated not as a happy mother but as a delinquent, not as a respectable woman but as a serf, and because she still saw Madame de Bouville as a harbinger of misfortune, Marie forgot to think and turned stubborn. Her great dark blue eyes shone with mingled fear and indignation.

'I shall keep my milk for my own son,' she said.

'We shall see about that, you wicked girl! Since you won't obey of your own accord, I shall call in the escort waiting outside and they'll remove you by force!'

The Mother Abbess intervened. The convent was an asylum she could not allow to be violated.

'I am not saying that I approve the conduct of my relation,' she said, 'but she has been committed to my care.'

'By me, Mother!' cried Madame de Bouville.

'That is no reason to come and do her violence within these walls. Marie will leave only of her own accord, or at the orders of the Church.'

'Or on those of the King! For you are a royal convent, Mother, and don't you forget it! I am acting in the name of my husband; if you want an order from the Constable, who is the King's tutor, and has just returned to Paris, or an order from the Regent himself, Messire Hugues will go and get them to seal it; we shall lose three hours, but I shall be obeyed.'

The Abbess took Madame de Bouville aside to inform her in a low voice that what Marie had said about the Pope was not altogether false.

'But what do I care!' cried Madame de Bouville. 'I've got to keep the King alive and I have no one to hand but her.'

She went out, and called to the men of her escort to seize the rebel.

'You are witness, Madame,' said the Abbess, 'that I have not given my consent to your being forcibly carried off.'

Marie, struggling between two of the escort as they dragged her across the courtyard, screamed: 'My child! I want my child!'

'That's right,' said Madame de Bouville. 'She must be allowed to take her child. By rebelling like this she has made us forget everything.'

A few minutes later, Marie, having quickly packed her clothes and clutching her newborn child to her, left the hospice in tears. Outside, two mule-litters were in readiness.

'Just look at her!' cried Madame de Bouville. 'You come and fetch her with a litter, as if she were a princess, and she screams and makes an appalling scene!'

Surrounded by the night, jostled by the trotting of the mules for a whole hour, in a box of wood and tapestry with loose curtains, through which the cold of November entered, Marie was thankful that her brothers had made her bring her big cloak when she left Cressay. How she had suffered from the heat under the heavy stuff when she arrived in Paris! 'Am I never to leave anywhere without tears and unhappiness?' she thought. 'What have I done that every hand should be against me?'

The baby slept, wrapped in a great fold of the cloak. Feeling this little life, so unconscious and untroubled, snuggling into the hollow of her breast, Marie gradually regained her calm. She was going to see Queen Clémence; she would talk to her of Guccio; she would show her the reliquary. The Queen was young; she was beautiful and pathetic because of her misfortunes. 'The Queen . . . it's the Queen's child I'm going to nurse!' Marie thought, realizing for the first time the strange and unexpected nature of this adventure, which Madame de Bouville's aggressive behaviour had presented in so odious a light.

The rattle of the drawbridge as it was lowered, the hollow sound of the horses' hooves on the planks, was followed by the clink of their shoes on the cobbles of a courtyard. Marie was told to get out of her litter; she passed through a group of armed soldiers, followed an ill-lit stone corridor, and saw a fat man in a coat of mail, whom she recognized as the Count de Bouville. All about Marie people were whispering; she heard the word 'fever' several times. Someone signed to her to walk on tiptoe; a hanging was raised.

In spite of illness the customs of the birth-chamber had been respected. But, since the season of flowers was over, only late and yellow foliage had been spread about the floor and it was already beginning to wither under foot. About the bed seats had been placed for visitors who would never come. A midwife was standing by, crushing aromatic herbs between her fingers. On the hearth, on iron trivets, grey-looking concoctions were boiling. The room was lit only by the fire and by the oil nightlight above the bed.

No sound came from the cradle, which was placed in a corner of the room.

Queen Clémence was lying on her back, her legs raised, humping the sheets, because of the pain she was suffering. Her cheekbones were red, her eyes bright. Marie noticed above all her long golden hair spread over the pillows, and the concentrated gaze which did not seem to see what it was fixed on.

'I'm thirsty, I'm very thirsty,' the Queen groaned.

The midwife whispered to Madame de Bouville: 'She has been shivering for more than an hour; her teeth have been chattering; and her lips turned purple like the face of someone dead. We thought she was dying. We rubbed her whole body; then her skin began to sweat as you can see. She has perspired so much that her linen must be changed; but we cannot find the keys of the linen-room, which were kept by Eudeline.'

'I will give them to you,' replied Madame de Bouville.

She led Marie into a neighbouring room, where a fire was also burning.

'You will live here,' she said. The royal cradle was brought in. Amid all the linen in which the King was wrapped he was hardly visible. He had a tiny nose, thick, closed eyelids, was puny and sleeping in a sort of flaccid immobility. One had to go very close to him to make sure that he was breathing. From time to time a tiny grimace, a sort of painful contortion, relieved the impassiveness of his features. Before this little being, whose father was dead, whose mother was perhaps to die, and who showed such slight signs of life, Marie de Cressay was assailed with an immense pity. 'I'll save him; I'll make him big and strong,' she thought.

As there was only one cradle, she laid her own child down beside the King.

2

Leave it to God

THE COUNTESS MAHAUT HAD been in a rage for the last twenty-four hours.

She let her rage and disappointment have full rein to Béatrice d'Hirson, who was helping her dress for the christening of the King.

'One might have thought, pining as Clémence was, that she would have miscarried! Many stronger than she do so. But no! She lasted out her nine months. She might even have had a still-born child. But not at all! Her brat's alive. It might at least have been a girl! But not on your life, it had to be a boy. My poor Béatrice, was it worth doing so much, running such great risks – and indeed they're not yet over – for fate to play such a trick on us?'

For Mahaut was now profoundly convinced that she had only murdered the Hutin to give the Crown of France to her son-in-law and her daughter. She almost regretted not having killed the wife at the same time as the husband, and all her hatred was now turned on the newborn child whom she had not yet seen, towards the baby to whom she was shortly to act as godmother and whose existence, hardly begun, was an obstacle to her ambitions.

This woman, powerful, immensely rich and despotic, had a truly criminal nature. Murder was her favourite method of bending fate to her own advantage; she liked contemplating her murders before she committed them, and afterwards she enjoyed the memory of them; she extracted from them all the excitements of fear, the pleasures of deception and the joys of secret triumph. If a first assassination did not have all the success she counted on, she began accusing fate of injustice, considered herself hard done by, and then began seeking the next victim who stood in her way and whom she might destroy.

Béatrice d'Hirson, reading the Countess's thoughts, said softly, lowering her long eyelashes: 'Madame, I have kept some of that excellent powder which served you so well for the King's sweets in the spring.'

'You've done well, you've done well,' replied Mahaut; 'it is always better to be provided; we have so many enemies!'

Béatrice, who was tall herself, had to raise her arms to arrange the Countess's chin-band and place her cloak about her shoulders.

'You will be holding the child, Madame. You may perhaps not have another opportunity so soon,' she went on. 'It's only a powder, you know, and hardly perceptible on one's finger.'

She spoke in a suave, tempting voice as if she were suggesting some delicacy.

'Ah, no!' cried Mahaut. 'Not during a christening; it might bring us bad luck!'

'Do you think so? You would be returning a soul without sin to Heaven.'

'Besides, God knows how my son-in-law would take it! I've not forgotten the expression on his face when I undeceived him about his brother's death, and the coldness with which he has since treated me. There are too many people whispering accusations against me. One king in the year is enough; let us for the moment bear with the one who has just been born.'

It was a small, almost secret cavalcade that left for Vincennes to make Jean I a Christian; and the barons who had prepared their ceremonial clothes, expecting to be summoned to a great occasion, were left to pay the cost.

The Queen's illness, the fact that the birth had taken place outside Paris, the darkness of winter, and the little pleasure taken by the Regent in being presented with a nephew, all resulted in the christening being dispatched rapidly as if it were some mere formality.

Philippe arrived at Vincennes accompanied by his wife Jeanne, Mahaut, Gaucher de Châtillon and a few equerries to hold the horses. He had omitted to inform the rest of the family. Besides, Valois was touring his fiefs to gather money; and Evreux had remained in Amiens to bring the Artois affair to a conclusion. As for Charles de La Marche, Philippe had had a lively altercation with him the day before. La Marche had asked his brother, in honour of the birth of the King, to give him a peerage and increase his appanage and revenues.

'But, Brother,' Philippe had replied, 'I am only the Regent; the King alone can give you a peerage – and then only at his majority.'

Bouville's first words, as he received the Regent in the forecourt of the manor, were to ask: 'No one is armed, Monseigneur? No one has a dagger, a stiletto, or a misericord?'

No one could tell whether his anxiety was directed towards the escort or the godfathers and godmothers.

'I am not accustomed, Bouville,' the Regent replied, 'to be escorted by unarmed equerries.'

Bouville, at once embarrassed and obstinate, asked the equerries to remain in the outer court. His zealous prudence began to annoy the Regent.

'I appreciate, Bouville,' he said, 'the zeal with which you have watched over the Queen's belly; but you are no longer Curator; it is to myself and the Constable that the duty of watching over the King now belongs. We leave you in charge, but do not abuse your powers.'

'Monseigneur! Monseigneur!' stammered Bouville. 'I had no intention of offending you. But there is so much gossip throughout the kingdom. Indeed, I but want you to see that I am faithful to my task, and that I am aware of the honour.'

He was not good at dissimulation. He could not help looking askance at Mahaut, and then immediately lowering his eyes.

'Everyone clearly suspects me and is afraid of me,' the Countess thought.

Jeanne de Poitiers pretended to notice nothing. Gaucher de Châtillon, who had not realized the implications of what was going on, dispelled the awkwardness of the moment by saying: 'Come on, Bouville, don't leave us to freeze; take us indoors.'

They did not go to the Queen's bedside. The news Madame de Bouville gave them was most alarming; the fever still had her in its grip, while she complained of appalling headaches and was shaken continuously by nausea.

'Her stomach is swelling again as if she had never been brought to bed at all,' explained Madame de Bouville. 'She cannot sleep, prays that the bells ringing in her ears may be silenced, and talks to us all the time as if she were addressing her grandmother, Madame of Hungary, or King Louis, her dead husband. It's sad to hear her so delirious and not be able to do anything to stop it.'

Twenty years as chamberlain to Philip the Fair had given the Count de Bouville a long experience of royal ceremonies. How many christenings had he not had to organize?

The ritual objects were handed to those taking part. Bouville and two gentlemen of the Guard placed long white napkins about their necks, holding the ends outstretched before them so that one might cover the basin of holy water, another an empty basin, and the third the cup containing the salt.

The midwife who had brought the child into the world took the chrisom to be placed about the child's head after the anointing.

Then the wet-nurse came forward, carrying the King. 'Oh, what a good-looking girl,' thought the Constable.

Madame de Bouville had found for Marie a rose-coloured velvet dress with a little fur at collar and cuffs, and she had long rehearsed the girl in the part she was to play. The baby was wrapped in a robe twice too long for it, over which had been placed a veil of violet silk falling to the ground like a train.

They moved towards the Château chapel. Equerries led the way, holding lighted candles. The Seneschal de Joinville came last, tottering even between his supporters. Nevertheless he had emerged a little from his usual torpor because the child was called Jean like himself.

The chapel was hung with tapestries and the stone font decorated with purple velvet. To one side was a table on which had been placed a covering of miniver; on top of this was a fine cloth, and on top of this again silk cushions. The few braziers did not suffice to dispel the damp cold.

Marie placed the child on the table and unswathed him. She was intent on making no mistakes; her heart was beating, and she was so excited that she could barely recognize the faces about her. Could she ever have imagined that she, a girl expelled from her family, would play so important a part, standing between the Regent of France and the Countess of Artois, at the christening of a king? Dazzled by this reversal of fortune, she was now full of gratitude to Madame de Bouville and had already asked her pardon for her refractoriness of the day before.

As she was unwrapping the swaddling clothes, she heard the Constable ask her name and whence she came. She felt herself blush.

The Queen's chaplain had blown four times on the body of the child, as it might be on the four branches of the Cross, to cast out the Devil from him by virtue of the Holy Ghost; then, spitting on his forefinger, he had smeared the child's ears and nostrils with saliva to signify that he must not listen to the voice of the Devil, nor breathe the temptations of the world and the flesh.

Philippe and Mahaut took up the little King, one by the legs and the other by the shoulders. The Regent, with his short-sighted eyes, gazed insistently at the child's minute sex, that pink grub which frustrated all his brilliant plans for the succession, that derisory symbol of male succession, that tiny but insurmountable barrier between himself and the crown.

'In any case,' thought Philippe to console himself, 'I shall be Regent for fifteen years. And in fifteen years many things can happen; shall I be alive myself in fifteen years' time? And will this child live till then?'

But to be Regent is not to be King.

The child remained perfectly quiet, even slept during the preliminary rites. He found his voice only when he was completely immersed in the cold water, but then he howled with the full force of his lungs, almost suffocating himself, and his tears mingled with the water of his baptism. While the other godfathers and godmothers, Gaucher, Jeanne, the Bouvilles and the Seneschal, held their hands over the little naked body, he was immersed three times, first with his head towards the east, then to the north, then to the south, to symbolize the sign of the Cross.[27]

He grew quiet again when he had been taken from the icy bath, and placidly accepted the consecrated oil with which his forehead was anointed. He was placed on the cushions and Marie de Cressay proceeded to dry him, while the rest of those present crowded as close as they could to the warmth of the braziers.

Suddenly Marie de Cressay's voice rang out through the chapel.

'Lord! Lord! He's dying, he's dying!' she screamed.

Everyone rushed to the table. The infant King had turned blue, and moment by moment his colour grew darker till it was almost black; his body was stiff, his arms contracted, his head twisted and his eyes had turned up, showing only the whites.

An invisible hand was stifling his insentient life amid the wavering candles and the anxious, bended heads.

Mahaut heard a voice murmur: 'She did it.'

She raised her eyes and encountered the gaze of the Bouvilles.

'Who can have done the deed so as to accuse me of it?' she wondered.

However, the midwife had taken the child from Marie's trembling hands and was trying to reanimate it.

'It's not certain he'll die, it's not certain,' she said.

The child stayed rigid, extended and dark in hue for nearly two minutes, which seemed to last an infinity of time; then, suddenly, he began jerking in violent spasms, his head bobbing in all directions, his limbs twisting; it seemed incredible that there could be so much force concealed in so puny a body. The midwife had to hold him tight to prevent him from falling out of her hands. The chaplain crossed himself as if he were in the presence of some manifestation of the Devil and began reciting the prayers for the dying. The child's face was contorted and he was slobbering; the black tint disappeared from his skin and was gradually replaced by a sort of icy pallor which was no less alarming. He then became still, urinated over the midwife's dress, and they thought he was saved; but his head immediately fell forward; he grew slack and inert; and now they believed he was really dead.

'It was high time he was baptized,' said the Constable.

Philippe was picking the hot wax from the candles off his hands.

And suddenly the little body waved its legs, uttered several cries, feeble but no longer distressful, and his lips worked in a movement of suction; the King was alive and hungry.

'The Devil fought hard before being expelled from his body,' said the chaplain.

'It is not usual', the midwife explained, 'for convulsions to seize on a child so early. It's because he was born with forceps; it does happen from time to time. And then he lacked the wet-nurse's milk for several hours.'

Marie de Cressay felt herself to blame, 'If only I had come at once, instead of arguing with Madame de Bouville,' she thought.

No one, of course, thought of blaming the immersion in cold water, nor made allusion to the family's splendid heredity, to the cripples, lunatics and epileptics flourishing on that glorious tree.

The reasons given by the midwife, and in particular the pressure on the brain by the forceps, were in any case sufficient.

'Do you think he's likely to suffer further seizures?' Mahaut asked.

'It is much to be feared, Madame,' replied the midwife. 'One cannot tell when a fit will come on him, nor how it will end.'

'Poor child!' said Mahaut loudly.

They took the King back to the Château and separated unhappily.

Philippe of Poitiers said no word during the whole journey back. When he reached the Palace, he allowed his mother-in-law to follow him and shut herself into the room with him.

'You only missed being King by very little just now, my son,' she said.

Philippe made no reply.

'Indeed, after what we have seen, no one would be surprised if the child were to die during the next few days,' she went on.

The Regent remained silent.

'Nevertheless, if he died, you would still be obliged to wait for Jeanne of Navarre's majority.'

'Oh, no, Mother! Oh no!' Philippe replied vehemently. 'We are no longer bound now by the law of July. The question °of Louis's succession is closed; it would be the question of little Jean's succession which would have to be considered. Between my brother and myself there would have been a king, and I should be my nephew's heir.'

Mahaut gazed at him in admiration: 'He has thought this out during the christening,' she thought.

'You have always dreamed of being king, Philippe; admit it,' she said. 'Even when you were a child you used to break off branches to make yourself sceptres!'

He raised his head a little and smiled at her, letting the silence run on. Then, grave again, he said: 'Do you know, Mother, that the Dame de Fériennes has disappeared from Arras, as have the men I sent to arrest her and deal with her to prevent her talking too much? It appears that she is held secretly in some castle of Artois, and they say that your barons are boasting of it.'

Mahaut wondered what Philippe intended by this warning. Did he merely wish to point out the dangers she ran? Or prove to her that he was protecting her? Or was it his manner of confirming his prohibition to resort to poison? Or, alternatively, was he, by making allusion to the supplier of the poison, giving her to understand that she had a free hand?

'Further convulsions might well kill him,' went on Mahaut.

'Leave it to God, Mother, leave it to God,' said Philippe, putting an end to the audience.

'Leave it to God, or leave it to me?' thought the Countess of Artois. 'He's prudent, even to the point of taking care not to damn his own soul; but he understood me very well. It's that fat idiot Bouville who'll give me most trouble.'

From that moment her imagination set to work. Mahaut had a crime in prospect; and that the victim was a newborn child excited her as much as if he had been the most ferocious of protagonists.

She began a careful campaign of perfidy. The King had been born unlikely to live; she told everyone so, and described, with tears in her eyes, the painful scene at the christening.

'We all thought he was going to die before our eyes, and indeed he very nearly did so. Ask the Constable who was there too; I've never seen Messire Gaucher, who is a brave man, turn so pale. Besides, everyone will be able to judge of the little King's weakness when he is presented to the barons, as must be done. It may even be that he is already dead, and that it is being concealed from us. For the presentation is unduly delayed, and no reason has been given us for it. It appears that Messire de Bouville is opposed to it because the unfortunate Queen – whom God keep! – is desperately ill. But after all the Queen is not the King!'

Mahaut's followers, such as her cousin Henry de Sully and her chancellor Thierry d'Hirson, spread her remarks.

The barons were becoming alarmed. For indeed, why was the solemn presentation being so long deferred? The private christening, Bouville's evasions, the impenetrable silence maintained at Vincennes: all seemed mysterious.

Contradictory rumours were going the rounds. The King was a cripple and they did not wish to reveal it. The Count of Valois had had him removed and taken secretly to Naples to place him in safety. The Queen was not ill; she had returned to her own country.

'If he's dead, we should be told so,' some were murmuring.

'The Regent has had him killed!' others asserted.

'What nonsense you're talking! The Regent's not that kind of man; but he's mistrustful of Valois.'

'It's not the Regent; it's Mahaut. She's preparing her blow, or has already carried it out. She will keep on saying that the King cannot live!'

While this ill-wind was blowing through the Court again, and people's nerves were overwrought with odious conjectures and infamous suspicions, with which everyone felt himself to be bespattered, the Regent remained impenetrably silent. He was absorbed in the administration of the kingdom, and if someone spoke to him of his nephew, he changed the subject to Flanders, Artois, or the collection of taxes.

On the morning of the 19th of November, since irritation was growing, a number of barons and masters of Parliament came in a delegation to have an audience with Philippe and make strong representations, demands almost, that he should agree to the presentation of the King. Those who were expecting a refusal or an evasive answer had an angry glint already in their eyes.

'But I desire it, Messeigneurs, I desire the presentation as much as you do,' said the Regent. 'But I am being opposed in the matter; it's the Count de Bouville who refuses it.'

Then, turning to Charles of Valois, who had returned forty-eight hours earlier from his county of Maine, where he had been organizing his finances, he said: 'Is it you, Uncle, who, in the interests of your niece Clémence, are preventing Bouville from showing us the King?'

The ex-Emperor of Constantinople, not understanding why this attack should have been made on him, turned purple in the face and cried: 'But, for God's sake, Nephew, what makes you think that? I have never desired or asked such a thing! I haven't even seen Bouville, or received any message from him, for several weeks. And I have come home especially for the presentation. I particularly desire that it should be made and that we should act in accordance with the customs of our fathers, as we haven't done for far too long.'

'Then, Messeigneurs,' said the Regent, 'we are all of the same mind and are agreed. Gaucher! You were at my brother's birth. I am right in thinking that it is the godmother whose duty it is to present the royal child to the barons, am I not?'

'Yes, of course, the godmother,' replied Valois, vexed that on a point of ceremonial someone other than himself should be consulted. 'I have attended all the presentations, Philippe; yours, which was a small one, because you were the second son, as well as Louis's and later Charles's. And my children were presented also on account of my crowns. It is always the godmother.'

'Very well,' went on the Regent, 'I shall inform the Countess Mahaut at once that she will shortly have to perform this office, and I shall give orders to Bouville to open Vincennes to us. We shall set out on horseback at midday.'

For Mahaut this was the opportunity for which she had been waiting. She allowed no one but Béatrice to dress her, and had a coronet placed on her head; the murder of a king deserved that much.

'How long do you think it will take for your powder to affect a child five days old?'

'That I cannot tell, Madame,' replied the lady-in-waiting. 'On the deer in your woods the result was manifest after one night. King Louis, on the other hand, resisted it for nearly three days.'

'I shall always have, as a resource,' said Mahaut, 'the wet-nurse I saw the other day, a handsome girl indeed, but who comes no one knows whence, and no one knows who placed her there. Doubtless, the Bouvilles . . .'

'I understand, Madame,' said Béatrice smiling. 'If the death should not appear natural, the girl could be accused and you could have her quartered.'

'My relic, my relic,' said Mahaut anxiously, touching her breast. 'Oh, yes, I've got it, that's all right.'

As she was leaving the room, Béatrice murmured: 'Whatever you do, Madame, do not blow your nose.'

3

Bouville's Trick

'Light roaring fires!' Bouville told the servants. 'Let the hearths flame red hot so that the warmth spreads to the corridors.'

He went from room to room, paralysing work in his efforts to hurry it on. He dashed out to the drawbridge to inspect the guard, ordered sand to be spread in the courtyards, then had it swept up because it turned to mud, and checked all the locks though none of them would be used. All this activity was merely to cheat his own anxiety. 'She's going to kill him, she's going to kill him,' he kept muttering to himself.

He met his wife in one of the corridors.

'The Queen?' he asked.

Queen Clémence had been given the last sacraments that very morning.

The Queen, whose beauty had become legendary in two kingdoms, was ravaged and disfigured by illness. Her nose was pinched, her skin had turned yellow, marked with red blotches the size of a two-*livre* piece; she stank appallingly;

her urine contained traces of blood; she breathed with greater and greater difficulty and groaned from the intolerable pains in her head and stomach. She was completely delirious.

'It's a quartan fever,' said Madame de Bouville. 'The midwife says that if she gets through the day she may live. Mahaut has offered to send Master de Pavilly, her personal physician.'[28]

'Not at any price, not at any price,' cried Bouville. 'None of Mahaut's people must be allowed to come in here.'

The mother was dying, the child was in danger, and more than two hundred barons were due to arrive with their escorts! What splendid confusion there would be in a little while, and what an easy opportunity for committing a crime!

'The child must not remain in a room next to the Queen,' Bouville went on. 'I cannot put enough men-at-arms to watch over him, and it's all too easy to slip behind the tapestries.'

'This is a fine time to think of it; where do you wish to put him?'

'In the King's room, to which all the entrances can be guarded.'

They looked at each other with the same thought; it was the room in which the Hutin had died.

'Prepare the room and light the fire,' Bouville insisted.

'Very well, my dear, I will obey you. But if you put fifty equerries about him, you cannot prevent Mahaut carrying the King in her arms for the presentation.'

'I shall be near her.'

'But if she has resolved to do it, she'll kill him under your very nose, my poor Hugues; and you'll notice nothing. A child five days old cannot struggle much. She'll take advantage of the crowd to plunge a needle into the weak part of his head, make him breathe poison or strangle him with a lace.'

'Well, what do you want me to do?' cried Bouville. 'I can't go to the Regent and say: "We don't wish your mother-in-law to carry the King because we fear she'll kill him."'

'No, you certainly cannot! We can but pray to God,' said Madame de Bouville as she went off.

Bouville, much disturbed, entered the wet-nurse's room.

Marie de Cressay was feeding both children at once. Both equally hungry, they clutched at her breasts with their little soft nails, and sucked noisily. Marie had generously given the King her left breast which was supposed to be the richer.

'What is the matter, Messire? You seem disturbed,' she asked Bouville.

He stood before her, leaning on his great sword, the black-and-white locks of his hair falling beside his cheeks, and his paunch extending the coat of mail, a sexagenarian archangel committed to the difficult protection of a child.

'He's so weak, our little King, so weak!' he said sadly.

'Oh, no, Messire, he's doing much better; look, he has almost caught up with mine. And the medicines they're giving me, though they upset my stomach a little, seem to be doing him good.'[29]

Bouville extended his great hand, tanned by the reins of horses and the pommels of arms; he gently stroked the little head on which a fair down was forming.

'He's not a king like others, you know . . .' he murmured.

Philip the Fair's old servant did not know how to express what he felt. For as long as he could remember or, indeed, his father had been able to remember, the monarchy, the kingdom, France itself, all that had been the basis of his functions and the object of his anxieties, had been merged with a long and solid chain of strong and adult kings, who exacted devotion and dispensed honours.

For twenty years he had pushed forward the faldstool on which sat a monarch before whom Christendom trembled. Never could he have believed that the chain would be reduced so soon to this tiny pink link, its chin smeared with milk, a link one could break with one hand.

'It's true enough', he said, 'that he has made a good recovery; except for the mark left by the forceps, which is already disappearing, one would have to look closely to distinguish him from yours.'

'Oh, no, Messire,' said Marie; 'mine is the heavier. Aren't you, Jean the Second, much heavier?'

She immediately blushed and exclaimed: 'Since they're both called Jean, I call my Jean the Second. Perhaps I oughtn't to.'

Bouville, with a gesture of automatic courtesy, stroked the second baby's head. His eyes moved from one to the other.

Marie thought that the fat man's gaze was attracted by her breasts, and she blushed the harder. 'When shall I stop blushing on every possible occasion?' she wondered. 'There's nothing immodest or provocative in giving a child the breast!'

At the moment Madame de Bouville came into the room, carrying the clothes for the King. Bouville took her aside and murmured: 'I think I've found a means.'

For some moments they conversed in low voices. Madame de Bouville nodded her head, deep in thought; twice she looked towards Marie.

'Ask her yourself,' she said at last. 'She doesn't like me.'

Bouville returned to the young woman. 'Marie, my child, you are going to render a great service to our little King to whom I see you are so attached,' he said. 'Here are the barons coming that he may be presented to them. But we fear the cold for him, because of the convulsions he was seized with at his christening. Imagine the effect it would have if he began writhing as he did the other day! It would soon be said that he cannot live, as his enemies are spreading it abroad. We barons are warriors, and we like the King to give proof of being robust even in his infancy. Your child is the stouter and looks the stronger. We would like to present him in the King's place.'

Marie looked anxiously at Madame de Bouville, who said quickly: 'This has nothing to do with me. It's my husband's idea.'

'Wouldn't it be a sin, Messire, to do a thing like that?' Marie asked.

'A sin, my child? But it's a virtue to protect one's king. And it would not be the first time that a healthy child was presented to the people in place of a weakly heir,' Bouville assured her, lying in a good cause.

'But won't people notice?'

'How should they?' cried Madame de Bouville. 'They're both fair; and at that age all children are alike, and alter from day to day. Who really knows the King? Messire de Joinville, who can see nothing, the Regent, who sees but little more, and the Constable, who knows more about horses than he does about infants?'

'Won't the Countess of Artois be surprised that he has no marks of forceps?'

'How could she see them under the bonnet and the crown?'

'Besides, it's a dull day. We shall almost have to light the candles,' Bouville added, pointing to the window and the sad November sky.

Marie made no further objection. At bottom, the idea of this substitution did her honour and she attributed to Bouville nothing but good intentions. She took pleasure in dressing her child as a king, swaddling him in silk, placing about him the blue cloak strewn with golden lilies and the bonnet on which had been sewn a tiny crown, clothes prepared before his birth.

'How beautiful my little Jean will be,' Marie said. 'Lord, a crown, a crown! You'll have to give it back to your King, you know, you'll have to give it back to him!'

She bounced her child up and down, as if he were a doll, before the cradle of Jean I.

'Look, Sire, look at your foster-brother, your little servant who is to take your place so that you will not catch cold.'

And she thought: 'Just imagine when I tell Guccio all this, when I tell him that his son is the King's foster-brother and that he was presented to the barons! What a strange life we lead, a life that I would exchange for no other! How lucky it was I fell in love with him, my Lombard!'

Her happiness was destroyed by a long groan from the adjoining room.

'My God, the Queen!' thought Marie. 'I had forgotten the Queen.'

An equerry entered the room, announcing the approach of the Regent and the barons. Madame de Bouville took up Marie's child.

'I'm taking him to the King's room,' she said, 'and will put him back there after the ceremony till the Court has left.

As for you, Marie, don't move from here till I return, and if anyone should come, in spite of the guard we're placing on the door, you must say that the child with you is yours.'

4

My Lords, Look on the King

THE BARONS HAD SOME difficulty in all crowding into the great hall; they were talking, coughing, stamping their feet and beginning to get impatient with having to stand so long. The escorts had invaded the corridors to see the spectacle; there were groups of heads in all the doorways.

The Seneschal de Joinville, who had been kept in bed until the last moment so as not to overtire him, was standing at the door of the King's chamber with Bouville.

'You must make the announcement, Messire Seneschal,' said Bouville. 'You are the oldest companion-in-arms of Saint Louis; the honour is yours by right.'

Ill with anxiety, his face running with sweat, Bouville was thinking: 'I could not do it. I could not make the announcement. My voice would betray me.'

At the end of the dim corridor he saw the Countess Mahaut appear, gigantic, looking still larger in her coronet and heavy state mantle. Never had Mahaut of Artois seemed to him so huge and so terrifying.

He dashed into the room and said to his wife: 'The moment has come.'

Madame de Bouville went to meet the Countess, whose heavy step rang on the flagstones, and handed her the light burden.

The place was dark; Mahaut did not look closely at the child. She merely thought that he had increased in weight since the day of the christening.

'Ah, our little King is doing well,' she said. 'I compliment you, my dear.'

'We watch over him very carefully, Madame; we do not wish to incur his godmother's reproaches,' replied Madame de Bouville, assuming her most polite manner.

'It's not before it was time,' thought Mahaut; 'he seems singularly healthy.'

She saw Bouville's face in the light from a window.

'What's the matter with you that you're sweating like that, Messire Hugues?' she asked. 'It can't be from the heat.'

'It's due to all the fires I've had lit. Messire the Regent gave me little time to make all the necessary preparations.'

Their eyes met; it was a bad moment for both of them.

'Let us move on,' said Mahaut; 'clear the way for me.'

Bouville gave his arm to the old Seneschal, and the two Curators moved slowly towards the great hall. Mahaut followed a few paces behind them. Now was the best opportunity and it might not occur again. The slowness of the Seneschal's advance permitted her to take her time. There were, indeed, equerries and ladies-in-waiting lining the walls, all gazing at the child in the dusk; but who would notice so brief and so natural a gesture?

'Now then! We must look our best,' said Mahaut to the

crowned child she was holding in the crook of her arm. 'We must do honour to the realm, and not dribble.'

She took her handkerchief from her purse and quickly wiped the little wet lips. Bouville turned his head; but the gesture was already accomplished, and Mahaut, concealing the handkerchief in the hollow of her hand, was pretending to arrange the child's cloak.

'We are ready,' she said.

The doors of the hall were opened and silence fell. But the Seneschal could not see the crowd of faces before him.

'Make the announcement, Messire, make the announcement,' said Bouville.

'What must I announce?' asked Joinville.

'The King, of course, the King!'

'The King . . .' murmured Joinville. 'It's the fifth King I shall have served, do you realize that?'

'Of course, of course, but make the announcement,' Bouville repeated nervously.

Mahaut, behind them, wiped the baby's mouth a second time to make certain.

The Sire de Joinville, having cleared his throat with a number of rasping coughs, finally made up his mind to make the announcement. In a grave and reasonably steady voice he said: 'My lords, look on the King! Look on the King, my lords!'

'Long live the King!' replied the barons, uttering the cry they had been denied since the burial of the Hutin.

Mahaut went straight to the Regent and to the members of the royal family gathered about him.

'But he's strong . . . he's rosy . . . he's fat,' said the barons as she passed by.

'What's this people have been saying about his being a weakling and unlikely to live?' murmured Charles of Valois to his son Philippe.

'Oh, the family of France is always valiant,' said La Marche in imitation of his uncle.

The Lombard's child looked well, indeed too well, to Mahaut's eyes. 'Couldn't he cry and writhe a little?' she thought. And she secretly tried to pinch him through the cloak. But the swaddling clothes were thick, and the child only made a happy little gurgling sound. The spectacle presented to his blue eyes, so recently opened, seemed to please him. 'The little wretch! He'll start cooing in a minute. But he'll be cooing less tonight, unless Béatrice's powder has lost its virtue!'

There were shouts from the back of the hall: 'We can't see him; we want to admire him!'

'Take him, Philippe,' said Mahaut to her son-in-law, handing him the baby. 'Your arms are longer than mine. Show the King to his vassals.'

The Regent took the little Jean by the body, and raised him high in the air so that everyone might see him. Suddenly Philippe felt a warm viscous liquid running over his hands. The child, seized with hiccups, was vomiting the milk it had sucked half an hour before, but the milk had become green and mixed with bile; his face had also become green, then quickly turned a dark, indefinable, alarming hue, while his neck twisted backwards.

There was a great cry of anguished disappointment from the crowd of barons.

'Lord, Lord,' cried Mahaut, 'the convulsions have seized him again!'

'Take him back,' said Philippe quickly, placing the child in her arms as if it were a dangerous package.

'I knew it!' cried a voice.

It was Bouville. He had turned purple, and his eyes moved in anger between the Countess and the Regent.

'Yes, you were right, Bouville,' said the latter. 'It was too early to present this sick child.'

'I knew it!' repeated Bouville.

But his wife pulled him quickly by the sleeve to prevent his committing an irreparable folly. Their eyes met and Bouville grew calmer. 'What was I about to do? I'm mad,' he thought. 'We've got the real one.'

But if he had taken every possible step to see that the crime fell on another's head, he had no plan ready to meet the case of the crime being actually committed. Mahaut, also, was taken aback by the speed with which it had happened. She had not expected the poison to act so quickly. She was uttering what she hoped were words of reassurance: 'Be calm, be calm! We thought the other day also that he was going to die; and then, as you saw, he recovered all right. It's a childish ailment, frightening to see, but it doesn't last. The midwife! Someone go and fetch the midwife,' she added, taking the risk in order to prove her good faith.

The Regent was holding his soiled hands away from his body; he was gazing at them with fear and disgust, and dared touch nothing with them.

The infant had turned blue and was suffocating. In the disorder and panic which followed no one very well knew what they were doing, nor what happened. Madame de Bouville rushed towards the Queen's room, but having almost reached it, abruptly stopped, thinking: 'If I call the midwife, she'll see at once that the child has been changed, and that he has not got the marks of the forceps. Above all, above all, let no one take off his bonnet!' She came running back, while the crowd were already moving towards the King's room.

No midwife's services were any longer of use to the child. Still wrapped in his lilied cloak, the tiny crown awry, he lay like a piece of jetsam, washed up on the huge silk coverlet of the bed. The whites of his eyes showing, his lips dark, his swaddling clothes defiled and his viscera destroyed, the infant, who had just been publicly presented as the King of France, had ceased to breathe.

5

A Lombard in Saint-Denis

'AND NOW WHAT ARE we going to do?' the Bouvilles asked each other.

They were hoist with their own petard.

The Regent had not lingered long at Vincennes. Assembling the members of the royal family, he had asked them to mount their horses and escort him to Paris in order to hold an immediate Council. At the very moment the Regent was leaving the manor, Bouville had had a last access of courage.

'Monseigneur!' he had cried, seizing the Regent's mount by the bridle.

But Philippe had immediately cut him short.

'Yes, yes, of course, Bouville; I am grateful to you for your sympathy in our affliction. We do not in any way blame you, you know that. It's the law of human nature. I will send you my orders for the funeral.'

And the Regent had left, spurring into a gallop as soon as he had crossed the drawbridge. At the pace he set, those accompanying him would have little opportunity for reflection on the way.

Most of the barons had followed him. Only a few remained, the less important and the idle, who hung about in little groups, discussing the event.

'You see,' said Bouville to his wife, 'I should have spoken out at once. Why did you prevent me?'

They were standing in a window-embrasure, whispering together, and hardly daring to confide their thoughts to each other.

'The wet-nurse?' went on Bouville.

'I've seen to her. I took her to my own room, locked the door, and placed two men outside it.'

'She suspects nothing?'

'No.'

'She'll have to be told.'

'Wait till everyone has gone.'

'Oh, I ought to have spoken out!' Bouville repeated.

Remorse at having failed to follow his immediate instinct tortured him. 'If I had shouted the truth out in front of all the barons, if I had produced proof on the spot . . .' But to do that he would have needed a character other than his own, needed to have been a man of the Constable's stamp for instance, and, above all, would have needed to have no wife behind him to pull him by the sleeve.

'But how could we know,' said Madame de Bouville, 'that Mahaut would do the deed so skilfully, and that the child would die before everyone's eyes?'

'We should in fact have done better,' Bouville murmured, 'to present the right one, and let fate take its course.'

'Oh, and didn't I say so!'

'Indeed, yes, I admit you did. It was I who had the idea and it was a bad one.'

For now, who on earth would believe them? How and to whom could they declare that they had deceived the assembly of barons by placing the crown on the head of the wet-nurse's child? Their action smacked of sacrilege.

'Do you realize the risk we run now if we fail to keep silent?' asked Madame de Bouville. 'Mahaut will poison us next.'

'The Regent was in concert with her; I'm sure of it. When he had wiped his hands, after the child had been sick over them, he threw the towel into the fire; I saw it. He would have us tried for committing a felony against Mahaut.'

From now on their greatest anxiety was to be for their own safety.

'Have you washed the child?' asked Bouville.

'I have, with one of my women, while you were seeing the Regent off,' replied Madame de Bouville. 'And now four equerries are watching over him. There is nothing to be feared in that quarter.'

'And the Queen?'

'I've told everyone to say nothing to her so as not to aggravate her illness. In any case she is in no state to understand. And I have told the midwives not to leave her bedside.'

Shortly afterwards the chamberlain, Guillaume de Seriz, arrived from Paris to inform Bouville that the Regent had been recognized King by his uncle, his brother, and those peers present. The Council had been brief.

'As regards his nephew's funeral,' said the chamberlain, 'our Lord Philippe has decided that it shall take place as soon as possible, in order not to distress the people too long with this latest death. There will be no lying-in-state. As today is Friday, and a burial may not be held on a Sunday, the body will be taken to Saint-Denis tomorrow. The embalmer is on his way already. I'll take my leave of you, Messire, for the King has commanded me to return as soon as possible.'

Bouville let him go without another word. 'The King . . . the King . . .' he kept muttering to himself.

The Count of Poitiers was King; a little Lombard was to be taken to Saint-Denis; and Jean I was alive.

Bouville returned to his wife.

'Philippe has been recognized,' he told her. 'What's going to happen to us, with this King left on our hands?'

'He must be made to disappear.'

'Oh, no!' cried Bouville in indignation.

'No, I don't mean that. You're losing your wits, Hugues!' replied Madame de Bouville. 'I mean he must be hidden.'

'But then he will not reign.'

'He'll live, at least. And perhaps one day . . . can one ever tell?'

But how was he to be hidden? Who could be trusted with him without rousing suspicion? To begin with, he had to continue to be fed.

'The wet-nurse. There is no one but the wet-nurse who can be any use to us,' said Madame de Bouville. 'Let's go and see her.'

They had been well advised to await the departure of the last barons before telling Marie de Cressay that her son was dead. For the cry she uttered pierced the manor walls. To those who heard it, and were aghast at the sound, it was later explained that it was the Queen who had screamed. Yet the

Queen, semi-conscious as she was, sat up in bed and asked: 'What's the matter?'

Even the old Seneschal de Joinville started out of the depths of his torpor.

'Someone's been killed,' he said; 'I heard the cry of someone having his throat cut.'

And Marie was saying over and over again: 'I want to see him! I want to see him! I want to see him!'

Bouville and his wife had to restrain her by force from rushing dementedly through the Château.

For two whole hours they did their best to calm and console her, and above all to justify themselves, repeating again and again explanations to which she paid no heed.

Bouville might well assert that it was no fault of his, that it was the criminal act of the Countess Mahaut. The words took unconscious root in Marie's memory, from which they were to be resurrected later; but at the moment they had no meaning.

From time to time she ceased sobbing, gazed straight before her, and then began suddenly to howl again like a dog run over by a wagon.

The Bouvilles thought she was losing her reason. She exhausted all their arguments: thanks to her involuntary sacrifice, Marie had saved the true King of France, the descendant of that illustrious line . . .

'You are young,' said Madame de Bouville, 'you will have other children. What woman has not lost at least one child in the cradle in her life?'

And she quoted the stillborn twins of Blanche of Castile, and all the children of the royal family who had died in the last three generations. How many mothers among the

Angevins, the Courtenays, the Burgundians, the Châtillons and the Bouvilles themselves had not been regularly bereaved and yet ended up happily with a vast family! Among the twelve or fifteen children that one woman might bring into the world, it was unusual for more than half to survive.

'But I understand very well,' went on Madame de Bouville. 'It's always harder to lose the first.'

'But you don't understand!' Marie cried through her tears, 'I shall never be able to replace this one!'

The child who had been killed was the child of love, born of a love and a faith greater than all the laws and restraints of this world; he had been the dream for which she had paid the price of two months' outrage and four months' cloister, the wonderful gift with which she had wished to present the man she had chosen, the miraculous plant in whom she had hoped to see flowering, every day of her life, her crossed yet marvellous love!

'No, you cannot understand!' she groaned. 'You have not been turned away by your family because of a child. No, I shall never have another!'

When one explains one's unhappiness, translates it into rational terms, it is because one has already admitted it to oneself. The shock, the almost physical pressure, was slowly giving way to the second stage of sorrow: the cruelty of awareness.

'I knew it, I knew it! When I didn't want to come here, I knew that disaster lay in wait for me!'

Madame de Bouville dared make no reply.

'And what will Guccio say when he knows?' said Marie. 'How shall I ever be able to break it to him?'

'He must never know, my child, never!' cried Madame de

Bouville. 'No one must know that the King lives, for those who missed their aim the first time would unhesitatingly try again. You are in danger yourself for you acted in concert with us. You must keep the secret until you are authorized to reveal it.'

And to her husband she whispered: 'Go and get the Gospels.'

When Bouville had returned with the great book, which he had taken from the chapel, they persuaded Marie to place her hand on it and swear to maintain absolute silence towards even the father of her dead child, in the confessional even, concerning the events that had taken place that day. Only Bouville or his wife could release her from her oath.

In her present condition Marie agreed to swear all that they asked. Bouville promised her a pension; but little she cared for money.

'And now you must keep the King of France, my child, and tell everyone that he is yours,' added Madame de Bouville.

Marie rebelled. She could no longer bring herself to touch the child in whose stead her own had been murdered. She wished to remain at Vincennes no longer; she wanted to escape, no matter where, and then to die.

'You'll die quickly enough, you may be sure of that, if you talk. Mahaut will see to it that you are poisoned or stabbed.'

'No, I shall not talk, I promise you. But for God's sake let me go!'

'You shall go, you shall go. But you cannot let that child die too. Don't you see he's hungry? Feed him today at least,' said Madame de Bouville, placing in her arms Queen Clémence's child.

When Marie held the baby to her, her tears fell faster

than ever. She felt the empty place at the other breast too keenly.

'Keep him. He will be as if he were yours,' insisted Madame de Bouville. 'And when the time comes to place him back on the throne, you will take an honoured place at Court with him; you will be his second mother.'

One lie more or less cost her nothing. But, in any case, it was not honours promised by the Curator's wife which could touch Marie, but the presence of the little life in her hands to which, unconsciously, she was to transfer her maternal feeling.

She placed her lips against the baby's downy head and, with a gesture that had become automatic, opened her bodice, murmuring: 'No, I cannot let him die, my little Jean, my little Jean . . .'

The Bouvilles heaved a sigh of relief. They had won, for the moment at least.

'She must not still be in Vincennes tomorrow, when they come to take her child away,' Madame de Bouville said in a whisper to her husband.

The next day Marie, who was prostrate and had left all decisions to Madame de Bouville, was taken back to the Convent of the Clarisses with the child.

To the Mother Abbess Madame de Bouville explained that Marie had been much shaken by the death of the little King, and that no attention should be paid to any absurdities she might utter.

'She gave us a considerable fright; she screamed and even failed to recognize her own child.'

Madame de Bouville insisted that Marie should receive no visitors and should be left in complete quiet and seclusion.

'If anyone comes to see her, do not let them in and send to warn me.'

That same day two lengths of gold cloth bespangled with lilies, two turkey sheets embroidered with the arms of France and eight ells of black *cendal* were brought to Vincennes for use in the burial of the first King of France who had borne the name of Jean. And, indeed, it was a child called Jean who was removed in a coffin so small that there was no need to place it on a vehicle; it was simply carried on the pack-saddle of a mule.

Master Geoffroy de Fleury, Bursar of the Palace, noted in his account book that the cost of the funeral amounted to one hundred and eleven *livres*, seventeen *sols* and eight *deniers*.

There was no long ritual procession or ceremony at Notre-Dame. They went straight to Saint-Denis where the burial took place immediately after the Mass. A narrow grave had been opened at the foot of the effigy of Louis X, which was still white and fresh in its newly carved stone; it was here, among the bones of the sovereigns of France, that the child of Marie de Cressay, Demoiselle of the Ile-de-France, and of Guccio Baglioni, Siennese merchant, was laid.

Adam Héron, First Chamberlain and Master of the Household, advanced to the edge of the little tomb and cried, looking at his master, Philippe of Poitiers: 'The King is dead, long live the King!'

The reign of Philippe V, the Long, had begun; Jeanne of Burgundy had become Queen of France, and Mahaut of Artois was triumphant.

Only three people in the kingdom knew that the real King was alive. One of them had sworn on Holy Writ to keep the secret and the other two were fearful that the secret would not be kept.

After that Saturday of 20 November 1316 all the sovereigns who reigned over France were no more than a long line of involuntary usurpers.

6

France in Firm Hands

TO GAIN THE THRONE Philippe V had used, within the monarchical constitution, the eternal process known in modern times as a *coup d'état*.

When, owing to his personal authority and the support of the clan surrounding him, he had found himself invested with the principal royal powers, he had persuaded the Assembly of July to ratify an act dealing with the succession; it might, eventually, favour his own ambitions, but only after considerable delay and after certain preliminary conditions had been fulfilled. But the death of the little King provided a new opportunity; Philippe, casting on one side the law he had himself established, immediately appropriated the Crown without submitting to the delay or awaiting the conditions.

Power obtained in these circumstances was naturally subject to menace, at least at the outset.

Busy consolidating his position, Philippe had little time to savour his victory or indulge in the self-satisfactions of achieved ambition. The summit he had reached was a perilous one.

There was much talk in the kingdom and suspicion was spreading. But the weight of the King's hand was known, and those likely to suffer from it gathered about the Duke of Burgundy.

The latter hurried to Paris to contest the accession of his future father-in-law. He demanded that the Council of Peers be summoned and that Jeanne of Navarre be recognized Queen.

Philippe made no attempt to use guile. For the regency he had offered his daughter and the county of Burgundy; to keep the throne he offered the separation of the two Crowns of France and Navarre, united so recently, and to give the inheritance of the little Pyrenean kingdom to his brother's suspect daughter.

But if Jeanne were considered worthy to reign over Navarre, she would also be worthy of reigning over France. At least this was the conclusion reached by Duke Eudes, who refused to yield. Force would therefore be the deciding factor.

Eudes galloped away to Dijon, whence, in the name of his niece, he issued a proclamation to all the lords of Artois, Picardy, Brie and Champagne, inviting them to withhold their obedience from the usurper.

He wrote in similar terms to King Edward II of England, who, in spite of the efforts of his wife Isabella, did his utmost to inflame the quarrel by taking the Burgundian part. In every division arising within the kingdom of France, the English King saw the prospect of emancipating Guyenne.

'Is this to be the sole result of my having denounced the adultery of my sisters-in-law?' thought Queen Isabella.

Seeing himself threatened in the north, the east and the south-west, anyone but Philippe the Long might perhaps have yielded. But the new King saw that he had several months in hand: the winter was no time for making war; his enemies would await the spring, if indeed they ultimately determined to put armies into the field. For Philippe the most urgent necessity was to be crowned and to clothe himself with the inalienable majesty conferred by coronation.

At first he wished to hold the ceremony at Epiphany; the Feast of the Kings seemed to him a good augury; and it was also the date his father had chosen to be crowned. But representations were made to him that the burgesses of Rheims would not have enough time to prepare for it; he accorded them a delay of three days. The Court would leave Paris on the 1st of January, and the coronation take place on Sunday the 9th.

Since Louis VIII, the first King not to have been elected during his predecessor's lifetime, the heir to the throne had never been so precipitate in repairing to Rheims.

But religious consecration was not enough for Philippe; he wished to add to it something that would fire the people's spirit in a new way.

He had often meditated the instructions of Egidio Colonna, Philip the Fair's tutor, the man who had formed the Iron King's thought. 'Considered in absolute terms,' Egidio Colonna had written in his treatise on the principles of sovereignty, 'it would be preferable that the King be elected; but the corrupt desires of men and their manner of acting must make heredity preferable to election.'

'I wish to be King with the consent of my subjects,' said Philippe the Long, 'and only on that basis shall I feel really worthy to rule them. And since some among the greater do not support me, I shall take the opinion of the smaller.'

His father had shown him the road by summoning, at the difficult crises of his reign, assemblies in which all classes, all the 'Estates' of the realm, were represented. He decided that two assemblies of this nature, but larger than former ones, should be held, one in Paris for the *langue d'oïl*, the other at Bourges for the *langue d'oc,* during the weeks following his coronation. And he used the phrase 'States General'.

The lawyers were set to drafting the bills to be presented to the Estates to ratify Philippe's accession to the throne by popular vote. The arguments of the Constable were naturally renewed to the effect that lilies could not spin wool and that the kingdom was too noble a thing to fall into the hands of women. There were other still stranger arguments: that there were, for instance, three intermediate generations between the venerated Saint Louis and Madame Jeanne of Navarre, while between Saint Louis and Philippe there were but two.

And this caused the Count of Valois to exclaim, not unjustifiably: 'In that case, why should I not be chosen, for I am separated from Saint Louis only by my father!'

Finally the councillors to Parliament, spurred on by Messire de Noyers, exhumed, though without much belief in it, the ancient code of the customs of the Salian Franks, before the conversion of Clovis to Christianity. This code contained nothing concerning the transmission of the royal powers. It was a fairly rough system of civil and criminal jurisprudence, and almost incomprehensible moreover, since it was over eight centuries old. A brief paragraph laid it down that the inheritance of land must be by equal division among the male heirs. That was all.

No more was necessary for certain doctors of secular law to construct a thesis and support the doctrine for which they were being paid. The Crown of France could go only to males, because the Crown implied the possession of land. And the best proof that the Salian Code had been applied since the beginning was clearly to be found in the fact that only men had indeed succeeded to it. Thus Jeanne of Navarre could be eliminated without the unprovable accusation of bastardy being even brought forward.

The doctors were masters of their own obscurity. No one thought of objecting that the Merovingian dynasty was not derived from the Salians, but from the Sicambres and the Bructeres; and no one, for the moment, thought of examining the documents on which the famous Salic Law was supposed to be based – this law which was to triumph in history after it had ruined the kingdom by a hundred years of war.

The adultery of Marguerite of Burgundy was to cost France dear.

But for the moment the central power was far from idle. Philippe was already reorganizing the administration, summoning important burgesses to his Council, and creating his 'Knights Pursuivant', thus rewarding those who had served him unremittingly since Lyons.

From Charles of Valois he bought back the mint at Le Mans, before buying the ten others scattered over France. From now on, all the coinage circulating in the kingdom would be minted by the King.

Remembering the ideas of John XXII, when he was still no more than Cardinal Duèze, Philippe prepared a reformed system of penal fines and chancellery dues. The lawyers would pay the dues into the Treasury every Saturday, and the registration of deeds would be subject to tariffs decreed by the Exchequer.[30]

He dealt with customs, provostships, captaincies of towns and the inland revenue as he had dealt with the chancelleries. The abuses and malversations, which had been freely indulged in since the death of the Iron King, were now sternly repressed. In every rank of society, in every national activity, in the courts of justice, in the ports, in the market-places and in the fairgrounds, it was felt and appreciated that France was now in firm hands – hands of twenty-three! Loyalty is not assured without favours. Philippe's accession was accompanied by considerable liberality.

The old Seneschal de Joinville had been taken back to his Château of Wassy, where he declared he wished to die. He knew that he had reached the very end of his life. His son, Anseau, who since Lyons had never left Philippe's side, one day said to the King: 'My father has told me that strange things occurred at Vincennes at the time of the little King's death; disturbing rumours have come to his ears.'

'I know, I know,' Philippe replied. 'I too have heard of certain curious events which took place during those days. Do you know what I think, Anseau? I don't want to slander Bouville, for I have no proof; but I sometimes wonder whether my nephew was not already dead when we went to Vincennes and whether another child was not presented to us.'

'Why should he have done that?'

'I do not know. Fear that he would be blamed; fear that he would be accused by Valois and others. For, after all, he alone had charge of the child and obstinately refused to show him, do you remember? But it's only a feeling and not based on anything factual. Anyway, it's too late now.'

He paused and then added: 'Anseau, I have put you down at the Treasury for a gift of four thousand *livres*, and this will show you how grateful I am for the help you have always been to me. And if on the day of the coronation my cousin, the Duke of Burgundy, as I believe, will not be there to put on my spurs, you shall have that office. You rank high enough as a knight for that.'

For riveting mouths, gold has always been the best metal; and Philippe knew that with some men the rivet must be jewelled.

There remained Robert of Artois's case to deal with; Philippe congratulated himself on having kept his dangerous cousin in prison during recent events. But he could not keep him in the Châtelet indefinitely. Coronation is generally accompanied by acts of clemency and the granting of pardons. On the pressing demand of Charles of Valois, Philippe pretended to show himself a kindly prince.

'It's entirely to please you, Uncle,' he said; 'Robert shall be given his freedom . . .'

He left the sentence in suspense and seemed to be calculating.

'. . . but only three days after my departure for Rheims,' he added, 'and he will not be allowed to go more than twenty leagues from Paris.'

7

Shattered Dreams

In his progress towards the throne Philippe the Long had not only stepped over two corpses, he had left in his path two other broken lives, two crushed women, one a queen, the other obscure.

On the day after the funeral of the false Jean I at Saint-Denis, Madame Clémence of Hungary, whom everyone had thought was going to die, slowly began to recover consciousness and return to life. Some remedy had at last proved efficacious; fever and infection left her body as if to give place to other qualities of suffering. The first words the Queen uttered were to ask for her son, whom she had barely had time to see. Her memory was merely of a little naked body being rubbed with rosewater and placed in a cradle.

When she was told, with every kind of excuse, that she could not be shown him at once, she murmured: 'He's dead, isn't he? I knew it. I felt it during my fever. That, too, had to happen.'

She did not suffer the violence of reaction that had been

feared. She was prostrated but without tears, her face expressing the tragic irony that people sometimes show after a fire, when contemplating the smoking ashes of their home. Her lips parted as if in laughter, and for a few moments they thought she was mad.

She had been subjected to all the outrages of misfortune; there were numbed places in her soul; and fate might strike once more without causing her greater suffering than she knew already.

Perhaps Bouville suffered even more: condemned to lie and powerless to console. Every friendly word that fell from the Queen's lips tortured him with remorse. 'Her child lives, and I may not tell her. When I think of the great happiness I could give her!'

Over and over again pity, and indeed simple honesty, all but carried the day. But Madame de Bouville, knowing him to be weak, never left him alone with the Queen.

At least he could half-console himself by accusing Mahaut, the real criminal.

The Queen shrugged her shoulders. What did she care whose hand the forces of evil had used against her?

'I have been pious, I have been kind, at least I think I have,' she said; 'I have done my best to follow the commandments of religion and to mend the ways of those who were dear to me. I have never wished harm to anyone. And yet God has tried me more than any of His creatures. I see the wicked triumphing.'

She neither rebelled nor blasphemed; she merely thought that there was some monumental error.

Her father and mother had died of the plague when she was barely two years old. While all the Princesses of her family, or nearly all, had found husbands before they were of marriageable age, she had had to wait till she was twenty-two. The unhoped-for husband, who had then presented himself, appeared to be the greatest in the world. She had come to this marriage with France, dazzled, bewildered by an unreal love and filled with every good intention. Before she had even reached her new country she had been nearly drowned at sea. After a few weeks she had discovered that she had married a murderer and succeeded a strangled queen. After ten months she had been left a widow and pregnant. Immediately removed from power, she had been put away on the pretence that it was for her safety. And now, for eight days, she had been struggling at the gates of death, only to discover, as she returned from that particular hell, that her child was dead, poisoned, no doubt, as her husband had been.

Could any more continuously disastrous fate be conceived?

'The people of my country believe in bad luck. They're right. I have bad luck,' she said. 'I must never undertake anything again.'

Love, charity, hope; she had exhausted all the reserves of virtue she possessed; and now faith also abandoned her. To what use had she put them? She had no longer anything to give.

During her illness she had suffered such torture, had been so certain of dying, that merely to find herself alive, able to breathe with ease, eat, gaze at walls, furniture and faces, seemed to her matter for surprise and provided her with the only emotion that her mind, now three-quarters destroyed, was still capable of knowing.

As her convalescence slowly progressed, and she gradually recovered her legendary beauty, Queen Clémence began to develop the tastes of a capricious old woman. It was as if beneath that exquisite form, the golden hair, the face from a reredos, the noble breast and slender limbs, which day by day regained their beauty, forty years had suddenly elapsed. From within her splendid body an old widow demanded the ultimate pleasures from life. She was to continue demanding them for eleven years.

Frugal from religion as much as from indifference in the past, the Queen now began to manifest curious tastes for rare and costly foods. Laden with jewels by Louis X, having despised them then, she now took pleasure in her caskets, eagerly counting the stones, calculating their value, and appraising their cut and water. Determined to alter a mounting, she would summon goldsmiths and design unwearable jewels.

She also spent long hours with drapers, ordered the most costly oriental stuffs, and wore them impregnated with scent.

If, when she left her apartments, she wore the white clothes of widowhood, in her own rooms her entourage were often surprised and embarrassed to see her crouching over the hearth in veils of an excessive transparency.

Her previous generosity now survived only in the degenerate form of absurd extravagance. The merchants had passed the word round and knew that no price would be questioned. Greed gained on her staff. And indeed Queen Clémence was well served! In the kitchens the servants quarrelled as to who should bring her a dish, because for some ornamental dessert, for some cream of nuts, for some 'golden water', newly invented, in which rosemary and cloves had been steeped in pomegranate juice, the Queen would suddenly produce a handful of coins.

She soon acquired a taste for singing and for having poems and romances read to her by attractive exponents. Her cold gaze no longer cared for any but young faces. A good-looking minstrel with an agreeable voice, who had entertained her for an hour, and whose eyes had responded to the sight of her body beneath its Cypriot veils, would be paid enough to make merry in the taverns for a whole month.

Bouville became alarmed at her expenditure; but he had not been able to avoid becoming one of its beneficiaries.

On the 1st of January, which remained the day of good wishes and presents, even though the official year began only at Easter, Queen Clémence gave Bouville an embroidered purse containing three hundred gold *livres*. The ex-chamberlain cried: 'No, Madame, I pray you; I do not deserve it!'

But it is impossible to refuse a queen's gift; even if that queen is ruining herself; even if one must maintain an odious lie in her presence.

The unhappy man, haunted by terror and remorse, foresaw that the Queen would have soon to face a disastrous financial situation.[31]

On this same day of the 1st of January, Bouville received a visit from Messer Tolomei. The banker found the ex-chamberlain grown astonishingly thin and grey. Bouville's clothes hung loosely on him, his cheeks were sunken, his glance had grown uneasy and his attention seemed to wander.

'The man is suffering from some hidden malady,' thought Tolomei, 'and I should not be surprised if he were to die soon. I must hasten to arrange Guccio's affairs.'

Tolomei knew the proper custom. On the occasion of the New Year he had brought Madame de Bouville a piece of cloth.

'To thank her,' he said, 'for all the care she has taken of the demoiselle who has given my nephew a son . . .'

Bouville wished also to refuse this present.

'Of course you must take it, of course,' Tolomei insisted. 'I should also like to talk to you a little about this affair. My nephew is shortly returning from Avignon where our Holy Father the Pope . . .'

Tolomei crossed himself.

'. . . has kept him until now to work on the accounts of his Treasury. He is coming to fetch his young wife and his son.'

Bouville felt faint.

'One moment, Messer, one moment,' he said; 'there is a messenger outside waiting for me to give him an urgent answer. Pray wait a moment for me.'

And he went off, the piece of cloth under his arm, to take counsel with his wife.

'The husband's returning,' he said.

'What husband?' asked Madame de Bouville.

'The wet-nurse's husband!'

'But she isn't married.'

'We must take it that she is! Tolomei is here. Look, he brought you this.'

'What does he want?'

'That the girl should leave the convent.'

'When?'

'I don't yet know. But soon.'

'Well, wait till you know, don't promise anything and come back and tell me.'

Bouville returned to his visitor.

'You were saying, Messer Tolomei?'

'I was saying that my nephew Guccio is due to arrive in

order to remove his wife and child from the convent in which you were kind enough to find them refuge. They no longer have anything to fear. Guccio is the bearer of a letter from the Holy Father, and will go to live in Avignon, I think, at least for a time; though I should have liked well enough to have kept them here with me. Do you know that I have not yet seen this little great-nephew of mine? I've been on the road, visiting my branches, and only got the news in a happy letter from the young mother. As soon as I got back, the day before yesterday, I took her some sweets; but at the Convent of the Clarisses they shut the door in my face.'

'The rule is very strict at the Clarisses,' said Bouville. 'And besides, on your demand, we gave definite instructions.'

'Nothing unfortunate occurred?'

'Oh, no, Messer; nothing that I know of. I would have informed you at once,' replied Bouville, who felt himself to be on thorns. 'When does your nephew arrive?'

'I expect him in two or three days' time.'

Bouville looked at him in fear.

'I must ask you to excuse me once again,' he said, 'but I've suddenly remembered that the Queen sent me for something and I have forgotten to take it to her. I'll be back in a moment.'

And he disappeared once more.

'The malady is in his head, for sure,' thought Tolomei. 'How pleasant to talk to a man who disappears every other second! As long as he doesn't forget that I'm here, too!'

He sat down on a chest, stroked the fur which edged his sleeve, and had time to calculate, to within about ten *livres*, the value of the furniture in the room.

'Here I am,' said Bouville, raising the hanging. 'You were talking to me of your nephew! You know that I am very attached to him. What a delightful companion he was during our journeys to Naples! Naples . . .' he repeated with nostalgia. 'Could one ever have imagined it . . .? The poor Queen, the poor Queen . . .'

He sank on to the chest beside Tolomei and wiped away the tears of memory with his spatulate fingers.

'And now I suppose he's going to weep on my shoulder!' thought the banker; but aloud he said: 'I have not referred to these disasters, but I know full well what you must have suffered. You have been much in my thoughts . . .'

'Oh, Tolomei, if you only knew! It was worse than anything you can imagine; the Devil took a hand in it . . .'

The sound of a little dry cough came from behind the tapestry; and Bouville stopped short on the verge of dangerous confidences.

'Someone's listening to us,' thought Tolomei, who hurriedly went on: 'At least in our affliction we have one consolation: we have a good King.'

'Indeed, indeed, yes, we have a good King,' Bouville replied without much enthusiasm.

'I was afraid,' went on the banker, leading Bouville away from the suspicious tapestry, 'I was afraid that the new King would be harsh to us Lombards. But not at all. It appears, indeed, that he has farmed out the taxes, in certain seneschalships, to members of our companies. But, returning to my nephew, who I must say has done very well, I should like him to be recompensed for all his trouble by finding his wife and his heir installed in my house. I am already preparing a room for the charming young couple. People speak ill of the younger generation. They say that they are no longer capable of sincerity, love or fidelity. But those two are very much in love, I can guarantee that. One has but to read their letters. And if the marriage was not made according to the rules, what does it matter? We can begin all over again, and I will even go so far as to ask you, if you will not be offended, to be a witness.'

'On the contrary, it is a great honour, a great honour,' replied Bouville, gazing at the tapestry as if he were searching for a spider. 'But there's the question of the family.'

'What family?'

'The wet-nurse's family, of course.'

'Wet-nurse?' repeated Tolomei, who did not understand the allusion.

For the second time the little cough sounded behind the tapestry. Bouville's expression changed, he muttered and stammered.

'The fact is, Messer . . . yes, I meant to say . . . yes, I wanted to tell you at once, but . . . being constantly disturbed, I forgot. Oh, yes, but I must tell you now . . . your . . . the wife of your nephew, since you assure me that they are married, we asked her . . . look, we were lacking a wet-nurse, and she willingly, very willingly indeed, on my wife's asking her, fed the young King, for the little time, alas, that he lived.'

'So she came here; you took her out of the convent?'

'And we took her back again! I was embarrassed to tell you about it . . . but there was so little time. And then it was all over so quickly!'

'But, Messire, don't be embarrassed. You did very well. That beautiful Marie! So she was wet-nurse to the King? What an astonishing piece of news, and what an honourable one! The only pity is that she did not need to feed him for longer,' said Tolomei, who was already regretting all the advantages he might have derived from such a situation. 'Then you will be able to get her out of the convent again without difficulty?'

'No, indeed! To get her out permanently, her family must consent. Have you seen her family again?'

'Never. Her brothers, who made such a fuss, seemed delighted to get rid of her and have never reappeared.'

'Where do they live?'

'At their house at Cressay.'

'Cressay, where is it?'

'Near Neauphle, where I have a branch.'

'Cressay . . . Neauphle . . . excellent.'

'Really, you're a very strange man, Monseigneur, if I may say so!' cried Tolomei. 'I confide a girl to your care and tell you all about her; you go and fetch her to feed the Queen's child; she lives here eight days, ten days . . .'

'Five,' corrected Bouville.

'Five days,' went on Tolomei, 'and you don't know where she comes from and barely what her name is?'

'Yes, I do know, I know it perfectly well,' said Bouville blushing. 'But at moments I have lapses of memory.'

He could not go running to his wife a third time. Why didn't she come to his rescue, instead of staying there hidden behind the tapestry, waiting to scold him later if he made a fool of himself! But she had her reasons.

'This Tolomei is the one man I fear in this business,' she had said to Bouville. 'A Lombard's nose is worth those of thirty hunting hounds. If he sees you alone, fool that you are, he'll suspect less, and I shall be better able to manage things afterwards.'

'Fool that you are . . . she's right, I've become a fool,' Bouville thought. 'Well, I used to know how to talk to kings and negotiate their business. I negotiated Madame Clémence's marriage. I had to deal with the Conclave and use guile with Duèze . . .' It was this thought that saved him.

'Did you say that your nephew is the bearer of a letter from the Holy Father?' he went on. 'Well, that makes everything easy. It'll be up to Guccio to go and fetch his wife and show the letter. We shall thus all be covered and no one will be able to reproach us or bring an action against us. The Holy Father! What more can we want? In two or three days, you said? We must hope that everything will turn out for the best. And thank you very much for that fine piece of cloth; I'm sure that my good wife will be delighted with it. Goodbye, Messer, and I remain always at your service.'

He felt more exhausted than if he had led a charge in battle.

As he left Vincennes, Tolomei thought: 'Either he's lying to me for some reason I do not know, or he's entering his second childhood. Anyway we shall have to wait for Guccio.'

Madame de Bouville, however, did not wait for anyone. She had her litter harnessed and went straight to the Faubourg Saint-Marcel. There she shut herself in Marie de Cressay's cell. Having killed her child, she had now come to demand of Marie that she should renounce her lover.

'You've sworn to keep the secret on the Gospels,' Madame de Bouville said. 'But will you be able to keep it from this man? Will you have the face to live with your husband' – she now agreed that Guccio was indeed graced with this quality – 'and let him believe that he is the father of a child that does not belong to him? It's a sin to conceal so grave a matter from one's husband! And when we are able to make truth triumph and they come to fetch the King to place him on the throne, what will you say to him then? You are too honest a girl, and your blood too noble, to consent to so villainous a thing.'

Marie had been asking herself these questions over and over again every hour of her solitude. She had thought of nothing else; and they were driving her mad. But she knew the answer! She knew that, as soon as she was once more in Guccio's arms, she would be able to keep nothing from him, not because 'it was a sin' as Madame de Bouville said, but because her love forbade her so atrocious a lie.

'Guccio will understand me; Guccio will absolve me. He will realize that it happened without my willing it; he will help me bear this burden. Guccio will say nothing, Madame; I can swear it for him as for myself!'

'One can only swear for oneself, my child. And a Lombard, what's more; you can imagine how quiet he'll keep about it! He'll turn it to his advantage.'

'Madame, you insult him!'

'No, I'm not insulting him, my good girl. I know the world. You have sworn not to talk, even in the confessional. It's the King of France you have in your keeping; and you will be relieved of your oath only when the time is ripe.'

'I pray you, Madame, take the King back and relieve me.'

'It was not I who gave him to you, it was the will of God. You have a sacred charge! Would you have betrayed our Lord the Christ if He had been given into your charge during the Massacre of the Innocents? That child must live. My husband must have you both under surveillance; you must be able to be found at any moment, and not go off to Avignon as I hear is proposed.'

'I'll get Guccio to agree to our living wherever you like; I assure you he won't talk.'

'He won't talk because you will never see him again.'

The battle, interrupted by the little King's feeding time, lasted the whole afternoon. The two women fought like two wild beasts in a cage. But little Madame de Bouville had the stronger teeth and claws.

'What are you going to do with me then? Are you going to shut me up here for the rest of my life?' Marie groaned.

'I should like that well enough,' thought Madame de Bouville. 'But her husband's due to arrive with a letter from the Pope . . .'

'Supposing your family agree to take you back?' she proposed. 'I think Messire Hugues might succeed in persuading your brothers.'

To return to Cressay, to a hostile family, accompanied by a child who would be considered the child of sin, when of all the children of France he was the most worthy of honour! To renounce all, to be dumb, grow old, with nothing to hope for but the contemplation of a monstrous fate and the desperate destruction of a love that nothing should have impaired! So many shattered dreams!

Marie rebelled; once more she found the strength which, against law and family, had urged her into the arms of the man of her choice. She refused bluntly.

'I shall see Guccio again, I shall belong to him, I shall live with him!' she cried.

Madame de Bouville slowly tapped the arm of her chair.

'You will never see this Guccio again,' she replied. 'For if he were to approach this convent, or any other refuge in which we may place you, if you spoke to him but for a single minute, that minute would be his last. My husband, as you know, is an active and redoubtable man when it is a question of safeguarding the King. If you insist on seeing this man again, you may succeed in doing so, but it will be with a misericord between his shoulders.'

Marie began to give way.

'The child is enough,' she murmured; 'the father must not be killed too.'

'It rests in your hands,' said Madame de Bouville.

'I did not know that at the Court of France people were so little sparing of others' lives. There's a fine Court, respected by the kingdom! I must tell you, Madame, that I hate you.'

'You are unjust, Marie. My task is a heavy one and I am protecting you against yourself. You will write what I shall dictate to you.'

Beaten, helpless, her head aching and her eyes dim with tears, Marie painfully traced phrases she would never have believed herself capable of writing. The letter was to be taken to Tolomei in order that he should give it to his nephew.

She declared in it that she felt great shame and horror for the sin she had committed; that she wished to devote herself to the child who was its fruit and never more succumb to the sins of the flesh; and that she despised him who had urged her to them. She forbade Guccio ever to try to see her again, wherever she might be.

She wanted at least to add a final sentence: 'I swear to you that I shall have no other man in my life but you, nor pledge my troth to another.' Madame de Bouville refused to allow it.

'He must not suppose that you still love him. Go on, sign, and give me the letter.'

Marie did not even see the little woman leave.

'He'll hate me, he'll despise me, and he'll never know that it was done to save his life!' she thought, as she heard the convent door slam to.

8

Departures

THE ARRIVAL AT THE Manor of Cressay, the following morning, of a courier wearing the lily on his left sleeve and the royal arms embroidered on his collar created considerable excitement. He was treated with elaborate courtesy and the brothers Cressay, on the basis of a short note demanding their presence urgently at Vincennes, imagined themselves to be on the point of being given a command, a captaincy at least, or perhaps even a seneschalship.

'It's not in the least surprising,' said Dame Eliabel; 'they will have remembered our deserts and the services we have rendered the kingdom during the last three centuries. This new King gives me the impression that he knows where to find brave men! Go on, my sons; put on your best clothes and set off as soon as possible. There's clearly some justice in this world, and it will be a consolation for the shame your sister has brought on us.'

She had not altogether recovered from the illness she had suffered in the summer. She was getting heavier, had lost her former activity, and no longer manifested her authority except by pestering her kitchenmaid. She had abandoned to her sons the management of the little estate, which was none the better for it.

The two brothers therefore set out, their heads filled with ambitious hopes. Pierre's horse was roaring so loudly when they arrived at Vincennes that this seemed likely to be its last journey.

'I have serious matters to discuss with you, my young sires,' said Bouville by way of greeting.

And he had them served with spiced wine and sweets.

The two boys sat on the edge of their chairs like country bumpkins and hardly dared raise the silver goblets to their lips.

'Ah, there's the Queen going by,' said Bouville. 'She's taking advantage of a rift in the clouds to take a breath of fresh air.'

The two brothers, their hearts beating, craned their necks to get a look at her through the green glass of the windows; they saw a white figure, in a great cloak, walking slowly and accompanied by several servants. They looked at each other and nodded their heads. They had seen the Queen.

'It's of your young sister I wish to speak with you,' went on Bouville. 'Would you be prepared to take her home? But you must know, in the first place, that she has been feeding the Queen's child.'

And he explained to them, in as few words as possible, as much as it was necessary for them to know.

'Oh, I've also got a good piece of news for you,' he went on; 'she does not wish to see that Italian who put her in the family way ever again. She is now aware of her sin, and that a girl of noble blood cannot lower herself to become the wife of a Lombard, however good-looking he may be. For he's a pleasing young man, it must be admitted, and intelligent . . .'

'But he's still only a Lombard,' interrupted Madame de Bouville, who this time was present at the interview. 'A man with no feudal links or loyalty, as indeed he has shown.'

Bouville lowered his head.

'And now I've got to betray you too, friend Guccio, my charming travelling companion! Have I got to end my days denying all those who have been my friends?' he thought. He fell silent, leaving it to his wife to conduct the negotiations.

The brothers were somewhat disappointed, particularly the elder. They had expected a miracle, and it was only a question of their sister. Was every single event in their lives to occur through her? They were almost jealous of her. Wet-nurse to the King! And such important personages as a Grand Chamberlain interested in her fate! Who would have thought it?

Madame de Bouville's cackling left but little time for reflection.

'The duty of a Christian', said Madame de Bouville, 'is to help a sinner to repentance. You must behave like proper gentlemen. Who knows whether it was not due to the Divine Will that your sister happened to be brought to bed at the right moment, though without great benefit, alas, since the little King is dead; but anyway she came to his rescue.'

Queen Clémence, to show her gratitude, was prepared to allow the wet-nurse's child an income of five hundred *livres* a year from her dower. And, over and above, an outright gift of three hundred *livres* would be paid at once. The money was there, in an embroidered purse.

The two Cressay brothers were unable to conceal their excitement. It was a fortune falling from the skies; the means of rebuilding the curtain wall of their tumbledown manor; the certainty of enough food all the year round; and the prospect of being able at last to buy suits of armour and equip a few of their serfs as valets of arms, so as to make a good showing when the banners were summoned! They would make their names on the field of battle.[32]

'Listen to me well,' went on Madame de Bouville; 'these gifts have been given to the child. If he were ill-treated or any misfortune should happen to him, the income would of course cease. Being the King's foster-brother confers a distinction on him you must respect.'

'Of course, of course I approve, since Marie repents,' said the bearded brother, his eagerness apparent, 'and since her repentance is conveyed to us by such high persons as yourselves, Messire, Madame. We must open our arms to her. The Queen's protection effaces her sin. And let no one, either noble or villain, mock her in my presence, for I shall kill him.'

'What about our mother?' asked the younger brother.

'I'll convince her all right,' replied Jean. 'I'm the head of the family since the death of our father, and don't let anyone forget it.'

'And of course you will have to swear on the Gospels,' went on Madame de Bouville, 'neither to listen to nor repeat anything your sister may say of the things she has seen here, for these are Crown matters and must remain secret. In any case she has seen nothing; she has fed the child and that's all! But your sister has a somewhat extravagant imagination, and is inclined to tell stories; she has certainly given you proof of it in the past. Hugues! Go and fetch the Gospels.'

With Holy Writ on one side of them, the purse of gold on the other, and the Queen passing in the garden, the brothers Cressay swore never to reveal anything concerning the death of King Jean I, to watch over, feed and protect their sister's child, and to close their door to the man who had seduced her.

'Oh, we swear it with all our hearts! Let him never appear again!' cried the elder.

The other showed less conviction in his ingratitude. He could not help but think: 'All the same, without Guccio . . .'

'We shall, moreover, keep ourselves informed as to whether you are faithful to your oath,' said Madame de Bouville.

She offered to go with the two brothers to the Convent of the Clarisses at once.

'That's giving you too much trouble, Madame,' said Jean de Cressay; 'we can go on our own.'

'No, no, I must go. Without my orders the Mother Abbess will not let Marie go.'

The bearded brother's expression turned gloomy. He was thinking.

'What's the matter?' asked Madame de Bouville. 'Do you foresee any difficulty?'

'The fact is, I should like first to buy a mule for our sister to ride.'

When Marie had been pregnant he had made her travel pillion from Neauphle to Paris; but now that she was making them rich he wanted her return to be more dignified. Besides, Dame Eliabel's mule had died the previous month.

'That's of no importance,' said Madame de Bouville; 'we'll give you one. Hugues! Go and have a mule saddled.'

Bouville accompanied his wife and the two Cressay brothers as far as the drawbridge.

'I wish I were dead, and no longer had to lie and be afraid,' thought the unhappy man, now thin and shivering, as he gazed out across the leafless forest.

'Paris! Paris at last!' thought Guccio Baglioni as he entered by the Porte Saint-Jacques.

Paris was sullen and cold; life, as always after the New Year festivities, seemed to have stopped, and more so than ever that particular January owing to the departure of the Court.

But the young traveller, returning after an absence of six months, did not notice the fog lying low over the roofs, or the few frozen passers-by; for him the town was sunlit with expectation, for the 'Paris at last!' which he repeated to himself over and over again, as if it were the happiest song in the world, meant: 'At last I shall see Marie again!'

Guccio wore a fur coat and a cape of camel's hair against the rain; at his belt he could feel the weight of a purse filled with good *livres* with the Pope's mark in their corners; he was wearing a gallant hat of red felt turned up at the back and forming a long point above the forehead. It would have been impossible to have been better dressed to please. Nor would it have been possible to feel a greater eagerness for life.

In the courtyard in the Street of the Lombards he leapt from his horse and, throwing his leg which was still stiff from the accident in Marseilles, ran to cast himself into Tolomei's arms.

'My dear Uncle, my good Uncle! Have you seen my son, how is he? And Marie, has she come through it all right? What did she say to you? When is she expecting me?'

Without a word Tolomei handed him Marie de Cressay's letter. Guccio read it twice, and then again. At the words 'Know that I have a great loathing for my sin, and never wish to see again him who is the cause of my shame. I want to redeem myself from this dishonour . . .' he cried: 'It's not true, it's not possible! She cannot have written this herself!'

'Isn't it her writing?' asked Tolomei.

'Yes.'

The banker placed his hand on his nephew's shoulder.

'I would have warned you in time, had I been able,' he said. 'But I received this letter only the day before yesterday, after going to see Bouville.'

Guccio, his eyes fixed and determined, his teeth clenched, was not listening. He asked for the address of the convent.

'The Faubourg Saint-Marcel? I'm going there,' he said.

He sent for his horse, which had hardly been unsaddled, crossed the town once more, though scarcely seeing it now, and rang the bell at the door of the Clarisses. He was told that the Demoiselle de Cressay had left the day before, in company with two gentlemen of whom one wore a beard. Brandish the Pope's seal, storm and bluster as he might, he could get no more information.

'The Abbess! I demand to see the Mother Abbess!' he cried.

'Men may not enter the cloister.'

In the end they threatened to send for the sergeants of the watch.

Breathless, grey and drawn, Guccio returned to the Street of the Lombards.

'It's her brothers, her idiot brothers, who have taken her back!' he told Tolomei. 'Oh, I've been away too long! That was a fine troth she pledged me, not to have lasted six months!

These ladies of the nobility, so the romances say, wait ten years for their knight when he has gone on a crusade. But you don't wait for a Lombard! That's what it is, Uncle, that and nothing else. Read the letter again! There's nothing in it but insults and contempt. They might have compelled her not to see me again, but not to give me a slap in the face like this . . . After all, Uncle, we are rich to the extent of tens of thousands of florins; the greatest barons come and implore us to pay their debts, the Pope himself took me for a counsellor during the whole Conclave, and now these country oafs dare spit on me from the height of their mud castle that could be knocked down with a shove of the shoulder! Those two mangy dogs have only to appear and their sister denies me. How wrong one can be to believe that a girl is different from her family!'

With Guccio sorrow quickly turned to anger and his innate pride helped him to fight despair. He had stopped loving, but not suffering.

'I don't understand it at all,' said Tolomei, distressed. 'She seemed so much in love, so happy to be yours. I would never have believed it possible. I now see why Bouville seemed so embarrassed the other day. He clearly knew something. But he must have warned the brothers after my visit. And yet, what with the letters she wrote me, I don't understand it at all. Do you want me to see Bouville again?'

'I don't want anything, I don't want anything any more!' cried Guccio. 'I've already too much importuned the great ones of the earth on behalf of that deceiving bitch. I even asked the Pope to protect her. In love, did you say? She merely cajoled you when she thought her own people would have no more to do with her and she saw no other recourse but us. And yet, we were really married! For though she was not lacking in impatience to give herself to me, she would not do so without a priest's blessing. You tell me that she spent five days with Queen Clémence as wet-nurse! Her head must have been turned at filling an office any chambermaid might have held in her place. I too have been close to the Queen, and helped her in another way! During the storm I saved her.'

His thoughts were no longer linked; he was incoherent with anger; and walking up and down the room throwing his leg must have covered a quarter of a league.

'Perhaps if you went and saw the Queen . . .'

'Neither the Queen nor anyone else! Let Marie go back to her muddy hamlet, where the manure's up to your ankles. No doubt they've found her a husband, a fine husband like those squalid brothers of hers. Some hairy, stinking knight who'll bring up my child, the cuckold! If she came on her knees to me, I wouldn't have her now, do you hear, I wouldn't have her!'

'I think if she came in at this moment, you'd talk in another tone,' said Tolomei gently.

Guccio turned pale and covered his eyes with his hands. 'My beautiful Marie . . .' He saw her in the room at Neauphle again; he saw her close to him; he could distinguish the golden lights in her dark blue eyes. How could such a betrayal have been concealed behind those eyes?

'I'm going away, Uncle.'

'Where to? Are you going back to Avignon?'

'I should cut a pretty figure there! I told everybody that I was coming back with my wife; I said she had every virtue. The Holy Father himself would be the first to ask me for news.'

'Boccaccio was telling me the other day that the Peruzzi

are undoubtedly going to farm the taxes in the seneschalship of Carcassonne.'

'No! Neither Carcassonne nor Avignon.'

'Nor Paris, of course . . .' said Tolomei sadly.

There comes a moment towards the evening of every man's life, however egotistical he may have been, when he feels weary of working for himself alone. The banker, having looked forward to the presence of a pretty niece and a happy family in his house, suddenly saw his own hopes disappear and in their place the prospect of a long and lonely old age.

'No, I must go,' said Guccio. 'I want nothing more to do with France, which grows fat on us and despises us because we are Italian. What has France given me, I ask you? A stiff leg, four months in the Hôtel-Dieu, six weeks in a church, and to cap it all, this! I ought to have known that this country would be no use to me. Do you remember how the day after my arrival I very nearly knocked down King Philip the Fair in the street? It was a bad omen! Not to speak of my sea voyages, in which I twice nearly perished, and of all the time spent counting coppers for villeins in the muddy town of Neauphle, because I believed myself in love.'

'All the same, you'll take away one or two good memories,' said Tolomei.

'What need of memories have I at my age? I want to go back to my own town of Sienna where there is no lack of pretty girls, the prettiest girls in the world people say when I tell them I'm Siennese. In any case they're not such bitches as the girls here! My father sent me to you to learn; I think I've learnt enough.'

Tolomei opened his left eye; it was a little misty under the eyelid.

'You may be right,' he said. 'Your sorrow will fade more quickly when you're far away. But regret nothing, Guccio. It's no bad apprenticeship you've served. You have lived, travelled, learned the miseries of the poor and discovered the weaknesses of the great. You have been to the four Courts which dominate Europe, those of Paris, London, Naples and Avignon. There are not many people who have been shut up in a Conclave! You've been broken in to business. I shall give you your share; it's a handsome sum. Love has made you commit a few follies, and you're leaving a bastard behind you as does everyone who has travelled much . . . And you're still only twenty. When do you want to leave?'

'Tomorrow, Zio Spinello, tomorrow if you don't mind. But I shall come back!' Guccio added in a furious voice.

'Indeed, I sincerely hope so, my boy! I hope you won't let your old uncle die without seeing you again!'

'I shall come back one day, and take away my child. For he is mine, after all, as much as he's the Cressays'. Why should I leave him to them? So that they may bring him up in their stables, like a mongrel hound? I'll take him away, do you hear, and that will be Marie's punishment. You know what they say in our country: the vengeance of a Tuscan . . .'

A terrific uproar on the ground floor cut him short. The house with its wooden beams shook to its foundations as if a dozen drays had entered the courtyard. Doors banged.

Uncle and nephew went to the spiral staircase which seemed to be resounding to the noise of a cavalry charge. A voice was shouting: 'Banker! Where are you, banker? I need some money.'

And Monseigneur Robert of Artois reached the top of the stairs.

'Just look at me, my banker friend, I've this moment come out of prison!' he cried. 'Would you believe it? My honey-sweet, my shortsighted cousin – the King, I mean, since it appears he is so – at last remembered that I was rotting in the gaol he threw me into, and he has now freed me, the kind fellow!'

'Welcome, Monseigneur,' said Tolomei without much enthusiasm.

And he leaned forward to look down the stairs, still doubting that the hurricane could have been caused by one man alone.

Lowering his head so as not to bang it against the lintel of the door, the Count of Artois entered the banker's study and went to a looking-glass.

'By God! I look like a death's-head!' he said, taking his face in his hands. 'Really, one might die of less! Just imagine it, for seven weeks I've only seen the day through a tiny window crossed with iron bars thick as a donkey's pizzle! Broth twice a day which looked like a colic before you even ate it. Luckily my Lormet had his own methods of supplying me with food, otherwise I should be dead by now. And the bed, if you can call it a bed! Because of my royal blood I was allowed a bed. I had to break the wood to be able to stretch out my legs! But have patience; my dear cousin will pay for it all.'

In fact, Robert had not lost an ounce of weight and prison had not affected his rock-like nerves. If his complexion was a little less high, his grey, flint-coloured eyes were shining more wickedly than ever.

'And a splendid freedom they've allowed me! "You're free, Monseigneur,"' the giant imitated the Governor of the Châtelet; '"but you may go no further than twenty leagues from Paris; but the office of the King's sergeants-at-arms must know where you are living; but the Captain of Evreux, if you go to your estates, must be informed!" In other words: "Stay here, Robert, walking the streets under the eyes of the watch, or go and moulder at Conches. But don't take a step towards Artois, and not a step towards Rheims! And above all, you're not wanted at the coronation! You might well sing a psalm unpleasing to certain ears!" And they've chosen a good day on which to release me. Neither too early, nor too late. The whole Court has left; there's no one at the Palace, no one at Valois's house . . . He's abandoned me all right, that cousin has! And here I am in a dead city, without even a farthing in my purse for supper tonight or for a wench to serve my amorous mood! Seven weeks, you know, banker! But no, you can't understand; that sort of thing doesn't worry you any longer. But mind you, I whored enough in Artois while I was there to keep me quiet for a bit; and there must be a lot of little knaves on the way in those parts who'll never know that they'll be able to say "grandfather" when speaking of Philippe-Auguste. But I've discovered a strange thing that the doctors and philosophers, the rats, might think on: why should man be furnished with a member which, the more work you give it, the more it asks to do?'

He laughed aloud, cracked an oaken chair as he sat down on it, and suddenly appeared to notice Guccio's presence.

'Well, young man, how are your love affairs going?' he asked, which meant no more, when he said it, than 'good day'.

'My love affairs! You may well talk of them, Monseigneur!' replied Guccio, somewhat annoyed at having been interrupted by a greater and noisier violence than his own.

Tolomei indicated to the Count of Artois with a look that the subject was untimely.

'What,' cried Artois with his usual tact, 'has a fair one forsaken you? Give me her address at once that I may hasten there! Come, don't look so sad; all women are whores.'

'Yes, indeed, Monseigneur, every one of them!'

'Well, let's sport with frank whores at least! Banker, I need money. A hundred *livres*. And I'll take your nephew out to supper with me, and make him forget his sorrow. A hundred *livres*! Yes, I know, I know, I already owe you a lot and you think I shall never pay you; but you're wrong. You'll see Robert of Artois more powerful than ever. Philippe can pull his crown down to his nose if he likes; it won't be long before I knock it off. Because I'm going to tell you something worth more than a hundred *livres*, something which will be very useful to you in judging whom to lend money to. How's regicide punished? Hanging, beheading, quartering? You'll soon have the opportunity of witnessing a delightful spectacle: my fat aunt Mahaut, naked as a whore, being pulled apart by four horses and her filthy guts spread out in the dust. And her niggling son-in-law'll keep her company! The pity of it is that they can't be executed twice. Because they've killed two, the villains! I said nothing while I was in the Châtelet; I didn't want someone to come and bleed me like a pig one fine night. But I've been keeping in touch with things. Lormet, my Lormet as always; he's a splendid fellow! But listen to me.'

After seven weeks of enforced silence, terrible talker that he was, he was catching up. And he drew breath only to talk the more.

'Listen to me carefully,' he went on. 'One: Louis confiscates the county of Artois from Mahaut in order to give it back to me; Mahaut immediately has him poisoned. Two: Mahaut, to cover herself, assists Philippe to the regency against Valois, who would have supported me in my rights. Three: Philippe gets his law of succession accepted which excludes women from the Crown of France, but not from the inheritance of fiefs, of course! Four: having been confirmed as Regent, Philippe can raise an army to dislodge me from Artois, which I was on the point of completely regaining. Not being a fool, I came and surrendered by myself. But Queen Clémence is about to be brought to bed; they want a free hand; they shut me up in prison. Five: the Queen gives birth to a son. No matter! They isolate Vincennes, hide the child from the barons, say that he won't live, fix things up with some midwife or wet-nurse whom they frighten or bribe, and kill the second king. After which he goes off and gets crowned at Rheims. That, my friends, is how you obtain a crown. And all this so as not to give me back my county of Artois!'

At the word 'wet-nurse' Tolomei and Guccio exchanged a brief but anxious glance.

'These are things everyone believes,' went on Artois, 'but which no one dares proclaim for want of proof. But I have the proof! I'm now going to produce a certain woman who furnished the poison. And then they'll have to make that Béatrice d'Hirson, who has served as the Devil's pander in this splendid game, sing a little by the application of the boot.'

'Fifty *livres*, Monseigneur; I can give you fifty *livres*.'

'Miser!'

'It's all I can do.'

'Very well. You'll then owe me the other fifty. Mahaut will pay you the lot, with interest.'

'Guccio,' said Tolomei, 'come and help me count out fifty *livres* for Monseigneur.'

He retired with his nephew into the next room.

'Uncle,' murmured Guccio, 'do you think there is any truth in what he said?'

'I don't know, my boy, I don't know; but I think you're quite right to leave. It might be a bad thing to get mixed up in this affair; it has a nasty smell. Bouville's strange manner, Marie's sudden flight . . . Of course, one cannot take everything this madman says for gospel; but I've often noticed that, when it's a question of crime, he's never very far from the truth; he's an expert in it and scents it from afar. Remember the adultery of the Princesses; it was he who exposed it, and he had already told us about it. As for your Marie,' said the banker, waving his fat hand in a gesture of uncertainty, 'she's perhaps less ingenuous and less frank than we believed. There's certainly some mystery here.'

'After her traitorous letter one can believe anything,' said Guccio, whose thoughts were straying all over the place.

'Believe nothing, seek nothing; leave. It's good advice.'

When Monseigneur of Artois had taken possession of the fifty *livres*, he would not be satisfied till Guccio agreed to take part in a little celebration he intended to hold on the occasion of his being freed. He needed a companion and would have got drunk with his horse rather than do so alone.

He insisted so much that Tolomei finally whispered to his nephew: 'Go, or we shall wound him. But hold your tongue.'

Guccio therefore finished his unhappy day in a tavern, whose owner paid tribute to the officers of the watch to be allowed to carry on some of the traffic of a brothel. Moreover, every word that was said in the place was reported to the office of the sergeants-at-arms.

Monseigneur of Artois was at his most typical: insatiable at the pitcher, prodigious in appetite, obstreperous, obscene, overflowing with human kindness towards his young companion, while he raised the whores' skirts in order to show everyone Mahaut's true likeness.

Guccio, encouraged to emulate him, did not neglect the wine. His eyes bright, his hair in disorder and his movements uncertain, he shouted: 'I know things too . . . Ah, if I were to tell you!'

'Tell me, tell me!'

But, drunk as he was, Guccio preserved an underlying prudence.

'The Pope . . .' he said. 'Oh, I know a lot about the Pope.'

Suddenly he burst into floods of tears on a whore's shoulder; then he slapped her face because he saw in her the image of all feminine betrayal.

'But I shall come back and I shall take him away!'

'Who, the Pope?'

'No, the child!'

The evening had become confused, vision uncertain, and the girls provided by the brothel-keeper had discarded their clothes, when Lormet came to Robert of Artois and whispered in his ear: 'There's a man outside, watching us.'

'Kill him!' the giant said casually.

'Very well, Monseigneur.'

Thus Madame de Bouville lost one of her servants; she had sent him to follow the young Italian.

Guccio was never to know that Marie, by her sacrifice, had

probably saved him from finishing up as a corpse floating on the waters of the Seine.

Sprawling in a dirty bed across the breasts of the girl whose face he had smacked, and who now showed herself understanding of man's sorrows, Guccio continued to insult Marie, imagining that he was avenging himself on her by taking this bought body in his arms.

'You're quite right! I don't like women either; they're all deceitful,' said the whore, whose face Guccio was never afterwards able to remember.

The next day, his hat pulled down over his eyes, his limbs weak, exhausted both in body and soul, Guccio took the road to Italy. He was taking with him a handsome fortune in the form of a letter of credit signed by his uncle; it represented his share of the profits in the business he had done during the last two years.

That same day King Philippe V, his wife Jeanne, and the Countess Mahaut, with all their suites, arrived in Rheims.

The gates of the manor of Cressay had already closed on the beautiful Marie, who was to live there, inconsolable, in a perpetual winter.

The real King of France was to grow up there as if he were a bastard. He was to take his first steps in the muddy courtyard among the ducks, play in the field with the yellow irises by the banks of the Mauldre, in that very field where Marie, as she walked through it, recalled again and again the face of her charming Siennese and the fleeting passage of her dead love. She was to keep her oath and for thirty years carry her secret; only at last to confess it, on her deathbed, to a Spanish priest who passed that way.

Marie de Cressay's destiny was a strange one. Crossed in

love, she was condemned to a life of solitude; but once in her whole life did she leave her native village and then only to be involved, in all innocence and helplessness, at the heart of a dynastic drama; while her confession, one day, was to trouble Europe.*

* The history of this confession, and the dramatic life of Clémence of Hungary's son, will be the subject of one of the volumes in the second series of *The Accursed Kings*.

9

The Eve of the Coronation

THE GATES OF RHEIMS, surmounted by the royal arms, had been freshly painted. The streets were hung with bright draperies, carpets and silks, the same indeed that had served a year and a half earlier for the coronation of Louis X. By the Archiepiscopal Palace three great halls had been quickly run up by carpenters; one for the King's table, another for the Queen's, and a third for the great officers, so that the whole Court might be feasted.

The burgesses of Rheims, at whose expense the coronation took place, found the cost somewhat heavy.

'If the occupants of the throne die as quickly as this,' they said, 'and we have the honour of crowning a king every year, we shall soon only be able to eat once in twelve months and have to sell our shirts to do so! Clovis is costing us dear by having had himself anointed here! If another town in the kingdom would care to buy the holy ampulla, we would certainly do a deal.' To the difficulties of finding the money was added the difficulty of finding, in midwinter, enough food for so many mouths. But the burgesses of Rheims had collected eighty-two oxen, two hundred and forty sheep, four hundred and twenty-five calves, seventy-eight pigs, eight hundred rabbits and hares, eight hundred capons, one thousand eight hundred and twenty geese, more than ten thousand hens and forty thousand eggs, without counting the barrels of sturgeons, which had to be brought from Malines, the four thousand freshwater crayfish, the salmon, pike, tench, bream, perch, carp, and the three thousand five hundred eels for making pies. They had collected two thousand cheeses, and hoped that the three hundred casks of wine, which was luckily a local product, would suffice to satisfy the thirsty gullets which would be banqueting there for three days or more.

The chamberlains, who had arrived in advance to organize the rejoicings, made singular demands. Had they not decided that at one single course three hundred roast herons should be served? These officers were very like their master, the King in a hurry, who ordered his coronation almost from one week to the next, as if it were a halfpenny Mass to mend a broken leg.

The pastrycooks had for days been building their almond-paste castles in the colours of France.

And the mustard! The mustard had not arrived! They needed sixty-two gallons. And then of course the guests couldn't eat out of the palms of their hands! They had made a mistake in selling off so cheaply the fifty thousand wooden bowls from the preceding coronation; it would have been more profitable to wash them and keep them. As for the four thousand pitchers, they'd either been broken or stolen. The seamstresses were hastily hemming two thousand six hundred ells of cloths, and it could be calculated that the total expense would amount to near ten thousand *livres*.[33]

But in fact the inhabitants of Rheims would get their money back, because the coronation had attracted great numbers of Lombard and Jewish merchants who paid tax on their sales.

The coronation, like all royal ceremonies, took place in a fairlike atmosphere. A continual spectacle was offered to the populace during these days, and people came from far to see it. The women dressed in new dresses; the gallants did not look glum at the sight of a jeweller's shop; brocades, fine stuffs and furs sold without difficulty. The clever made fortunes, and the shopkeepers who served their customers competently could make in a single week enough to keep them for five years.

The new King was lodged in the Archiepiscopal Palace, before which a crowd was permanently gathered to watch for the appearance of the Sovereign or marvel at the Queen's coach which was covered in brilliant scarlet.

Queen Jeanne, surrounded by her ladies-in-waiting, supervised, with a woman's delighted excitement, the unpacking of the twelve trunks and four chests, the coffer containing shoes and the coffer containing spices. Her wardrobe was certainly the finest that any woman in France had ever had. There was a special dress for every day and almost every hour of this triumphal journey.

The Queen had made her solemn entry into the town dressed in a coat of cloth of gold lined with ermine, while shows, mystery plays and entertainments were taking place all along the streets for the benefit of the royal couple. For the supper on coronation eve, which was to take place shortly, the Queen would wear a dress of violet velvet trimmed with miniver. For the morning of the coronation she had a dress of turkey cloth of gold, a scarlet cloak and a vermilion cape; for dinner a dress embroidered with the arms of France; for supper a dress of cloth of gold and two different mantles of ermine.

The following day she was to wear a dress of green velvet, and later another of azure *camocas* with a squirrel cape. She would never appear in public wearing the same dress, nor even the same jewels.

These marvels were laid out in a room whose decorations had also been brought from Paris: white silk hangings embroidered with thirteen hundred and twenty-one golden parrots, and in the centre the great arms of the Counts of Burgundy showing a lion gules; the baldaquin, counterpane and cushions were decorated with seven thousand silver trefoils. On the floor had been placed carpets with the arms of France and of the county of Burgundy.

Jeanne went several times into Philippe's room to show him the beauty of some stuff or the perfection of some creation.

'My dear Sire, my well-beloved,' she cried, 'how happy you are making me!'

Though little inclined to be emotionally demonstrative, she could not help tears coming to her eyes. She was dazzled by her own fate, particularly when she remembered that she had but recently been in prison at Dourdan. What an astounding reversal of fortune in less than eighteen months! She thought of the dead Marguerite, she thought of her sister Blanche of Burgundy, who was still shut up in Château-Gaillard. 'Poor Blanche, who loved finery so much. What pleasure today would have given her!' she thought, as she tried on a golden belt encrusted with rubies and emeralds.

Philippe was anxious, and his wife's enthusiasm tended to depress him; he was examining the accounts with his Bursar.

'I am delighted, my dear, that all this pleases you,' he ended by saying. 'You see, I am following the example of my father, who, as you know, was very careful in his expenditure though he was never stingy when it was a matter of the royal majesty. You must show off these beautiful clothes well, because they are for the people who provide them by their labour, as much as they are for you; and take great care of them, for you will not be able to have others for some time. After the coronation we shall have to economize.'

'Philippe,' Jeanne asked, 'won't you do something for my sister Blanche on this day?'

'I have, I have. She is being treated as a princess again, but with the reservation that she does not go outside the walls of her prison. A difference must be made between Blanche who sinned, and you, Jeanne, who were always pure though falsely accused.'

As he said these last words, he looked at his wife with a gaze which revealed more anxiety for the royal honour than any certainty of her love.

'Besides,' he added, 'her husband is far from pleasing me at the moment. He is a bad brother to me!'

Jeanne realized that it would be useless to insist and that it would be to her advantage never to open the subject again. As long as Philippe was King, he refused to free Blanche.

Jeanne withdrew and Philippe returned to the examination of the long sheets of figures Geoffroy de Fleury was presenting for his inspection.

The expenses were not limited merely to the clothes of the

King and Queen. Philippe had, indeed, received a few presents. For instance, the grey robe he was wearing that day had been given him by his grandmother, Marie of Brabant, the widow of Philippe III; and Mahaut had given the figured cloth for the dresses of the little Princesses and the young Louis-Philippe. But it was little among so much.

The King had had to provide new clothes for his fifty-four sergeants-at-arms and their commander, Pierre de Galard, the Master of the Crossbowmen. Adam Héron, Robert de Gamaches, Guillaume de Seriz, the chamberlains, had each received ten ells of striped cloth from Douai to make themselves stylish coats. Henry de Meudon, Furant de la Fouaillie and Jeannot Malgeneste, the huntsmen, had been given new liveries, as had all the archers. And as twenty knights were to be armed after the coronation, there were another twenty robes to give! These presents of clothes were customary gifts; and precedent also demanded that the King should add to the shrine of Saint-Denis a golden lily set with emeralds and rubies.

'What's the total?' Philippe asked.

'Eight thousand five hundred and forty-eight *livres*, thirteen *sols*, and eleven *deniers*, Sire,' replied the Bursar. 'Perhaps you might ask for the dues normally paid at a happy accession?'

'My accession will be all the happier if I impose no new taxes. We'll manage some other way,' said the King.

At this moment the Count of Valois was announced. Philippe raised his hands towards the ceiling: 'That's what we've forgotten in our calculations. You'll see, Geoffroy, you'll see! That uncle will cost me more by himself than ten coronations! He's come to do a deal with me. Leave me alone with him.'

How splendid Monseigneur of Valois was! Embroidered, bedizened, doubled in size by his furs which opened on a robe sewn with precious stones! If the inhabitants of Rheims had not known that the new King was young and thin, they might have taken him for the King himself.

'My dear Nephew,' he began, 'you see me much distressed, much distressed on your account. Your brother-in-law of England is not coming.'

'For a long while now, Uncle, the King of England has not attended our coronations,' Philippe replied.

'Of course; but they send a representative, some relation or great lord of their Court to occupy their place as Duke of Guyenne. But Edward has sent no one; he thereby confirms the fact that he does not recognize you. The Count of Flanders, whom you thought you had won over with your treaty last September, is not here either, nor is the Duke of Brittany.'

'I know, Uncle, I know.'

'As for the Duke of Burgundy, don't let's mention him; we knew very well that he would let you down. But, on the other hand, his mother, our Aunt Agnès, entered the town a while ago, but I do not think that she has come with the purpose of giving you her support.'

'I know, Uncle, I know,' Philippe repeated.

The unexpected arrival of the last daughter of Saint Louis worried Philippe more than he liked to say. At first he had thought that the Duchess Agnès had come to negotiate. But she showed no haste to put in an appearance, and he had determined not to take the first step himself. 'If the people, who acclaim me when I appear, and who believe that I am to be envied, only knew of the hostility and danger around me!' he thought.

'Indeed,' went on Valois, 'out of the six lay peers who should hold your crown tomorrow, you have precisely none.'[34]

'But I have, Uncle; you're forgetting the Countess of Artois and yourself.'

Valois violently shrugged his shoulders.

'The Countess of Artois!' he cried. 'A woman holding your crown when you yourself, Philippe, you yourself, have only reached your position by excluding women!'

'Holding the crown is not wearing it,' said Philippe.

'Did Mahaut help you to become King that you should increase her importance in this way! You'll but lend more credit to all the lies that are going about. Don't let's bring up the past, Philippe, but is it not really Robert who should occupy the peer's seat for Artois?'

Philippe pretended not to have heard his uncle's last words.

'At all events the ecclesiastical peers are here,' he said.

'They're here, they're here,' said Valois, shaking his rings. 'But there are only five out of the six who should be here. And what do you think they'll do, those peers of the Church, when they see that on the side of the kingdom there is but one hand – and what a hand! – raised to crown you?'

'But, Uncle, do you count for nothing?'

It was Valois's turn to ignore the question.

'Even your own brother is cool towards you,' he said.

'It's no doubt because Charles', replied Philippe softly, 'does not fully realize, my dear Uncle, on what good terms we are, and he may think that he is serving you by doing me an ill-office. But you may be reassured; his arrival is announced for tomorrow.'

'Why don't you give him a peerage at once? Your father

did it for me, and your brother Louis for you; I should feel less alone in supporting you.'

'Or less alone in betraying me,' thought Philippe, who went on: 'Is it for Robert, or for Charles, that you have come to plead, or did you want to talk to me of yourself?'

Valois fell silent for a moment, lolled back in his chair, and contemplated the diamond glittering on his forefinger.

'Fifty or a hundred thousand?' Philippe wondered. 'I don't care a damn about the others. But I need him, and he knows it. If he refuses and makes a scandal, I may have to postpone my coronation.'

'Nephew,' said Valois at last, 'you can see that I have not stood aloof and that I have even spent a lot of money on my clothes and my suite to do you honour. But if the other peers are absent, I think I shall have to withdraw. What would be said, if I were seen alone at your side? That you had bought me, precisely that.'

'I should deplore that, Uncle, I should deplore it very much. But there it is; I cannot oblige you to do something which displeases you. Perhaps the time has come to give up the custom by which the peers raise their hands to the crown.'

'Nephew! Nephew!' cried Valois.

'And if there must be consent by election,' Philippe went on, 'perhaps it should be asked, not of the six great barons, but of the people, Uncle, who provide men for the armies and money for the Treasury. It will become the duty of the Estates, whom I shall summon.'

Valois could not contain himself; leaping from his chair, he began shouting: 'You're blaspheming, Philippe, or you've gone mad! Has there ever been a king elected by his subjects? Your Estates are a splendid innovation! These ideas come straight from Marigny, who was born of the lower orders and did your father so much injury. I am telling you that, if you begin like this, in fifty years' time the people will manage without us; they'll choose some rich burgess for king, some doctor of parliament, some grocer who has made a fortune by thieving. No, Nephew, no; this time I've made up my mind; I shall not hold up the crown of a king who is only of his own making, and who is prepared to act in such a way that the crown must soon become the perquisite of clod-hoppers!'

Purple in the face, he was striding up and down the room.

'A hundred thousand or fifty thousand?' Philippe was still wondering. 'What sum must he be bribed with?'

'Very well, Uncle, don't hold it,' he said. 'But let me send for my Bursar at once.'

'Why?'

'To get him to alter the lists of donations I am to seal tomorrow, in celebration of my happy accession; you head that list for a hundred thousand *livres*.'

The thrust told. Valois stood there flabbergasted, his arms outstretched.

Philippe realized he had won and, though the victory had cost him dear, he had to make an effort not to smile at the sight of his uncle's face. The latter quickly managed, however, to cover his embarrassment. He had been cut off in the middle of his rage; he continued with it. Anger was with him a method of trying to confuse other people's reasoning, when his own arguments were weak.

'To begin with, Eudes is at the bottom of all the harm,' he said. 'I blame him very much for it and I shall write to him! And what right had the Count of Flanders and the Duke of

Brittany to take his part and refuse your summons? When the King summons you to hold his crown, you come to do so! Am I not here myself? The barons, indeed, are overstepping their rights. And there lies the danger of authority passing to the little vassals and the burgesses. As for Edward of England, what faith can be placed in a man who behaves like a woman? I shall therefore be at your side to set them an example. And what you contemplated giving me I shall accept out of a sense of justice. For it is only just that those who are loyal to the King should be treated in a different manner from those who betray him. You govern well. As to this gift which marks your esteem for me, when are you going to sign it?'

'At once, Uncle, if you so wish. But it will bear tomorrow's date,' replied King Philippe V.

For the third time, and always by means of money, he had silenced the Count of Valois.

'It is certainly time I was crowned,' said Philippe to his Bursar, when Valois had left. 'If I had to do any more negotiating I think next time I should have to sell the kingdom.'

And when Fleury showed surprise at the enormous sum promised, the King added: 'Don't worry, don't worry, Geoffroy, I have given no date as to when the donation is to be paid. He'll only get it a little at a time. But he'll be able to borrow on it. Now let's go to supper.'

The ceremonial demanded that after the evening meal the King, surrounded by his officers and the chapter, should go to the cathedral to meditate and pray. The church was already prepared, the tapestries hung, the hundreds of candles in their places, and the great dais raised in the choir. Philippe's prayers were short; nevertheless, he spent a considerable time in being instructed for the last time on the sequence of the ritual and the gestures he would have to make. He verified that the side doors were locked, inquired into the security arrangements, and asked where everyone was sitting.

'The lay peers, the members of the royal family and the great officers of State are on the dais,' it was explained to him. 'The Constable remains at your side. The Chancellor stays at the Queen's side. The throne, opposite yours, is that of the Archbishop of Rheims, and the seats placed about the high altar are for the ecclesiastical peers.'

Philippe wandered slowly about the dais, and turned down the corner of a carpet with his foot.

'How strange it is,' he thought. 'I was here only last year for my brother's coronation. And I paid no attention to all these details.'

He sat down for a moment, but not on the royal throne; a superstitious fear prevented his occupying it yet. 'Tomorrow I shall really be King.' He thought of his father, of the line of his ancestors, who had preceded him in this church; he thought of his brother, killed by a crime of which he was innocent but by which he was now profiting; he thought of the other crime, the murder of the child, which he equally had not ordered but of which he was the silent accomplice, almost the inspirer. He thought of death, his own death, and of the millions of men who were his subjects, of the millions of fathers, sons, brothers whom he would govern until then.

'Are they all like me,' he wondered, 'criminals if they had the opportunity, innocent only because they are powerless, and ready to make use of evil to accomplish their ambitions? And yet, when I was at Lyons, my only desire was for justice. But is that certain? Is human nature really so detestable, or is it royalty which makes us like this? Is the discovery that one is so impure and so besmirched the tribute one must pay to rule? Why did God make us mortal, since it is death that makes us so detestable, through the fear we have of it, and through the use we make of it? Perhaps someone will try to kill me tonight.'

He watched the great shadows wavering in the high windows between the pillars. He felt no repentance, only a lack of happiness at being King.

'This no doubt is what is called an orison, and why we are counselled to come to the church the night before the coronation.'

He judged himself clearly for what he was: a bad man, with the gifts of a very great king.

He was not sleepy; he would gladly have stayed there much longer meditating on himself, human destiny, the origins of human actions, and asking himself the greatest questions in the world, those that can never be answered.

'How long will the ceremony last?' he asked.

'Two full hours, Sire.'

'Well, we must try to get some sleep. We must be fit tomorrow.'

But when he had returned to the Archiepiscopal Palace he went to the Queen's room and sat on the edge of her bed. He talked to his wife of things that seemed to have but little importance; he talked of people's places in the cathedral; he was concerned about his daughters' clothes.

Jeanne was already half-asleep. She had to struggle to give him her attention; she discerned in her husband a nervous tension, a sort of mounting uneasiness against which he was seeking protection.

'My dear,' she asked him, 'do you want to sleep with me?'

He seemed to hesitate.

'I cannot; the chamberlain has not been warned,' he replied.

'You are King, Philippe,' Jeanne said smiling; 'you can give your chamberlain what orders you please.'

He took some time to make up his mind. This young man who knew how to control his most powerful vassals by means of arms or money felt embarrassed at informing his servant that, owing to unforeseen desire, he was going to share his wife's bed.

Finally he called one of the housemaids who slept in the adjoining room and sent her to warn Adam Héron that he need not wait for him nor sleep that night outside his door.

Then, among the parrots of the hangings, beneath the silver trefoils of the baldaquin, he undressed and slipped between the sheets. And his great uneasiness, from which all the soldiers of the Constable could not protect him, because it was a man's uneasiness and not a king's, was calmed at the touch of this woman's body, her long firm legs, her soft belly and warm breasts.

'My darling,' Philippe murmured into Jeanne's hair, 'my darling, answer me, have you deceived me? Do not fear to answer me, for even if you did deceive me once, you are forgiven.'

Jeanne clasped his long body, so spare and so strong, feeling the bones beneath her fingers.

'Never, Philippe, I swear it,' she replied. 'I was tempted to do so, I confess it, but I never yielded.'

'Thank you, darling,' Philippe whispered. 'Nothing is lacking to my kingship.'

Nothing more was lacking to his kingship, because he was in truth like every man in his kingdom; he needed a woman, and one that should be his own.[35]

10

The Bells of Rheims

A FEW HOURS LATER, lying on a state bed decorated with the arms of France, Philippe in a long robe of vermilion velvet, his hands joined at his breast, was awaiting the bishops who were to lead him to the cathedral.

The first chamberlain, Adam Héron, also sumptuously clothed, was standing by the bed. The pale January morning spread a milky glow over the room.

There was a knock at the door.

'Whom do you want?' asked the chamberlain.

'I want the King.'

'Who wants him?'

'His brother.'

Philippe and Adam Héron looked at each other in surprise and vexation.

'All right. Let him come in,' said Philippe, sitting up a little.

'You've got very little time, Sire,' said the chamberlain.

The King signed to him that the audience would not last long.

The handsome Charles de La Marche was in travelling clothes. He had just arrived in Rheims and had only stopped for a moment to see his uncle Valois. There was anger apparent both in his expression and the way he walked.

Angry though he was, the sight of his brother dressed in vermilion and lying in a hieratic pose impressed him. He halted for a moment, his eyes wide in astonishment.

'How he would like to be in my place,' Philippe thought, then aloud he said: 'So here you are, my good brother. I'm grateful to you for having understood your duty and for giving the lie to the wicked talk which had it that you would not be at my coronation. I am grateful to you. But you must hurry and get dressed, for you cannot appear like that. You'll be late.'

'Brother,' replied La Marche, 'I must first talk to you on an important matter.'

'On an important matter, or something which is merely important to you? The important thing at the moment is not to keep the clergy waiting. In a minute the bishops will be here to fetch me.'

'Well, they'll have to wait!' cried Charles. 'Everyone in turn gets you to listen to him and gets something out of you. I seem to be the only person to whom you pay no attention; this time you'll listen to me!'

'All right, Charles, let's talk,' said Philippe, sitting on the edge of the bed. 'But I warn you that we shall have to be brief.'

La Marche made a gesture with his head which seemed to say: 'We shall see, we shall see.' He took a chair, doing his best to look important and hold his head high.

'Poor Charles,' thought Philippe, 'he wants to ape the

manners of our uncle Valois, but he hasn't the presence.'

'Philippe,' went on La Marche, 'I have asked you over and over again to confer a peerage on me, and increase my appanage and my revenues. Have I asked you, or haven't I?'

'What a family!' Philippe murmured.

'And you've always refused to listen to me. But I'm asking you now for the last time; I've come to Rheims, but I shall attend your coronation only if I am given a peer's place. If I'm not, I shall go away again.'

Philippe looked at him for a moment in silence, and beneath that glance Charles felt himself diminish and dissolve, lose all self-assurance and all importance.

In the presence of their father, Philip the Fair, the young Prince had in the old days felt the same sensation of his own insignificance.

'One moment, Brother,' said Philippe, rising to his feet and going to speak to Adam Héron, who had withdrawn into a corner of the room.

'Adam,' he asked in a low voice, 'have the barons who went to fetch the holy ampulla from the Abbey of Saint-Rémy returned?'

'Yes, Sire, they are already at the cathedral with the clergy of the abbey.'

'Very well, then deal with the town gates as at Lyons.'

He made three almost imperceptible movements of the hand, which signified: portcullises, bars, keys.

'On the day of the coronation, Sire?' murmured Héron in stupefaction.

'Exactly, on the day of the coronation. And make haste.'

The chamberlain left the room and Philippe came back to the bed.

'Well, Brother, what were you asking of me?'

'A peerage, Philippe.'

'Oh, yes, a peerage. Well, Brother, I'll give you one, I'll give you one with pleasure; but not at once, because you have made your request too well known. If I yielded now, it would be said that I was acting not because I wished but because I was constrained to it, and everyone would think that he had a right to behave as you do. You must know that there will be no more appanages created or augmented before an ordinance has been promulgated declaring that no part of the royal domains is alienable.'[36]

'But you no longer need the peerage of Poitiers! Why don't you give it to me? You must admit that my position is insufficient!'

'Insufficient?' cried Philippe, who was beginning to lose his temper. 'You were born the son of a king, you're the brother of a king; do you think that your position is insufficient for a man of your intelligence and capacities?'

'My capacities?' said Charles.

'Yes, your capacities, which are limited. The moment has come when you must be told so to your face, Charles. You're a fool; you always have been and you don't get any better as you grow older. When you were no more than a child you already seemed to everyone so stupid, so backward in intelligence, that our mother herself despised you, sainted woman that she was! She called you "the goose". Do you remember, Charles? "The goose." You were one and you've remained one. Our father used to make you sit on his Council; what did you learn there? You used to gape at the flies, while the affairs of the realm were being discussed, and I can't ever remember your uttering a remark which did not make either our father or Messire Enguerrand shrug his shoulders. Do you think that I want to make you more powerful because of the great help you'd be to me, when for the last six months you've done nothing but conspire against me? You had everything to gain from taking another road. You think you've got a strong character, and that people will bend to your will? No one has forgotten the pitiful figure you cut at Maubuisson, when you were bleating: "Blanche, Blanche!" and crying at the injury done you before the whole Court.'

'Philippe! Is it your place to say that to me?' cried La Marche, sitting bolt upright, his features contorted. 'Is it your place when your wife . . .'

'I won't hear a word against Jeanne, not a word against the Queen!' Philippe interrupted, raising his hand. 'I know that to do me an injury, or to feel less alone in your misfortune, you continue to spread your lies.'

'You have acquitted Jeanne, because you wanted to keep Burgundy, because, as always, you have put your interest before your honour. But perhaps my unfaithful wife can still also serve her turn.'

'What do you mean?'

'I mean what I say!' replied Charles de La Marche. 'And I tell you, too, that if you want to see me at the coronation, I insist on sitting in a peer's place. A peerage, or I go!'

Adam Héron came into the room and informed the King, by a nod of the head, that his orders had been passed on. Philippe thanked him in the same manner.

'Go then, Brother,' he said. 'There is only one person who is necessary to me today: the Archbishop of Rheims, who will crown me. And you're not the Archbishop, I imagine? So go; go if you wish.'

'But why', cried Charles, 'does our uncle Valois get what he wants, whereas I never do?'

Through the half-opened door could be heard the chanting of the approaching procession.

'When I think that if I were to die it would be this fool who would be Regent!' Philippe thought. He put his hand on his brother's shoulder.

'When you have injured the kingdom for as many long years as our uncle has, you can demand the same price. But, thank God, you're less assiduous in your folly!'

He glanced at the door, and the Count de La Marche went out, pale, a prey to impotent rage, only to meet a great crowd of clergy.

Philippe went back to the bed and lay down in the same position, his hands clasped, his eyes shut.

There was a knocking at the door; this time it was the bishops knocking with their crosiers.

'Whom do you want?' said Adam Héron.

'We want the King,' replied a grave voice.

'Who wants him?'

'The ecclesiastical peers.'

The doors were opened and the Bishops of Langres and Beauvais entered, their mitres on their heads, their reliquaries about their necks. They went up to the bed, helped the King to rise, presented him with holy water, and, while he knelt on a silken cushion, said prayers.

Adam Héron placed about Philippe's shoulders a cape of vermilion velvet matching his robe. Then, suddenly, there broke out a quarrel over precedence. Normally the Duke-Archbishop of Laon took the place at the King's right. But at that time the see of Laon was vacant. The Bishop of Langres,

Guillaume de Durfort, was supposed to replace him. But Philippe chose the Bishop of Beauvais for the place. He had two reasons for doing this: on the one hand, the Bishop of Langres had somewhat too openly welcomed the ex-Templars into his diocese, giving them places as clerks; on the other hand, the Bishop of Beauvais was a Marigny – a relation of the great Enguerrand and of his brother, the Archbishop of Sens – and Philippe wished to do homage, if not to the Bishop himself, at least to his name.

It therefore happened that the King found himself with two prelates on his right and none on his left.

'I am a duke-bishop; it is for me to be on the right,' said Guillaume de Durfort.

'The see of Beauvais is more ancient than that of Langres,' replied Marigny.

Their faces began to grow red beneath their mitres.

'Messeigneurs, the King decides,' said Philippe.

Durfort obeyed and changed places.

'One discontented man the more,' thought Philippe.

Amid crucifixes, candles and the smoke of incense, they went down into the street where the whole Court, the Queen at its head, was already formed up in procession. They walked to the cathedral.

There was great cheering as the King passed by. Philippe was somewhat pale and screwed up his shortsighted eyes. The earth of Rheims seemed suddenly to have become strangely hard beneath his feet; he felt as if he were walking on marble.

At the doors of the cathedral there was a halt for more prayers; then, to the sound of the organ, Philippe advanced up the nave towards the altar, the great dais and the throne on which, at last, he took his seat. His first gesture was to indicate to the Queen the seat prepared for her on the right of his own.

The church was crowded. Philippe could see nothing but a sea of coronets, embroidered breasts and shoulders, jewels and chasubles glittering in the light of the candles. A human firmament was spread at his feet.

He turned his eyes upon his more immediate neighbourhood, looking to right and left to see who was on the dais. Charles of Valois was there and Mahaut of Artois, monumental, shimmering in brocades and velvets, as she smiled at him; Louis of Evreux was sitting a little further away. But Philippe did not see Charles de La Marche, nor Philippe of Valois, whose father was also searching for him.

The Archbishop of Rheims, Robert de Courtenay, weighed down with sacerdotal ornaments, rose from his throne opposite the royal throne. Philippe rose too and went to kneel before the altar.

Throughout the singing of the *Te Deum* Philippe was wondering: 'Have the gates been properly closed? Have my orders been faithfully carried out? My brother is not the man to stay hiding in a room while I'm being crowned. And why is Philippe of Valois absent? What are they plotting? I should have left Galard outside to be in a better position to command his crossbowmen.'

But while the King was anxious, his younger brother was paddling in a marsh.

When he had left the royal chamber in a rage, Charles de La Marche had gone at once to the Valois lodging. He had not found his uncle there because he had already gone to the cathedral, only Philippe of Valois, who was finishing dressing and to whom he breathlessly related what he called his brother's 'felony'.

The two cousins were somewhat similar, with the difference that Philippe of Valois was physically bigger and stronger than Charles; as regards their intelligence, they complemented each other in vanity and folly.

'If that's the case, I shan't attend the ceremony either; I'll leave with you,' declared Valois the younger.

Thereupon they assembled their escorts and went proudly to one of the town gates. Their pride, however, had had to yield before the sergeants-at-arms.

'No one may enter or leave. The King's orders.'

'Even Princes of France?'

'Not even Princes; the King's orders.'

'Ah, he wants to coerce us!' cried Philippe of Valois, who was now making the affair his own. 'Well, we'll get out all the same!'

'How do you propose to do that, since the gates are closed?'

'Let's pretend to go back to our lodgings, and leave it to me.'

They thereupon indulged in a schoolboy trick. The equerries of the young Count of Valois were sent to find ladders and these they quickly placed at the end of a blind alley at a place where the walls appeared to be unguarded. And then the two cousins, their bottoms in the air, scaled the wall, not for one moment imagining that on the further side lay the Vesle marshes. They let themselves down into the fosse with ropes. Charles de La Marche lost his foothold in the muddy, icy water; he would have been drowned if his cousin, who was six feet tall and had strong muscles, had not fished him out in time. Then they went off, like a couple of blind men, groping across the marshes. There was soon no question of their giving up. Going on or going back amounted to the same thing. They were risking their lives and it took them three full hours to get out of the mire. The few equerries who had followed them were floundering about them and did not hesitate to curse them aloud.

'If ever we get out of here,' cried La Marche to keep up his courage, 'I know what I shall do. I shall go to Château-Gaillard!'

Young Valois, dripping with sweat in spite of the cold, looked his stupefaction across the rotting reeds.

'Do you still care for Blanche?' he asked.

'I no longer care for her at all, but I want some information from her. She is the last person who can say whether Louis's daughter is a bastard or not, and whether Philippe was a cuckold like me! With her evidence I shall be able to disgrace my brother in my turn, and have the crown given to Louis's daughter.'

The clamour of the bells of Rheims came to their ears.

'When I think, when I think it's for him they're ringing!' said Charles de La Marche, up to his waist in mud, pointing a hand towards the town.

In the cathedral the chamberlains had unclothed the King. Philippe the Long, standing before the altar, had nothing on his body but two shirts, one over the other, one of fine linen next to the skin, the other of white silk, wide open at the breast and under the arms. The King, before being invested with the insignia of his majesty, was presenting himself to his assembled subjects as an almost naked man, and one, indeed, who was shivering.

All the emblems of coronation were laid out on the altar, under the guardianship of the Abbot of Saint-Denis, who had brought them. Adam Héron took from the Abbot's hands the hose, long silken garments embroidered with lilies, and helped the King to put them on, as also the shoes, also of embroidered cloth. Then Anseau de Joinville, in the absence of the Duke of Burgundy, fastened the gold spurs to the King's feet, and then immediately removed them again. The Archbishop blessed the great sword which was supposed to be that of Charlemagne, and fastened it to the King's side with the baldric while reciting: 'Accipe hunc gladium cum Dei benedictione . . .'*

'Gaucher, come here,' said the King.

Gaucher de Châtillon came forward and Philippe, unfastening the baldric, handed him the sword.

Never had a constable, in the whole history of coronations, better deserved the honour of holding for his sovereign the symbol of military power. This gesture was more than the accomplishment of a rite; they exchanged a long look. The symbol had become fused with the reality.

With the point of a golden needle the Archbishop took from the holy ampulla, which the Abbot of Saint-Rémy held out to him, a drop of the oil which was said to have been sent down from Heaven and, with his finger, mixed it with the chrism laid ready on a paten. Then the Archbishop anointed Philippe, touching him on the top of the head, on the breast, between the shoulders and in the armpits. Adam Héron fastened the hooks and eyes which closed the shirts. The

---

* 'Receive this sword with God's blessing, to resist all your enemies by virtue of the Holy Spirit . . .'

King's shirt would later be burnt, because it had been touched with the holy oil.

The King was then clothed with the vestments from the altar: first the vermilion satin cotta embroidered with silver thread, then the blue satin tunic edged with pearls and strewn with golden lilies, and over that the dalmatic of the same material, and over that again the *soq*, a great square mantle fastened on the right shoulder by a golden clasp. Each time Philippe felt a greater weight on his shoulders. The Archbishop performed the anointing of the hands, slipped the royal ring on to Philippe's finger, placed the heavy gold sceptre in his right hand, and the hand of justice in his left. After genuflecting before the tabernacle, the prelate finally took up the crown, while the Great Chamberlain began calling the roll of the peers present: 'The magnificent and puissant Lord, the Count . . .'

At that very moment a high imperious voice sounded in the nave: 'Stop, Archbishop! Do not crown that usurper; it is the daughter of Saint Louis who commands you.'

There was a great stirring among the congregation. All heads turned in the direction whence the cry had come. On the dais and among the officiating priests there were anxious looks. The crowd parted.

Surrounded by a few lords, a tall woman with a still-beautiful face, a firm chin and clear, angry eyes, the narrow coronet and veil of a widow surmounting a mass of almost white hair, advanced towards the choir.

As she went by there were whisperings of: 'It's the Duchess Agnès; it's she!'

People craned their necks to look at her. They were surprised that she was still so young in appearance and that her step was so firm. Because she was the daughter of Saint Louis, people thought of her as someone belonging to another age; she was looked upon as an ancestress, a broken shadow in a castle in Burgundy. But now she suddenly appeared as she really was, a woman of fifty-seven, still full of vigour and authority.

'Stop, Archbishop!' she repeated, when she was but a few paces from the altar. 'And listen, all of you. Read, Mello!' she added to her councillor who attended her.

Guillaume de Mello unfolded a parchment and read: 'We, most noble Dame Agnès of France, Duchess of Burgundy, daughter of Monsieur Saint Louis, in our name and in that of our son, the most noble and puissant Duke Eudes, address you, barons and lords here present or without in the realm, in order to prevent the Count of Poitiers, who is not the legitimate heir to the Crown, from being recognized King, and to demand that the coronation shall be postponed until such time as have been recognized the rights of Madame Jeanne of France and of Navarre, daughter and heir to the late King and of our daughter.' The anxiety on the dais increased, and uneasy murmurs began to come from the back of the church. The congregation was crowding forward.

The Archbishop seemed embarrassed by the crown, not knowing whether he should replace it on the altar or continue with the ceremony.

Philippe stood still, his head bare, impotent, weighed down with forty pounds of gold and brocades, his hands encumbered by Power and Justice. He had never felt so helpless, so threatened and so alone. It was as if a steel gauntlet were gripping him in the hollow of his chest. His calm was terrifying. To make a gesture, to say a word at this moment was to begin an argument, cause a riot, and doubtless fail. He remained frozen within the matrix of his ornaments, as if the battle were taking place on some lower level.

He heard the ecclesiastical peers whispering: 'What should we do?'

The Bishop of Langres, who had not forgotten the snub he had received that morning, was of the opinion that the ceremony should be stopped.

'Let us retire and discuss the matter,' proposed another.

'We cannot, the King is already the anointed of the Lord. He is King; crown him,' replied the Bishop of Beauvais.

The Countess Mahaut leaned towards her daughter Jeanne and murmured: 'The bitch! She deserves to die for it.'

There was poison in the air.

With his saurian eyes the Constable signed to Adam Héron to continue the roll.

'The magnificent and puissant Lord, the Count of Valois, Peer of the Realm,' announced the chamberlain.

All eyes then turned on the King's uncle. If he responded to the call, Philippe had won. For it was the support of the lay peers, the real power, that Valois embodied. If he refused, Philippe had lost.

Valois showed no alacrity and the Archbishop, who as a Courtenay was his relation by marriage, was visibly awaiting his decision.

Philippe then at last made a slight movement; he turned his head towards his uncle; and the look he gave him was worth a hundred thousand *livres*. The Burgundian would never pay so much.

The ex-Emperor of Constantinople rose to his feet, his face expressionless, and came to take his place behind his nephew.

'How right I was not to be mean with him,' thought Philippe.

'The noble and puissant Dame Mahaut, Countess of Artois, Peer of the Realm,' called Adam Héron.

The Archbishop raised the heavy circle of gold surmounted at the front by a cross and said at last: 'Coronet te Deus.'

One of the lay peers had then at once to take the crown and hold it over the King's head, while the other peers placed on it a symbolic finger. Valois was already putting out his hands; but Philippe with a gesture of his sceptre, stopped him.

'You, Mother, hold the crown,' he said to Mahaut.

'Thank you, my son,' murmured the giantess.

By this spectacular choice she received thanks for her double regicide. She was taking her place as the first peer of the realm, and the possession of the county of Artois was confirmed to her for ever.

'Burgundy will not yield!' cried the Duchess Agnès.

And, gathering her suite, she marched off towards the doors, while Mahaut and Valois slowly led Philippe back to his throne.

When he had taken his seat on it, his feet resting on a silken cushion, the Archbishop removed his mitre and came to kiss the King on the mouth, saying: 'Vivat rex in aeternum.'

The other peers followed him, repeating: 'Vivat rex in aeternum.'

Philippe felt weary. He had won his last battle, after seven months of unceasing struggle for the supreme power, which no one could now dispute with him.

The bells shattered the air as they rang out his triumph; outside the people were cheering, wishing him glory and long life; all his adversaries were defeated. He had a son to assure his line, a happy wife to share his sorrows and his joys. The kingdom of France was his.

'How weary I am, how very weary!' Philippe thought.

To this King of twenty-three, who had imposed himself on the kingdom by his own tenacious will, who had accepted the benefits of crime, and who possessed all the gifts of a great monarch, nothing, indeed, seemed to be lacking.

The days of chastisement were about to begin.

Historical Notes

1. Charles of Valois (see preceding volumes), second son of Philippe III and Isabella of Aragon, younger brother of Philip the Fair, was nominated at the age of thirteen, by Pope Martin IV, to receive the throne of Aragon which had been withdrawn from his uncle Pierre of Aragon, who had been excommunicated after the massacre of the Sicilian Vespers. Crowned as a matter of form in 1284, during the disastrous campaign conducted by Philippe III, the Bold, who was to die immediately afterwards, Valois never occupied his throne and finally renounced it in 1295.

   Later, having married as his second wife Catherine de Courtenay, titular heiress to Byzantium, he bore, from 1301 to 1313, the title of Emperor of Constantinople.

   The relationship between Charles of Valois and Clémence of Hungary is among the most complicated that have ever existed; Valois was cousin to Clémence, because they were both descended, one in the third and the other in the fourth generation, from Louis VIII of

France. He was also her uncle twice over: in the first place because he had married as his first wife Marguerite of Anjou-Sicily, Clémence's aunt, and secondly because he married Clémence off to his nephew, Louis X.

But he was also related to the Anjou family in another way, having in 1313 married his eldest daughter by Catherine de Courtenay, Catherine of Valois, to Philippe, Prince of Taranto, the brother of his first wife. He was thus also great-uncle by marriage to Queen Clémence.

It was owing to the Valois–Taranto marriage that the titular crown of Constantinople, which was part of Catherine of Valois's inheritance, had had to be abandoned by Charles to his son-in-law Prince Philippe.

2. These quotations are from the *Elixir des Philosophes* by Cardinal Jacques Duèze, Pope John XXII. This work, besides a dictionary of the principal terms of alchemy, contains curious recipes, such as the following for 'purifying' a child's urine: 'Take it and put it in a jar and let it remain for three days or four; then pour it out gently; let it stand again till the solids sink to the bottom. Then heat it well and skim it until it is reduced to a third; then strain it through felt and keep it well stoppered against the corruption of the air.'
3. It was not until about the middle of his pontificate, in 1325, that Jacques Duèze (John XXII) began to proclaim in sermons and studies his theory of the beatific vision. One may, however, well suppose that he had been interested in the subject for a long time.

His theory was passionately argued among all the theologians in Europe, arguments which lasted several years and nearly brought about a schism. The University of Paris condemned John XXII's theories and the question arose of deposing the 'Pope of Cahors', as he was derisively called. Duèze retracted on his deathbed, the day before his death, doubtless anxious to preserve the unity of the Church. He was ninety years of age.

Among other propositions put forward by this strange and fascinating Pontiff must be noted that concerning the legislative powers of the Pope. According to him a Pope might modify all legislation created by his predecessors; he considered, indeed, that Popes, being men, were incapable of knowing or foreknowing everything, and that their laws were thus subject to the consequences of change in the world, which necessitated new rules of conduct.

John XXII also pronounced himself against the Immaculate Conception of the Virgin Mary, but considered that if Mary had been conceived with original sin, God had purified her before birth but at a moment, he added, difficult precisely to determine.

It was also he, if Viollet-le-Duc's opinion is correct, who added the third crown to the tiara of which, indeed, no trace is to be found in the papal effigies before his reign.

4. The sovereign lords of Viennois bore the name of 'Dauphin' because of the dolphin which ornamented their crests and their arms, from which arose the name of Dauphiné, given to the whole region over which they exercised sovereignty, and which included: Grésivaudan, Roannez, Champsaur, Briançonnais, Ambrunois, Gapençais, Viennois, Valentinois, Diois, Tricastinois and the Principality of Orange.

At the beginning of the fourteenth century the sovereignty was exercised by the third dynasty of the Dauphins of Vienne, that of La Tour du Pin. It was not until the end of the reign of Philippe VI of Valois, by the treaties of 1343 and 1349, that the Dauphiné was ceded by Humbert II to the Crown of France, on condition that the eldest son of the Kings of France should henceforth bear the title of Dauphin.

5. Most authors give the figure of twenty-three for the Cardinals at the Conclave of 1314–16. We make the number twenty-four.

The party of the 'Romans' consisted of six Italians: Jacques Colonna, Pierre Colonna, Napoléon Orsini, François Caetani, Jacques Stefaneschi-Caetani, Nicolas Alberti (or Albertini) de Prato, one Angevin from Naples, Guillaume de Longis, and finally a Spaniard, Lucas de Flisco (sometimes called Fieschi), brother of the King of Aragon. These Cardinals had been created before the pontificate of Clement V and the installation of the Papacy at Avignon; the hat had been conferred on them between 1278 and 1303, during the reigns of Nicolas III, Nicolas IV, Célestin V, Boniface XVIII and Benoît XI.

All the others had been created by Clement V. The party called 'Provençal' comprised: Guillaume de Mandagout, Bérenger Frédol the elder, Bérenger Frédol the younger, the native of Cahors, Jacques Duèze and the Normans, Nicolas de Fréauville and Michel du Bec.

Finally the Gascons, who were ten in number, were Arnaud de Pélagrue, Arnaud de Fougères, Arnaud Nouvel, Arnaud d'Auch, Raymond-Guillaume de Farges,

Bernard de Garves, Guillaume-Pierre Godin, Raymond de Got, Vital du Four and Guillaume Teste.

In preceding volumes we have mentioned the death of Clement V, the aggression of Carpentras and the vagrant Conclave.

6. Until the middle of the twelfth century the town of Lyons was under the power of the Counts de Forez and de Roannez, under the purely nominal suzerainty of the Emperor of Germany.

After 1173, the Emperor having recognized the sovereign rights of the Archbishop of Lyons, Primate of the Gaules, Lyonnais was separated from Forez and the town was governed by ecclesiastical power with rights of justice, minting coinage and raising troops.

This rule displeased the Commune of Lyons, which was composed exclusively of burgesses and merchants, who struggled to emancipate themselves for more than a century. After several unsuccessful rebellions, they appealed to King Philip the Fair who, in 1292, took Lyons under his protection.

Twenty years later, on 10 April 1312, a treaty was concluded between the Commune, the Archbishop and the King, uniting Lyons permanently to the kingdom of France.

In spite of the claims made by Jean de Marigny, Archbishop of Sens, who controlled the diocese of Paris, the Archbishop of Lyons succeeded in keeping the Primacy of the Gaules, the only one of his prerogatives which remained to him.

By the end of the Middle Ages, Lyons had approximately 24 tavern-keepers, 32 barbers, 48 weavers, 56 tailors, 44 fishmongers, 36 butchers, grocers and sausage-makers, 57 shoemakers, 36 bakers, 25 fruit merchants, 87 lawyers, 15 goldsmiths or gilders, and 20 drapers.

The town was administered by the Commune, which consisted of burgesses engaged in business who elected, on the 21st of December each year, twelve Consuls, always notable men and selected from among the rich families; this consular body was called the 'Syndical'.

7. The family of Varay, drapers and money-changers, was one of the oldest and most considerable in Lyonnais.

   Thirty-one of its members bore the title of Consul; some were frequently re-elected, and one of them as many as ten times. There were eight members of the Varay family among the fifty citizens whom the inhabitants of Lyons chose as their leaders, in 1285, in the struggle against the Archbishop and to achieve annexation by France.

8. The 'Knights Pursuivant', created by Philippe V at the beginning of his reign, were nominated by the King to accompany him and advise him; some of them were always with him on all his journeys.

   Among them are to be found close relations of the King, such as the Count of Valois, the Count of Evreux, the Count de La Marche, the Count of Clermont; great lords such as the Counts de Forez, Boulogne, Savoy, Saint-Pol, Sully, Harcourt, and Comminges; great officers of the Crown such as the Constable, the Marshals, the Master of the Crossbowmen, as well as other personages, such as members of the Secret Council or 'the Council which governs', jurists, administrators of the Treasury, ennobled burgesses and personal friends of the King.

There are to be found such names as Mille de Noyers, Giraud Guette, Guy Florent, Guillaume Flotte, Guillaume Courteheuse, Martin des Essarts, Anseau de Joinville.

These knights more or less foreshadowed the 'Gentlemen of the Chamber' instituted by Henri III and kept in being until the reign of Charles X.

9. The Roman Church has never, as its adversaries have contended, sold absolution. But it has, and this is quite a different matter, made sinners pay for the bulls given them to prove that they had received absolution for their sin.

These bulls were necessary when the sin or crime had become public knowledge and proof had to be produced of having been absolved in order to be readmitted to the sacraments.

The same principle was applied in civil law for letters of reprieve and remissions granted by the King; the delivery of these letters and their being recorded in the registers were taxed. This very ancient custom dated from the Franks before even their conversion to Christianity. John XXII's idea was, through his Book of Taxes and by the creation of the Holy Apostolic Penitentiary, to codify and make general this usage; it was an idea which brought in considerable revenues to the Church, as is proved by the flourishing condition of the pontifical treasury at this Pope's death.

Members of the clergy were not alone in being affected by these bulls; the laity was also taxed. The tariffs were calculated in *gros*, one of which was worth about six *livres*.

Thus parricide, fratricide, or the murder of a relation among laymen was taxed between five and seven *gros*, as was incest, the rape of a virgin, or the theft of sacred objects. The husband who beat his wife or made her miscarry was fined six *gros,* and seven if the wife had her hair torn out. The heaviest fine, twenty-seven *gros,* was imposed for the forgery of apostolic letters, that is to say the Pope's signature.

The fines increased with time, in proportion to the devaluation of the coinage.

But, once again, it was not a question of buying absolution; it was a question of duty being raised for registering and furnishing the authentic proof.

The innumerable pamphlets put into circulation after the Reformation to discredit the Roman Church were all based on this wilful confusion.

It is, moreover, a remarkable fact that at the precise period when John XXII created the Holy Penitentiary, King Philippe V, on his side, was reorganizing the functioning of the royal chancellery and revising the tariffs.

10. The Predicant Friars, or Dominicans, were also called Jacobins because of the Church of Saint-Jacques which had been given to them in Paris, and about which they had established their community.

    The monastery at Lyons, where the Conclave of 1316 was held, had been built in 1236 on a site behind the Hôtel of the Templars. The monastery extended from the present Place des Jacobins to the Place Bellecour.

11. Geoffroy Coquatrix (without doubt from the term *coquatier,* an egg and poultry merchant), who first married Marie La Marcelle, then Jeanne Gencien, kept until his death, in 1321, all the posts he had accumulated under three reigns, and for which he never rendered any

accounts. It was only the son of Charles of Valois, Philippe VI, who, after 1328, asked for these accounts from Geoffroy Coquatrix's heirs; but he had to give up and ultimately absolved the sons from having to justify their father's administration, though they had to forfeit a sum of fifteen thousand *livres*.

12. These arguments were first used in the States General of February 1317, and again at the deaths of Philippe V and Charles IV, when the succession to the throne of France was involved in somewhat similar circumstances. There is little doubt that the Constable Gaucher de Châtillon, who lived and held his appointment until 1329, played a preponderant part in denying the throne to women.
13. It is generally forgotten that the Capet monarchy was originally elective and that this preceded, or at least coexisted with, its hereditary character.

At the accidental death of the last Carolingian, Louis V the Slothful, who died at the age of twenty after a reign of a few months, the Dukes and Counts elected one of their number. They chose Hugues, Duke of France, whose father Hugues the Great, Count of Paris, Duke of France and Burgundy, had in fact exercised the powers of government during the last reigns.

Hugues Capet (that is to say Hugues the Head, Hugues the Chief) immediately associated his son Robert II with the throne by having him elected as his successor and crowned in the same year as himself. Almost the same procedure was followed during the five following reigns, up to and including that of Philippe-Auguste. As soon as the eldest son of the King was nominated heir-presumptive, the peers had to ratify the choice and the newly elected heir was crowned during his father's lifetime.

It was only at the time of Louis VIII, two hundred and twenty-seven years after Hugues Capet, that the formality of a preliminary election was abandoned.

Louis VIII inherited the Crown of France at the death of Philippe-Auguste, on 14 July 1223, exactly as he would have inherited a fief. It was on that 14th of July that the French monarchy became truly hereditary.

At the time of Philippe the Long's regency the new custom was less than a century old.

14. In the genealogies the Christian name of Louis is generally given to the son of Philippe V, who was born in July 1316. But in the accounts of Geoffroy de Fleury, Bursar to Philippe the Long, who began to keep his books in that year, precisely on the 12th of July, when he assumed his functions, the child is mentioned by the name of Philippe.

    Other genealogists mention two sons of whom one was born in 1315 and was therefore conceived while Jeanne of Burgundy was a prisoner at Dourdan; this seems incredible when one considers the efforts Mahaut made to reconcile her daughter and her son-in-law.

    The child who was the fruit of this reconciliation probably received several Christian names, among them both Philippe and Louis; and, since he lived but a short while, the latter-day chroniclers probably became confused.

15. Blanche of Castile's seizure of power was not, however, without its difficulties. Though nominated by an act of King Louis VIII, her husband, as guardian and regent,

Blanche was opposed by the violent hostility of the great vassals who disliked the idea of the kingdom being in the hands of a woman.

But Blanche of Castile was a woman of different stamp from Clémence of Hungary. Moreover, she had been Queen for ten years and had twelve children. She triumphed over the barons, thanks to the support of Count Thibaud of Champagne, who was said to be her lover. It was even whispered that she used him to poison her husband; but there are no real grounds for this suspicion.

16. There is a remarkable similarity between the madness of Robert of Clermont and that which attacked King Charles VI, who was his nephew in the fifth generation on the male side, and in the fourth generation on the female side.

In both cases the madness began with a wound, with cranial traumatism in the case of Clermont, without traumatism in the case of Charles VI, though in each case the madness became dangerous; they both had periods of frenzy followed by long periods of calm in which their behaviour appeared normal; they were both obsessed with a love of tournaments which they could not be prevented from organizing and in which they themselves took part, though sometimes in a state of delirium. Clermont, mad and dangerous as he was, had permission to hunt all over the royal domain. He also appeared in Philip the Fair's army during one of the campaigns in Flanders, as Charles VI, who had been mad for twenty years, took part, during his reign, in the siege of Bourges and in all the battles against the Duke of Berry.

Clermont died on 7 February 1317, a month after Philippe V's coronation.

17. The accustomed cries at the beginning of a tournament.
18. These two children were later to marry each other and receive the Crown of Navarre.
19. Children's toys and games have scarcely altered since the Middle Ages. They already had balls of various sizes made of leather or cloth, hoops, tops, dolls, hobby-horses and quoits. They played at blind-man's-buff, prisoners' base, counting each other out, tag, hot cockles, hide-and-seek and leapfrog, and also at puppets. Little boys in rich families also had imitation suits of armour made to measure: helmets of light steel, coats of mail, blunt swords, the ancestors of the modern soldier or cowboy suits.
20. The second daughter of Agnès of Burgundy, Jeanne, married to Philippe of Valois, future Philippe VI, was lame like her first cousin, Louis I of Bourbon, son of Robert of Clermont.

There was also lameness in the collateral branch of Anjou, since King Charles II, grandfather of Clémence of Hungary, had the byname of 'the Lame'. There is a tradition, recapitulated by Mistral in the *Iles d'Or,* which has it that, when the ambassador of the King of France, the Count de Bouville, came to ask Clémence's hand in marriage for his master, he demanded that the Princess should undress before him so that he might make sure her legs were straight.

Jeanne of Burgundy's infirmity was accompanied by a pathological cruelty which, when she came to the throne, earned her the name of 'the Bad Queen of France' or 'the Lame Queen'.

The list of her victims is a long one. It is possible that Marguerite of Burgundy (who seems to have been affected, amid all the defects of her family, only with excessive sensuality) had been credited with a great many of the cruelties inflicted by her younger sister.

Among other examples, Jeanne endeavoured to get rid of Archbishop Jean de Marigny by preparing him a poisoned bath. She also forged death sentences which she sealed with the King's seal. Philippe VI, having on one occasion discovered her in the act, whipped her so violently with birch-rods that he nearly killed her.

When she died of plague in 1349, the populace with considerable satisfaction saw in it the punishment of Heaven.

21. The hauberk *(broigne)* was a garment of leather, cloth or velvet, on which were sewn steel rings, and which had replaced the coat of mail properly so called. On the hauberk, to reinforce it, had begun to appear pieces of steel called 'plates' – from which derives the name plate armour – which were forged to the shape of the body and articulated like the tails of crayfish.

22. Mahaut drew up a detailed list of the thefts and damage committed in her castle of Hesdin, a list which contained no fewer than a hundred and twenty-nine articles.

    She began a lawsuit in the Court of Justice in Paris to obtain damages, which were partially accorded her by a judgment of 9 May 1321.

23. Philippe V was called the Long, the Tall, or the Myope.

24. There are three methods of election in the Conclave:

1. By secret scrutiny, completed if necessary by a second scrutiny called 'of accession'; the majority must consist of two-thirds of the votes.
2. By delegation, if the Cardinals unanimously appoint some among them to elect the Pope in the name of them all.
3. By 'inspiration' or 'acclamation'.

Some authors assert that Jacques Duèze was elected by delegation; this opinion may have been based on the numerous negotiations which his election involved. But in fact Duèze was elected by an ordinary vote, since there were the regulation number of four tellers whose names are known.

25. Miniver is the fur of a kind of squirrel, grey on the back and white underneath.
26. It was the custom at that time, in royal and princely families, to give children several godmothers and godfathers, sometimes as many as eight altogether. Thus Charles of Valois and Gaucher de Châtillon were both godfathers to Charles de La Marche, the third son of Philip the Fair. Mahaut was a godmother to this Prince, as she was to many other children in the family. Her selection to carry the posthumous child of Louis X to the font had, therefore, nothing surprising about it; not to have chosen her would, on the other hand, have been an insult.
27. Baptism at this period was always performed on the day after birth.

Total immersion in cold water was practised only until the beginning of the fourteenth century.

A synod, held at Ravenna in 1313, decided for the first

time that baptism might also be given by aspersion, if there was a shortage of holy water, or if it was feared that total immersion would imperil the child's health.

But it was really only in the fifteenth century that the practice of immersion disappeared.

If to this form of baptism are added the deplorable hygienic conditions in which childbirth took place, it is easy to understand why the mortality among newborn children was so high during the Middle Ages.

28. Queen Clémence was suffering, so it would appear, from puerperal fever.
29. When a newborn child showed signs of illness, medicines were not given to the child but to the wet-nurse.
30. These dispositions included not only the registering of private deeds but the granting of patents, authorizations for foreigners to reside or trade, and the warrants for royal offices. According to the ordinance of 1321, it is to be noted for instance that deeds concerning Lombards and Jews were subject to the same tariffs: eleven *sous* for a letter with a plain label, seven *livres* and ten *sous* for a letter with a double label, and nine *livres* if the seal affixed to these labels was in green wax, the colour reserved for the royal seal. The letters of appointment to office were charged fifty-one *sous* for bailiffs and seneschals, six *sous* for sergeantries or minor offices. Even the gifts or revenues granted by the sovereign had to be certified by a document which was taxed.
31. The signs of mental derangement grew rapidly worse. Jean XXII, who had always protected Clémence since she was a Princess of Anjou (did he not go so far as to grant, when he heard of her lying-in, twenty days' indulgence to

those who prayed for her and for her son?), was compelled, in the following month of May, to take the young widow to task by letter, telling her that she must live in seclusion, chastity, humility, be simple in the table she kept, modest in her speech and clothing, and not show herself only in the company of young men. At the same time he approached Philippe V to fix Clémence's dower, which was a matter of some difficulty.

On several occasions the Pope wrote again to Clémence exhorting her to reduce her private expenditure and asking her firmly to pay her debts, particularly that to the Bardi of Florence. Finally, in 1318, she had to make a retreat lasting several years in the Convent of Saint Mary of Nazareth, near Aix-en-Provence. But, before doing so, she was compelled, in order to satisfy the demands of her creditors, to make a deposit of all her jewels.

When she died, ten years later, in the Hôtel of the Templars in Paris, which Philippe V had given her in exchange for the Château of Vincennes, all her personal possessions were sold by auction.

32. The brothers Jean and Pierre de Cressay were to be armed knights by Philippe VI of Valois, twenty years later, in 1346, on the battlefield of Cressay (Crécy), on the eve of the famous English victory.

33. These figures are taken from the accounts of the coronation of Philippe VI, twelve years later. Neither prices nor quantities had much varied. On the other hand, all the details of the dresses and decorations given in the course of the chapter concerning the coronation of Philippe V are taken from the account books of his Bursar.

34. The electors of Hugues Capet – from which derives their

title of peer, that is to say, equal to the King – had been: the Duke of Burgundy, the Duke of Normandy, the Duke of Guyenne, the Count of Champagne, the Count of Flanders and the Count of Toulouse.

No one either descended from or holding the titles of the six original lay peers was present at Philippe V's coronation.

35. A few months later, in September 1317, the Pope wrote to Queen Jeanne's confessor giving him the power to absolve her 'of all the sins she had confessed three years earlier'. It seems unlikely that Philippe V could have asked his friend Duèze for this official absolution if he had not firmly believed in the innocence of his wife, at least as far as adultery was concerned.

36. Five centuries later, in his speech of 21 March 1817, in the Chamber of Peers, concerning a finance act, Chateaubriand brought forward in argument this ordinance of Philippe the Long's, promulgated in 1318, by which the domains of the Crown had been declared inalienable.